TEAROOM
mysteries

Dear Reader,

Writing about Jan's and Elaine's Christmas season made me think about gifts. One gift that I've enjoyed for the past several years is writing for Guideposts. The editors and staff have provided me with excellent guidance and friendship, as well exciting opportunities to write stories like this one.

I was recently blessed with another gift: the opportunity to collaborate with author Amy Woods in writing the Tearoom Mysteries volume you hold in your hands. Amy's strong story and talented prose meshed well with my own writing style. I believe that our story, like the perfect blend of tea leaves, turned out just right.

In this story, the tearoom is full of holiday spirit and intrigue when a food critic arrives to review Tea for Two. That's when trouble starts brewing, giving Jan and Elaine a pastry-laced mystery to solve for Christmas. So settle in with your favorite cup of tea, while visions of sugar plums dance in your head, and enjoy *O Christmas Tea*.

Kristin Eckhardt

Tearoom Mysteries

Tearoom for Two
Tea Rose
To a Tea
Crosswords and Chamomile
Burning Secrets
O Christmas Tea

TEAROOM
mysteries

O Christmas Tea

AMY WOODS
with Kristin Eckhardt

Guideposts
New York

Tearoom Mysteries is a trademark of Guideposts

Published by Guideposts Books & Inspirational Media
110 William Street
New York, New York 10038
Guideposts.org

Acknowledgments

Every attempt has been made to credit the sources of copyrighted material used
in this book. If any such acknowledgment has been inadvertently omitted or
miscredited, receipt of such information would be appreciated.

Scripture quotations are taken from *The Holy Bible, New International Version.*
Copyright © 1973, 1978, 1984, 2011 by Biblica, Inc. Used by permission of
Zondervan. All rights reserved worldwide. www.zondervan.com

Cover and interior design by Müllerhaus
Cover illustration by Ross Jones, represented by Deborah Wolfe, Ltd.
Typeset by Aptara, Inc.

Printed and bound in the United States of America
10 9 8 7 6 5 4 3 2 1

O Christmas Tea

CHAPTER ONE

Morning fog was just beginning to lift from its perch atop Chickadee Lake as Jan Blake sipped the last drops of tea from her cup, closing her eyes to savor a quiet moment as the liquid warmed her within. Thick gray clouds hung low in the sky, but Jan, who had lived in Central Maine all her life, did not need those to sense the probability of oncoming snow.

"It won't warm up much today, Earl Grey," she warned the large, long-haired cat at her side.

Earl Grey opened one green eye, briefly acknowledging his human companion before returning to the all-important task of napping away the day, tucked snugly in his chair inside the screened-in porch at the back of the home of Jan and her cousin Elaine Cook. The stray cat had adopted their Victorian tearoom, Tea for Two, as his own home ever since they had purchased the building earlier that year. With the onset of cold weather, the cousins had created a small shelter to keep their outdoor feline tenant warm, since he wasn't allowed inside due to food-service laws. Jan had contacted an outdoor cat organization for a recommendation on how to make it. A Styrofoam cooler, covered with Mylar and filled with straw, made an excellent shelter with a small door cut for entry and exit. The straw, she'd learned, was dry and didn't hold moisture like hay.

They also had purchased a heated water bowl so he always would have access to fresh water, and Jan fed him daily and scooped the litter box they'd placed in one corner of the porch. During the late spring, summer, and early fall, there was no need for it, but they had decided that during the colder months it was prudent to offer him a protected potty spot so he wouldn't choose a random corner of the porch for his needs.

Jan grinned and stood up, stretching her arms before collecting her teacup and saucer. She pushed her glasses higher on her nose. "All right, sir," she said, nodding at the now sleeping tomcat. "It's back to work for me. Stick to the porch today and you'll stay warm."

Earl Grey tucked his tail in tighter, encircling all four limbs, and continued to snooze as Jan headed back inside to check the progress of the morning baking.

Most mornings at Tea for Two were pleasantly busy, thanks to word-of-mouth recommendations to tourists and a handful of faithful locals, but this day was particularly so as they awaited the arrival of a special guest—a Miss Clara Hill—the renowned food critic of Portland's most circulated newspaper. Reviews from Clara were known to elevate the popularity of up-and-coming eateries, and though business was going well for Tea for Two, Jan couldn't help the excited nervousness that had begun to tickle her stomach like butterfly wings upon waking that morning.

Jan took a steadying breath of crisp December air, then pushed open the kitchen door, welcoming the rich scents of maple syrup, butter, and flour that greeted her. The kitchen was her favorite spot in the house. It boasted granite countertops, a work island with built-in storage, gleaming appliances, and rich walnut cupboards. Over time, she'd decorated it with old kitchen utensils and tins, and a blue Fiesta bowl filled with lemons near the coffeemaker added a bright splash of color.

Their server, Rose Young, looked up at Jan, hand paused over a mixing bowl. "How's the weather out there?" Rose asked.

Jan smiled at the question as she removed her hat and then gloves, stuffing one into each coat pocket before hanging up her outerwear. "If I had to guess, I'd say there's a good chance it's going to snow this afternoon."

"Oh, don't mind the *guess* part of that statement," Elaine's voice carried from the pantry. "Jan's too humble to point out that she never guesses and her forecasts are more reliable than the weather girl on the news."

Rose laughed, the pleasant sound reminding Jan how thankful she was that they'd hired the young woman, whose temperament was as golden as the wheat-colored hair she usually wore in a braid. The past few months had been hard on Rose since the death of her mother, and on occasion Jan sensed her vulnerability. Yes, Rose was a grown woman, but she had still needed her mother, and the loss had taken its toll.

Jan supposed that was part of the reason she'd taken Rose under her wing recently, and had begun teaching her how to bake all of the pastries that customers so loved ordering to accompany their tea.

But that day, Rose was nothing but smiles as she continued stirring the wet ingredients for Jan's favorite maple brownies. Jan stopped to wash her hands at the sink, then walked over to join Rose at the counter.

"You're in a good mood," Jan told her.

"I am," Rose said, then took a deep breath. "And I wanted to tell both of you—I've been thinking about something." She looked nervously between Jan and Elaine. "I've been so inspired by both of you, working here. And…I think I am going to go to culinary school. I know it's a big step, and I'd have to find one that has night classes so I can still work here, but you two have shown me how much I love cooking and baking and after all this time, I think I've finally realized that's the career path I want to follow."

"I think that's wonderful," Jan exclaimed, glancing over at Elaine.

"We couldn't be more proud of you," Elaine told her.

Rose blushed. "Well, I haven't decided for certain, but I'll start looking into it."

Elaine smiled. "We're behind you all the way."

"That means more than you know," Rose said, a slight quaver in her voice as she turned her attention back to the mixing bowl. "Being a nurse was wonderful because it allowed me to serve, but it wasn't right for me. With a culinary degree, I can serve in a different way."

"What a wonderful idea." Jan watched her, so touched that Rose had shared her career aspirations with them. She did have baking talent and Jan looked forward to watching that talent flourish.

Rose looked up at Jan. "I'm just about ready to mix this in with the dry ingredients."

"Perfect," Jan answered, rubbing her hands together. "We're right on time."

Rose nodded rapidly, betraying a little of the tension she must have been feeling.

"Don't you worry, Rose," Jan said. "You're doing great."

The younger woman sighed. "I still can't believe you're letting me make your special recipe," she said, chuckling nervously.

"Nonsense. You've been baking regularly for months now and these brownies will be just the thing for Miss Hill to try," Jan responded.

"Absolutely," Elaine said, joining Jan and Rose in the main part of the kitchen. Elaine's blue eyes sparkled above her cerulean sweater as she set a can of diced tomatoes and an onion on the counter before pulling a slow cooker down from an upper cabinet. "They're all the rage with the regulars, so if our food critic wants a taste of local flavor, she's certainly come to the right place."

"I sure hope so," said Rose, carefully adding a little of the wet ingredients at a time to the dry already in the spinning stand mixer. "Though I still wish you would have made today's batch, Jan. I'm so nervous I'm afraid I might forget something and ruin our chances at a good write-up."

Jan gave Rose's shoulder a gentle squeeze. "I have complete faith in you, Rose. Besides, if you do decide to go to culinary school, you can tell them you've cooked for a famous foodie." She'd meant to encourage Rose, but the young woman's cheeks suddenly lost their rosy shade.

5

"You're scaring her, Jan," Elaine teased. "Why don't you let her handle the brownies while you come on over and help me with this stew?"

"All right, but let me know if you need me, Rose."

"Will do," Rose called, her voice sounding a little less anxious than before.

Jan and Elaine had decided to put together a beef stew that morning and let it cook all day, as they were certain time would fly with their visitor and they'd both be hungry and too worn out to put something together when dinner rolled around. Taking a quick glance at the inventory Elaine had already gathered, Jan pulled a pound of round steak from the fridge, along with carrots and celery. She grabbed a couple of potatoes from the pantry and began washing the vegetables while Elaine rubbed the meat with olive oil, salt, and pepper.

The cousins worked so well together, both in tasks related to the tea shop and in life in general, Jan thought, tickled. When Elaine had first approached her with the idea of buying a large house on Chickadee Lake and turning it into a tearoom, Jan, having lived as a widow for a decade by that time, had not been able to envision such a different lifestyle.

But now she wouldn't trade it for anything. It was nice to come home to a warm house where she knew she wouldn't have to be alone very often. And baking for her community brought a new kind of joy into her world; she found satisfaction in comforting and nourishing the locals, many of whom she'd come to think of as extended family.

Though, never in her wildest dreams would she have imagined that Tea for Two would draw the attention of a food critic as well known and regarded as Clara Hill.

When Elaine had first gotten the telephone call from Clara's assistant, asking if they would entertain a review of their tearoom, Jan had given in to her curiosity and done a little research of her own. What she'd found had both pleased her and served to make her more nervous at the idea than she already had been, as Miss Hill's articles were exceptionally detailed and well written, and seemed to be very fair. The critic's write-ups were never unkind, but always extremely honest, making readers, at least in Jan's experience, either ecstatic to try out the eatery in question, or very, very certain they were not missing anything by passing it up.

In other words, Jan mused with a deep sigh, a review from Clara Hill had the power to potentially make or break a budding establishment like Tea for Two.

Silently, she passed her worries on to God, praying that He would be by her side as He had been every day of her life, a reminder that, like a balm, soothed her instantly.

When she and Elaine finished preparing the vegetables and meat for stew, Jan turned the slow cooker to low and went to check on Rose.

"All set," Rose said, brushing floured hands against her apron. She picked up an empty banana peel from the counter and tossed it into the garbage can before washing her hands. "The brownies are in the oven and Miss Hill should be here in"—she glanced at the wall clock—"less than an hour."

Jan nodded and glanced around anxiously, wishing for something to occupy her hands. She'd risen early to get some of the baking out of the way before Rose came in, and she and Elaine had already completed their morning routine of checking that each table in the parlor was set to receive customers. Evidently they had just been too efficient for their own good that morning. Finally, she settled for wiping down the counters. By the time she'd finished, they were squeaky clean, and Elaine had made a pot of oolong tea for the three of them and set out a jar of honey at the kitchen table.

"Everything is ready for Miss Hill." Elaine brushed a loose strand of brown hair from her eyes as she slid into a chair. "Don't worry," she said as Rose eyed her mug. "I made decaf. I didn't think we needed any help waking up, seeing as how we're already just bundles of nerves."

The three women broke into laughter, and Jan felt the tension in the room dissipate as they all managed to relax a little.

"Truer words have never been spoken," Rose added, sipping her tea. "I suppose all we can do now is wait."

"Wait and pray," Jan said. "But no use worrying ourselves too much."

Rose and Elaine nodded, and Jan noticed the apples of Rose's cheeks had returned to their usual pretty pink.

"We serve tea and pastries to so many people every day, and if the regulars' constant return is any indication, I think we're doing well enough," Jan said.

"Exactly," Elaine agreed. "We'll give Clara the very best treats we have to offer. If she enjoys our tearoom, that will be lovely. If not, we'll still get up the next day and get to work." She added a teaspoon of sugar to her cup and stirred. "Besides, it's a simple breakfast. What could possibly go wrong?"

AN HOUR LATER, the tearoom was bustling with activity as Rose served brownies, scones, muffins, and the cookie of the day, a chocolate shortbread, while Jan wandered the parlor, chatting with guests and pouring tea.

Suddenly, the parlor door opened, bringing a gust of frigid wind. "She's here," Jan whispered discreetly as she passed Rose on her way to greet Clara Hill, whose shoulder-length dark, wavy hair, green eyes, and slim stature she recognized from the photo that always accompanied the food critic's byline in the Portland paper.

Jan brushed imaginary crumbs off her apron as she approached. "Good morning and welcome to Tea for Two," she said holding out an arm. "May I seat you?"

The woman smiled warmly and Jan was pleased to see that the smile reached her eyes. "Good morning to you as well. I'm Clara Hill from the *Portland Pelican*," Clara answered, offering a hand. "I believe I spoke with your cousin Elaine on the phone."

Jan nodded, shaking Clara's outstretched hand. "Jan Blake. It's so nice to have you with us today."

"And yes, a seat would be lovely."

Jan smiled, hoping her features didn't betray her nervousness. "Right this way." She took a deep breath as she led Clara farther into the parlor, stopping at a cozy table for two near the fireplace. "How is this?" she asked.

"Wonderful." Clara wrapped her purse strap around the back of the chair and sat down, picking up a menu.

Jan hovered, suddenly unsure of what to do with herself. Normally she would give a customer a few minutes to peruse the menu before she asked about an order, but in that moment, she froze.

Clara smiled up at Jan, her green eyes friendly. "Please don't be nervous. I'm just like any other guest," she said. "I know it probably feels a little strange, knowing I'll write about my experience here, but I'd love it if you'd try not to let that bother you too much."

Relief flooded through Jan and the two women giggled at the same time. "I'm so glad you said that. For a second there, I'd almost forgotten what I'm meant to be doing, but you've put me more at ease."

Clara grinned. "How about this?" she suggested, folding her menu and placing it neatly on the table. "Why don't you tell me your favorite things on the menu, and I'll start there?"

"Well, a lot of our customers have fallen in love with the cinnamon spice tea we're carrying over the fall and winter seasons. It's a nice blend of nutmeg, cinnamon, orange peel, and sweet cloves." As she spoke, Jan's apprehension began to fade and she felt a little more like her usual self. "The aroma just makes me think of Christmastime."

"Sold," Clara said. "I'd love a cup of that. I had my breakfast earlier, but I'd like something to go with my tea. I'd be thrilled to have something sweet."

Jan hesitated, not wanting to toot her own horn about her maple brownies. But she had to admit they were a customer favorite, and Clara did not need to know who'd created the recipe to enjoy them, after all.

"Our white maple brownies are popular with the regular customers, and they would definitely fix your sweet tooth right up. How does that sound?" Jan clasped her hands together in front of her apron, surprised to discover that she looked forward to reading the critic's commentary on her specialty. Perhaps, if Miss Hill didn't enjoy the treats, she might give insight into how they could be made even better. Jan was happy with the recipe, and the brownies had a growing fan base in Lancaster, but she believed there was always room for improvement.

"White maple brownies it is, then," Clara said, her voice cheerful and enthusiastic.

There was something open and discerning about the young woman that made a person want to please her palate, and Jan could see why Clara had gained her reputation for being honest and fair, but also a little intimidating.

"I'll have that right out." Jan gave a little nod and turned toward the kitchen to put together Clara's order. Out of the corner of her eye, she saw Rose attending to a couple who appeared to be in their midthirties. She and Rose had served the regulars quickly and everyone seemed to be at ease, enjoying their orders. Confident that all was going smoothly, Jan left the parlor and passed through the entrance hall and into the kitchen.

"How's it going out there?" Elaine asked, busy at the stove with a large kettle.

"So far, so good. Miss Hill arrived a few minutes ago and ordered the cinnamon spice tea and maple brownies. Rose has everything else under control at the moment, so I'm going to gather Clara's tea and food and bring it on out."

Elaine turned off one of the burners and lifted the kettle, settling it on a trivet. She disappeared into the pantry, returning a moment later with the cinnamon spice tea canister. "So what was she like? Did she seem nice?"

"Yes, very nice, actually. She's kind and has a pretty face to go with her personality, and she seemed relaxed and happy to be here."

"Not at all what I was expecting," Elaine said. "For some reason, I'd pictured her with a very stern expression and a pad and pen out, taking notes."

Jan gave a little chuckle. "It is an interesting job, isn't it?" she mused, placing loose tea leaves into a steeper ball and pouring water over them in an individual pot. She'd chosen her favorite, a white ceramic one with little hand-painted bluebells—not an antique, but sweet and pretty nonetheless. "It can't be easy to have restaurateurs so nervous around you all the time. I know I was. She called weeks ago to schedule a time to stop by, and still I had goose bumps covering my arms."

Elaine laughed. "Just remember, it's all in God's hands. Whatever happens, we'll make the best of it."

While the tea steeped, Jan arranged two maple brownies on a plate that matched the teapot, placing a tiny jar of fresh maple syrup next to everything else on a silver tray. As soon as the tea was ready, she added it along with a cup and saucer, then stood back to survey the arrangement. Pleased, she set off toward the parlor, almost bumping into Rose as she passed through the door.

"*Oof!*" Rose said, moving quickly out of the way. "That was a close one. Sorry, Jan, I had my mind on Miss Hill out there."

"No problem," Jan said with a smile. "I'm a little distracted myself."

"I've got an order of green tea for the couple at that table—who were in no mood for small talk. So I'm on my way in to get that ready and I'll be right back out there to help you. Is that her order?" Rose asked. "I hope she likes the brownies. I tried a nibble of one myself—just to make sure the batch came up okay—and it was divine, as ever."

"Yes, this is it." Jan clutched the tray tighter, easing carefully past Rose into the hallway. "Just a little while longer and we can rest easy."

Jan sent up another silent prayer and braced herself before returning to the parlor. Clara had gotten up from the table and was busy admiring the antique tea sets on display in a cabinet in a corner of the parlor. As soon as she saw Jan approaching with a tray, she returned to her table near the fire.

"You have a beautiful collection here, Ms. Blake," Clara complimented, turning to face Jan. "It must have taken a great deal of work to put all this together."

"It's a hobby of mine and Elaine's. I suppose it is work in a way, but it's something we both enjoy." Jan placed the tray carefully on the table, setting the teacup and saucer at Clara's place just as she sat down.

"This looks fabulous," Clara commented, spreading a napkin in her lap.

Jan finished up and stood, her hands curled nervously at her sides. "And here we have everything you might need in the way of sweetening," she said, motioning to a lazy Susan at the center of the table. "If you like."

Clara smiled. "I think I'll try a sip plain first so I can get an unhindered taste of all the flavors."

"I'll leave you to it then," Jan said. "Please let us know if there's anything else you need."

"Absolutely."

"Enjoy."

Though her instinct was to hurry, Jan tried her best to walk away at a normal pace. She checked on the regulars, and noticed a few new customers among them. Emmaline Cribbs and Pearl Trexler were there, enjoying a cup of tea together. Maureen Oakley had brought her youngest grandson and was giving him tiny nibbles from her cranberry scone.

As Jan walked through the parlor she smiled at Dr. Tyson McInnes and his wife, Claudia, as they sat at a corner table working on a crossword puzzle together.

Then she stopped a table where a young couple, Marisa and Sven, sat. They told her they were traveling through Maine on their honeymoon. She chatted with them about local sights to see, such as the lighthouses and the preserved granite fort in nearby Prospect, before moving on.

Jan waved to two tourists whose names she learned were Irene Kelly and Scott Landon—Rose had already served them—then checked on how River White was enjoying his cinnamon spice tea and brownie before making her way back to the kitchen. Once again, she and Rose passed each other, the younger woman carrying a full tray this time.

"Did it go all right?" Rose asked, eyes wide in anticipation of Jan's answer.

"I think so." Jan lowered the empty silver tray to her side. "It remains to be seen how she likes everything. She said to think of her like any other customer, so I'm doing my best not to give her any special treatment."

"Well, I'll stop by her table and check on her once I drop off these orders."

"Sounds great."

Once she'd entered the kitchen, Jan released an audible sigh of relief. Elaine came in from her office next to the kitchen.

"Unless our famous critic has left so soon, that sigh's a little premature, don't you think?" Elaine teased.

"I'm just celebrating the fact I didn't drop the tray into Miss Hill's lap."

Elaine chuckled. "Oh, come now. I'm sure you did just fine. She'll be finished in no time, and on her way to write us a positive review. I'm certain of it. It's out of our hands now."

"And thank goodness for that."

Jan was just about to grab a pitcher of water from the refrigerator when she heard a loud noise, like feet pounding on the wood floor outside the kitchen. Her heart lurched into her throat, knowing Rose wouldn't run down the hallway unless something wasn't right.

A few seconds later, her concern was validated, as Rose rushed in, pink-cheeked, her tray hanging listlessly at her side.

"Call an ambulance and come quick!" Rose gasped, the words rushing from her in a panicked jolt. "Something terrible has happened."

Jan bolted from where she stood in front of the fridge, letting the door slam loudly shut. "What is it?" she asked, rushing to Rose's side.

The younger woman's eyes swam back and forth as she worked to calm herself and gather her thoughts. "It's the food critic, Miss Hill," Rose blurted. "She's passed out!"

CHAPTER TWO

Elaine stood freezing in the morning air, a hand over her mouth as she watched a MaineGeneral ambulance carry Clara Hill off to the hospital. "I still can't believe this is happening." She turned to her side to face Jan and Rose, who were as stunned and immobile as she.

"This is just awful," Rose said, tears swimming in her eyes. "And what if it's my fault? I'm the one who made the brownies today, and she's the only customer who ate one so far this morning."

"Don't say such things, Rose," Jan soothed, rubbing her hands together. "This can't possibly be your fault. You made the same brownies we've baked together hundreds of times, and River bit into his just as Clara began to have her reaction."

She pointed to River White, a reporter for *The Penzance Courier*, who stood a few feet away with a group of customers, all of who had followed the stretcher outside, no doubt curious about what had happened to their fellow diner.

"See, River's fine, and everyone else is okay. No one knows yet what happened to Clara, but the paramedics had her conscious and breathing, and you heard them say she'll probably be all right. Take heart."

Rose nodded, taking a few deep breaths as she blinked back the burgeoning tears.

Elaine reached out to their employee and gave her a quick hug. She was a little shaky herself and had been fervently praying for the past half hour as the medics had worked to help poor Clara.

Now Elaine regretted her carefree words that morning when she'd asked what could possibly go wrong, but no one could have imagined that the food critic would have passed out cold right there in the tearoom where they'd served her goodies only moments before.

"I have an idea," Jan said, suddenly moving to action. "Rose and I will follow the ambulance into Waterville and stay there until we figure out if Clara will be all right. It's the right thing to do, and we'll need to see that her bills are covered." She turned to Rose, placing a hand on each of her shoulders. "Would that make you feel a little better?"

Rose nodded and Elaine's heart eased just a tad.

"That sounds like a good idea," Elaine said. "I'll stick around here and speak to the police." She looked past Jan and Rose at the street, where a state trooper truck pulled up. "And here they are now."

Jan nodded and tucked an arm around Rose's shoulder. "We'll text you once we hear any news."

The two women walked away, headed toward Jan's blue Camry, and suddenly Elaine felt very much alone.

She waved as Trooper Benson's truck pulled up, then wrapped her arms around herself, wishing she'd thought to grab a scarf and hat along with the gloves she always kept in her coat pocket. The wind had picked up and the temperature was dropping steadily; as ever, Jan's prediction would prove spot-on and there would likely be snow before nightfall.

Daniel Benson, a Maine state trooper in his early thirties, shut his truck door and approached the small cluster of customers gathered a few feet away from Elaine. "Hey, folks, we appreciate your concern, but we'd like you to leave for now while we conduct our investigation."

Elaine stepped toward them. "Of course, there will be no charge for anyone's breakfast, due to the circumstances. And the tearoom will open again as soon as we're given the all-clear."

There was some quiet chatter among the customers as they dispersed, heading for their vehicles. River hesitated, but a pointed glance from the trooper soon sent him on his way.

After they'd all left, Daniel approached Elaine, tucking his hands in his pockets as he walked. Though she and Jan had worked with him before and she was comfortable around Daniel, his sandy hair and blue eyes giving him a gentler appearance than he might have liked as a law enforcement professional, Elaine couldn't help the apprehension that rose within, settling like a lump in her throat.

"Good morning, Mrs. Cook," he greeted, holding out a palm.

Elaine shook his uncovered hand, its cold seeping through her glove. "Not so good, really," she answered.

Trooper Benson nodded solemnly, his eyes tender. "It's too cold to talk out here, don't you think? Why don't we go on inside and have something hot to drink?"

"That sounds like a fine idea," she agreed.

Once indoors, Elaine led Daniel to the office to wait while she made tea for them both. After she'd set up the hot beverages on a small table near the desk, she found she was too on edge to drink hers, but Daniel sipped his eagerly, probably chilly from his morning rounds.

"Now there's nothing to be nervous about at this point, Mrs. Cook, so why don't we just start at the beginning and you can tell me what happened."

Elaine nodded, pulling in a deep breath. As she relayed the morning's events with as much clarity and thoroughness as she could, Trooper Benson calmly removed a small notebook and pen from his pocket and began writing a few things down. Elaine had to force herself not to look at the scrawled words as his hand moved across the page, but it was difficult. After the terrible chaos of hearing Rose's panicky voice announcing that Clara had passed out, calling 911 to get paramedics to the tearoom, and calming the other worried customers before she was able to close up shop, the gravity of what had happened finally began to sink in.

Elaine pushed back the tears that sat poised behind her eyes, and tried to focus on the trooper's gentle but probing questions.

When she'd retraced the morning—waking up, helping Jan and Rose with the baking, making the stew, serving tea and pastries to the regular customers—nothing stood out to either Elaine or Daniel.

"As far as I can tell, it was like any other morning," she concluded, taking a sip of tepid tea. "That's just the thing—nothing stands out at all."

Trooper Benson nodded, folding the cover over his notepad and returning it to his pocket. "You've done very well, Mrs. Cook, and remember that you're not being charged with anything at this time."

Elaine nodded, trying to take comfort in his words, even as her mind wandered over the disaster the awful event could cause.

Their business had been doing so well. Word of mouth had spread about their unique selection of teas and Jan's wonderful baking, and things had been going really great. Plus, even though she and her cousin had been nervous, there had also been an underlying sense of excitement surrounding Clara's review, and the possibilities a good one might have brought.

She swallowed over the growing lump in her throat.

Now that all could disappear. Something may have poisoned the food critic, after all. After the experience she'd had, what could Clara Hill possibly have to say about Tea for Two that wouldn't drive customers away for good?

Oh, this is just dreadful.

At times like these, Elaine told herself to turn to God. She often needed a little reminder that she wasn't alone when hardships came along. Even as she had that thought, she felt a gentle nudging in her heart to hand her worries over to the One who could calm raging storms, and, taking advantage of the quiet moment as Trooper Benson drained the last of his tea, she did just that.

"I know it might seem like nothing unusual occurred. We just need to figure out what happened to Miss Hill, so that *if* something was contaminated, by whatever means, we can prevent the same thing from happening to anybody else."

"Yes, I understand. It's just that I can't for the life of me figure out what caused Clara to collapse. We've served Jan's maple brownies to practically everyone in town at one point or another, and the same goes for all of our tea blends. The only relatively new tea is the cinnamon spice, which we've had for a month or so, and another customer had the same thing this morning and seems fine, so it couldn't possibly be that."

Trooper Benson held up a hand. "So another customer consumed the same tea as Miss Hill?"

"Yes, in fact, Jan and Rose helped me make a list while we were waiting for the ambulance." She reached into her pocket and pulled out a slip of paper. "River White had the cinnamon spice tea and a white maple brownie, which he only took one bite of; Maureen Oakley was here with her grandson and had a cranberry scone and white tea. The McInneses had chocolate shortbread cookies and mint tea."

She took a breath, still stunned by what had happened. "Emmaline and Pearl each had the orange-spiced black tea and the chocolate shortbread cookies. And two of the guests— Irene and...Scott, I think their names were—had the green tea without anything to eat. The honeymoon couple, Marisa and Sven, had pumpkin bread and chai tea. Of course Clara had the cinnamon spice and a maple brownie."

"Thank you, Mrs. Cook. I know this is hard on you," Daniel said.

"Also, when I spoke to the paramedic about the ingredients we use, she agreed that there aren't any common irritants in the pastries or the tea." Elaine put a hand to her forehead. "I'm just at a complete loss as to what might have caused such a thing to happen. We feel awful about it. Just awful."

"Well, whatever it is, we'll all work together to figure it out, all right, Mrs. Cook?"

She nodded, not feeling all right at all.

"In the meantime, let's head into the kitchen and, if you don't mind too much, I'll take a few samples of the tea and food."

"No, not at all," Elaine said, standing. She gathered the tea things, glad for something to do with her hands, and followed the trooper out of the office. Back in the kitchen, she set the tea tray near the sink while Daniel retrieved evidence bags from his truck.

Trooper Benson returned with a sealed box of bags, along with a pair of disposable, plastic-looking gloves, which he pulled on. "I'll gather all the...evidence"—he seemed to hesitate over the word, which hung heavy in Elaine's ears too—"from the kitchen and tearoom and get it to the police lab as soon as possible." He scanned the kitchen. "I'll need several samples—including the leaves in the canister that the cinnamon spice tea originated from—as well as the actual brownie that Miss Hill was eating when she became ill."

"Take what you need," Elaine said. "Please let me know if there's anything I can do to help."

Trooper Benson nodded and got to work, and Elaine followed him around the kitchen and back into the parlor, feeling for all the world like a lost puppy, wishing there was some way she could make herself useful. Oddly, she envied Jan and Rose at that particular moment—at least they would be on hand at the hospital if Clara needed anything, though they would probably be doing a lot of sitting around and waiting as well. She hadn't thought until now to recommend that they bring something to read, or cross-stitch for Jan.

She sighed. Perhaps when Daniel left, she would make use of the time in the closed shop to do some office work and dust the curio cabinets in the parlors. As it was, she stood in the hallway, rubbing her hands together as she waited for Trooper Benson to finish up.

Finally, he emerged from the parlor, now holding several labeled evidence bags with samples from the kitchen, including tea leaves and small pieces of the white maple brownies their customers so loved. It saddened her to see the pastry like that.

"I think I'm all set here," Daniel said, tucking the bags into an envelope and then placing it in a coat pocket. Elaine realized suddenly that she hadn't offered to take the man's outerwear when he'd come into the house, a testament to how distraught she felt by the morning's events.

"Are you sure you wouldn't like a blueberry muffin to take on the road with you, Trooper?" Elaine asked, not realizing until she'd spoken the words how the offer might come across under the circumstances. Surely Daniel wouldn't want a baked good that could possibly be tainted. But his answer surprised her.

"I'd love one, Mrs. Cook." He gave her a sympathetic smile and her heart warmed. It was sweet of him to give Tea for Two a vote of confidence, and she wouldn't forget it.

Elaine told him to wait right there while she returned to the kitchen and wrapped a muffin in plastic. Daniel took it gratefully when she brought it out and handed it to him.

"Thank you so much, Mrs. Cook." He held up the muffin before putting it into his pocket. "This will be an excellent morning snack to munch on during my drive to Augusta."

"It's no trouble at all, Trooper Benson."

Halfway out the door, he turned back. "Try not to lose too much sleep over this. There's no telling what Miss Hill might have come in contact with that caused her reaction—possibly not even something from here—and I'll keep you updated on anything we find, all right? And, if you wouldn't mind asking Rose and Jan to contact me about giving a statement as soon as they're able? But in any case, the tearoom will need to remain closed until it's determined that there is no contamination and that the food and facilities are safe for customers."

All she could do was nod as he left. There wasn't anything else to say. Once again, all they could do now…was wait.

Half an hour later, Elaine heard a car pull up out front.

Probably a customer, she thought, grabbing a coat to greet the visitor and pass on the news that Tea for Two was closed for the rest of the afternoon, at the very least.

But when she opened the front door, she was pleasantly surprised to see the car belonging to her longtime friend Nathan Culver pulling to a stop.

Even more surprising than the sight of his vehicle was the little kick her heart gave at the promise of his company—a bright spot in an otherwise bleak morning.

She stood on the porch and waved as Nathan got out of his car. In his late fifties, the antiques auctioneer who'd been her childhood friend was a comfortable sort of handsome. That day in particular, she welcomed his twinkling blue eyes and gray-sprinkled light-brown hair. He looked casual but sharp in a navy-blue overcoat and khaki slacks.

Nathan gave a warm smile as he approached, stopping to pat Earl Grey, who'd evidently roused himself from his usual nest on the screened-in porch. The lazy cat leaned into their guest's hand, closing his eyes as Nathan scratched behind his ears, a favorite spot.

"Good morning," Elaine called, trying hard to inject a little cheerfulness into the words.

"Hi there," Nathan greeted, joining her on the porch. "I heard the bad news and thought I'd stop by to see how you all are holding up." His words held questions.

Elaine's lips formed a thin line as she pondered how to begin to explain it all. Best to start simply. "We've certainly had better days."

She quickly filled him in on what had happened, realizing suddenly that they were standing out in the cold. A chaotic morning could really wreak havoc on one's social skills, she realized.

"Would you like to come in?"

Nathan shook his head. "Sorry to say I've got an appointment in half an hour, so I can't stay long."

Elaine grinned. "It's just as well, probably. Between sitting with Rose and Jan this morning, and then going over everything with the state trooper, I've had more tea in one morning than I usually do in a week."

Nathan laughed. "Well, in that case, I'll be on my way." He smiled affectionately. "I certainly don't want to be the cause of you standing out here in below freezing temperatures."

His concern for her made Elaine's cheeks warm.

"But before I go, would you agree to have dinner with me tomorrow evening?"

Elaine hesitated. She very much enjoyed Nathan's company and his friendship, but lately, she'd begun to wonder if he might not like to be something more, and at the bottom of her heart, she just wasn't sure she was ready for their relationship to progress to anything beyond friendship. While her husband, Ben, had been gone for a while now, she still ached at his loss and missed him terribly.

It was something she'd have to pray about and consider at length, perhaps when things settled down here and she had some time.

"So what do you say?"

Looking at Nathan's cheerful, carefree smile, she decided that maybe she was overthinking things. Possibly her old friend just wanted to have dinner and chat. It might not mean anything at all.

"I hope you'll say yes, Elaine. There's something important I'd like to talk to you about." He gazed at her hopefully, waiting for her answer.

Surely a dinner between friends would be fine.

"All right, Nathan, yes. If things have cleared up here by tomorrow evening, I'll have dinner with you."

Then again, her instincts that morning had been somewhat less than precise.

CHAPTER THREE

Later that afternoon, Jan and Rose sat in the waiting room of MaineGeneral, munching on a very sad lunch of pretzels and coffee from the vending machine.

Finally, after what had only been an hour or so, but what seemed like days, a doctor emerged from the room Clara Hill had been admitted to. He carried a clipboard and had pulled his face mask down so that it no longer covered his mouth, but try as she might, Jan was unable to read much into his expression. As soon as he stood before her and Rose, he held out a hand and gave the two of them a friendly smile.

"Hi there. I'm Dr. Albert Ross. Are either of you ladies kin of Miss Hill?"

Jan and Rose exchanged glances.

"No, we're...well, acquaintances only, really," Jan responded.

The doctor's eyes narrowed in question.

"We just want to make sure that Clara is okay. I'm afraid she was drinking tea at our tearoom this morning when she became ill."

"Of course, I can't share too much with you about her condition without her consent, but if you'd like to see her, it's visiting hours now, and I'm happy to report that she's awake and doing fine."

Jan closed her eyes, saying a quick prayer of thanks, and Rose gave a little audible gasp of relief before she caught herself.

"We're so glad to hear it, Dr. Ross. And yes, if it's all right, we'd love to go in and visit with her for a moment."

"Absolutely," he said, stepping aside. "It's just this way."

When they entered Clara's hospital room, Jan was beyond pleased to see that the color had returned to the food critic's cheeks and she was sitting up in the hospital bed, taking a sip of water.

"Well, hello there," Clara said, giving them a more cheerful greeting than Jan felt they deserved.

"Hello, Miss Hill," Jan answered. Rose gave a tentative little wave from where she stood near the door behind her boss. "I'm so happy to see you're doing much better. How do you feel?"

Clara set down the water glass and folded her hands on her lap. "As good as can be expected, I guess."

"Have they figured out what happened?" Jan asked, but before Clara could respond, Rose interjected.

"Oh, Miss Hill, if it was something we served, I take full responsibility and we are so very sorry. I can't imagine what it might have been. Jan and I have made those brownies so many times and practically everyone in Lancaster has eaten them more than once, and I just..."

Clara held out a hand, motioning for Rose to slow down. "It's all right. I don't blame either of you for anything." She hesitated a moment, as if catching her breath, then continued. "The doctors aren't certain, but they think it might have been an unusual reaction to something that irritated my system, which could have happened anywhere at any time. Although the only thing I'm allergic to is latex." She looked at Jan. "Do you use latex gloves for food preparation?"

"No, we don't," Jan told her. "Only nonlatex gloves."

Rose continued to worry an invisible spot on her lavender sweater. Jan's heart went out to her, knowing Rose's reaction to what had happened to Clara might have been more acute in light of the recent loss of her mother.

"Actually, I'm fortunate that I was in the tearoom when it happened." Clara's brows knit together. "If I'd been alone, I might not have fared so well…" Her voice trailed off and she almost seemed to forget that Jan and Rose were in the room with her.

Jan wondered if any medicine they might have given Clara was making her sleepy. She took a step closer to get her attention. "Do the doctors know what might have caused the reaction?"

Clara shook her head. "No, but they suggested that I start the process of looking closely at my environment and such to figure out what caused me to pass out."

Jan pulled up a nearby chair, careful not to touch any of the medical equipment or tubes near Clara's hospital bed. She motioned at the chair next to her so that Rose would take a seat, hoping it might relax her fidgeting.

"If you wouldn't mind too much," Jan broached hesitantly, "I'd like to ask you a little more about that."

"That would be fine with me," Clara said, "except there's not much to tell."

"You mean, you've never had anything like that happen to you before, that you know of?"

"Well, no. And we spoke about the possibility that I might have contracted some sort of short-term bug or something, but the doctors have all but ruled that out."

Jan nodded.

"And I don't have any cardiac problems or brain tumors, thank God, according to the tests I've had. The paramedics reported that my blood pressure dropped dangerously low, which concerns me, of course. So I'm back to square one, with no clue what happened or why."

Jan sat back in her chair, working to put all the pieces from that morning together. Trouble was, just like Clara's medical history—or lack thereof—there weren't many pieces to work with. She loved solving puzzles, but first there had to be something to solve. From where they sat, she didn't see much of anything.

It seemed she would just have to look closer.

Clara shrugged her shoulders. "They've given me a cortisone shot, and I'm feeling a little better now. And they're setting me up with an epinephrine pen prescription when I check out, which they said should be in just a few hours. I'll make sure to pick one up before I leave town."

"Will you be on your way soon?" Rose asked.

"No, I planned to stay a few days and the doctor told me to take it easy for a while. The town is beautiful with all its Christmas lights. And it looks like it may snow anyhow. As long as the doctor says I'm okay, I don't see any reason not to enjoy a long weekend here as I'd initially set out to do."

"Well, I'm sure you aren't eager to visit us again," Rose said quietly. "But I know Jan would agree when I say that you're welcome back at the tearoom any time."

"Absolutely," Jan agreed, giving Rose a nod. "And anything you'd like is on the house."

"Except white maple brownies," Rose said, quickly covering her mouth at her own awkward joke.

"Yes, that's probably best," Clara agreed quietly. "At least until we figure out what caused me to pass out." She stared down at her hands, her fingers moving nervously over the blanket.

"Your full recovery is all that matters now, Miss Hill," Jan said, meaning every word.

Jan turned to Rose, whose features had relaxed considerably after hearing that Clara was doing okay and that she didn't seem to blame anyone at Tea for Two for her troubles.

Unfortunately, Jan couldn't rest as easily. Whether or not Miss Hill chose to write a review, word still traveled fast in a small town like Lancaster, and it wouldn't take long for locals and tourists alike to hear about the food critic's adverse reaction, possibly linked to a handmade treat from their tearoom.

Their business and, more importantly, their reputations, were still at risk.

Jan's mouth went dry. It was her and Elaine's livelihood, and Rose's too. They still needed to get to the bottom of this and reassure folks that their tea and food did not pose any danger to the community.

The room had grown quiet.

"We should probably be going," she said to Rose, standing up and slipping her purse strap over her shoulder. "I'm sure Miss Hill would like to get a little rest."

Rose took the cue and stood as well, giving Clara one last smile before walking to the door. Jan made a mental note to be extra encouraging to Rose over the next few weeks as they baked together. She had a strong feeling it would take some time to build the young woman's confidence back up.

As the two women were exiting the hospital, they ran into River White.

"River!" Jan called, walking toward him. The thirty-something reporter was hovering near the nurse's desk and his face blanched when he spotted her. "What are you doing here?"

He set his shoulders back, taking a little too long to answer such a simple question.

Jan tried to resist becoming annoyed at his presence in the hospital, suspiciously close to Clara's room after the incident earlier, but it was an awfully difficult feat.

"Just came in for a quick check," he said, looking completely normal to her. "After I had tea this morning at your shop, I felt a little queasy."

It was Jan's turn to look surprised, and then her heart sank. "Oh no. I'm terribly sorry to hear that. Do you think it might be the same thing that caused Clara to get sick?" Having a very popular food critic ill, possibly at their hands, was bad enough. It had never occurred to her that things might get worse, but if River had symptoms, that could mean other customers might as well.

Oh no, this is just awful, she thought, mentally making a list of all the people who'd stopped in for tea and breakfast that morning. She felt fine, and Rose and Elaine hadn't complained of any stomach troubles. Then again, they'd only had oolong tea…

"Can't say for sure, but I may not be the only one who was feeling a little off when I left," River continued. "Though, as far as I know, no one got as sick as Clara from the *Pelican*."

Jan placed a hand on the counter of the nurse's desk, to steady herself. Rose reached out to grasp her elbow.

"Jan, are you all right?"

"Yes, yes, I'm fine," she assured Rose.

She asked River if he could recall anyone else feeling ill, but he seemed suddenly preoccupied with the camera that hung perpetually around his neck.

"I don't really remember," he said.

Jan doubted that was entirely true, but she wasn't going to force him to share. She couldn't even be sure that he was really there to get a physical; it was just as likely he'd followed the ambulance to chase a story…one she wasn't keen on seeing in the *Courier* the next day.

The best she could do was try to get him to pass on the information, and to do the same herself. "Well, River, if you do remember anything, I'd encourage you to let the police know. Trooper Benson is on the case; I imagine you've got his number." Elaine had texted her the update while they'd been waiting to see Clara.

River nodded, but didn't agree to anything.

Jan was beginning to feel a little queasy herself, but it had nothing to do with tea or white maple brownies.

CHAPTER FOUR

A date with Nathan.

Elaine closed her eyes and pressed her fingers into her lids before opening them again. She opened the front door and stopped to hang her coat up, then, noticing that her apron was still on, untied the strings at her back and removed it.

It seemed like such a simple thing—dinner with a friend. Normally, the idea would not have given her pause, but this time Nathan had said there was *something important* he wanted to talk to her about, and she had a feeling what that something might be.

She really enjoyed Nathan's company. He loved the Lord, was kind, was a good listener, and he made her laugh, but was she ready for anything beyond the friendship they'd shared since childhood? Elaine had a strong sense he would want to speak with her about that very thing when they dined together. In her heart, she knew that he'd begun to see their relationship in a different light, but she was afraid he'd bounded down the path ahead of her, and she would need time to catch up.

It was so difficult to know the right answer, if there was such a thing. Any other morning, she would have spent the hours working and imagining their upcoming dinner, pondering what she would like to say should he bring up the future of their relationship. Unfortunately, on this particular day, things were far too chaotic to think about much of anything apart from the terrible morning incident.

So her personal life would just have to wait, Elaine thought, making her way up the house's old wooden stairs. Despite everything, she grinned at the way the floorboards creaked beneath her footsteps, comforted by their age and durability. The weathered planks were a reminder of a phrase her grandmother liked to offer up in difficult times: *This too shall pass.*

Elaine knew the saying to be true, and she trusted that God would give her and her cousin the courage and strength required to face whatever happened from there on out. She and Jan would do everything they could to see Clara Hill back to health, and if the food critic's illness tarnished their tearoom's reputation, they would find a way to recover...somehow.

That was one of the beautiful things about aging: with the passage of time came a certain peace she'd never experienced as a younger woman. It was only with the steady movement of the calendar, experience, and increased growth in her relationship with God that Elaine had fully learned to trust His plan, to listen carefully for the still, small voice she knew would speak if only she had the courage to ask, and the patience to wait for an answer.

In her bedroom, Elaine changed from her work clothes into a fresh sweater set in a soft shade of blue, not unlike the hue of the sky over the lake on spring mornings. Then she completed the outfit with a pair of navy slacks, ran a brush through her windblown hair, and dabbed on a little lipstick, hoping the effort would soften any visible signs of the stress she still felt, and likely would continue to experience until she got word that Clara was okay.

For the time being, she needed to get out of the house and get some fresh air before she jumped out of her skin. The breakfast things left out in the kitchen and parlors would save until later in the afternoon, when Elaine hoped she'd have some good news that might make her feel a little better. If she hadn't heard from the police lab by then, she would throw herself into tidying up.

After a quick last glance in the mirror, Elaine headed back downstairs and grabbed her coat and purse. She had no destination in mind—just the hope that a drive would help clear her head. Only then could she start the process of going over each moment of that morning, right down to even the tiniest of details, to find out what happened to their poor customer, and to clear the tearoom's name.

A PLEASANT-SOUNDING BELL jingled a soft tune when Elaine opened the door of her favorite antique shop, Oldies But Goodies.

"Hello there!" called out Fiona Latimore, the shop's owner, as she walked over to greet Elaine.

"Good morning, Fiona," Elaine answered. "How are you?"

Fiona smiled. A single woman in her early sixties, she had opened the store two decades ago, following a long, successful career as a traveling photojournalist. Fiona had seen much of the world, and collected a menagerie of treasures, as well as several brilliant antique-finding contacts, along the way. Her store specialized in unique pieces from around the globe, chosen more for their beauty and stories than for their monetary value. One never knew what could be found among the shelves, and it was always such fun to wander through the stock and breathe in the scents of exotic spices, various kinds of worn wood, and the pages of books printed in many languages.

"Business is good and I'm well," Fiona replied, wiping her hands on a dusty red-and-white-checkered apron. "And you? How's the tearoom?"

Elaine did her best to smile, not wanting the other woman to worry. She knew word would get around town soon enough, but Fiona was a regular customer of the tearoom and, more importantly, a friend, and Elaine didn't want to burden her with the events of that morning. Neither would she lie, so Elaine chose to answer only one of the questions Fiona had asked.

"I'm doing pretty well," Elaine responded.

Fiona's smile lit up her pretty brown eyes. She had long hair, brown tinseled with gray here and there, twisted into a bun at the base of her neck. Her skin was weathered in a not unpleasant way, speaking to Fiona's years of travel under the sun.

"Is there anything in particular you're looking for this morning?" Fiona asked, pushing a strand of loose hair back into her bun. "I've just been marking up some new items in between attempting to keep the dust bunnies from multiplying and taking over the place. It's an uphill battle, as I'm sure you know."

Elaine laughed, glad for a little humor. "Yes, curio cabinets are especially good at housing the pesky creatures, aren't they?"

Fiona grinned and swept an arm over the store. "That they are. And, as you can see, I'm surrounded by those very things."

The two women giggled.

"Well, I'll get back to work and let you browse," Fiona said, turning to leave. "Be sure to let me know if I can help with anything."

Elaine opened her mouth to speak, then paused. Just before Fiona walked away, she said, "Actually, there is one thing I'd like to ask you about."

"Absolutely," Fiona said, shifting back to face Elaine.

Elaine hesitated, still unsure if saying anything about Clara Hill passing out at the tearoom was the right thing to do. She hadn't consulted with Jan about it yet, and, until the police were able to run their tests and Clara recovered at the hospital, there really wasn't too much to say. But after a few seconds, she decided it was probably best to tell a friend and patron of the shop before anyone else heard from the customers who'd been there that morning. It was a small town and people would talk, even if they didn't mean any harm, so it might help if she went ahead and said something about it before rumors got out of hand. She would tell her cousin, and Elaine was sure Jan would understand.

"You see," she started, nervously folding her fingers into her purse straps, "something happened at the shop this morning…something bad, and, well, I was wondering if you'd yet heard anything about it."

Fiona's eyes softened, tiny crinkles forming at their corners. "I did hear something, but not directly."

Elaine's eyebrows rose. "Oh?"

Fiona shoved the dusting cloth she'd been holding into a front pocket of her apron. "There was a couple in here browsing this morning, a little after breakfast time—a man and woman who looked about midthirties or so, and I suppose they seemed a little"—she seemed to be searching for the right word—"out of place."

Elaine stopped fiddling with her purse and folded her hands in front of her, listening intently.

"We get tourists in Lancaster all the time, but there was something different about them."

"What do you mean?" Elaine asked.

Fiona tilted her head. "They were dressed very formally, for one thing; the woman was wearing a fancy skirt suit, probably designer of some sort, though I wouldn't know the name, and the man was equally formally dressed. It was as if they were about to attend a very important business meeting." Fiona held out a hand. "I certainly don't mean any of that to be judgmental, just that it's not the sort of dress you'd expect from people out browsing for antiques."

Elaine nodded. Fiona's description rang a bell in her memory that she couldn't quite place.

"And I wasn't eavesdropping, but they were talking fairly loudly about their breakfast as though they wanted to be overheard."

There was a sinking feeling in Elaine's stomach as Fiona continued to talk.

"The man mentioned that someone had been sick and had to be taken by ambulance to MaineGeneral, and the woman was speculating as to what might have happened. I believe she even said the person was possibly poisoned."

Elaine pulled in a deep breath.

"I recall thinking it was an odd conversation to have while shopping, but I didn't think much of it. After all, people do get food poisoning sometimes, and I didn't want to ask them to elaborate further. To be honest, they both made me a little uncomfortable, though I couldn't put my finger on why, and I was sort of hoping they'd finish their shopping and move along."

"Did they say where they'd eaten breakfast?" Elaine asked quietly, not looking forward to the answer.

Fiona's eyes dropped to the floor.

"It's okay, Fiona. I already know."

"They did. They said they'd eaten at your tearoom and that someone—a woman—had been poisoned."

Fiona looked ashamed, so Elaine reached out and squeezed the woman's shoulder, not knowing what to say.

"I didn't want to worry you, Elaine. I love the tearoom and I know you and Jan would never allow anything bad to happen to a customer. I was certain what they were saying was just a silly story. They seemed to want attention, so I didn't put any merit into what they'd said."

"That's very kind of you, Fiona, but unfortunately"—Elaine swallowed before meeting her friend's eyes—"at least part of what they're saying is true."

Fiona brought a hand to her mouth. "Oh no." She moved a few steps closer, wringing her hands. "I'm so sorry, Elaine. Is there anything I can do? Will things be all right?"

Despite fresh unease at the news spreading about the tearoom, Elaine felt her features soften over Fiona's display of kindness. "I believe so, eventually. At least, I hope they will. I'd like to clear things up a little though."

"Of course," Fiona said.

"The couple that you mentioned sounds familiar and I'm fairly certain that they did have breakfast at Tea for Two this morning, or at least they had tea. I only caught their first names, Irene and Scott, and that they are from out of town, but I don't know what brought them to Lancaster. So they were there when another customer, a food journalist, became ill."

Fiona's forehead was creased in concentration.

"The main thing is, we don't know much at this point. Miss Hill, the journalist, was taken to the hospital…that part is correct. But it's not yet clear what made her sick, and I'm sad to hear that conclusions have already been drawn that are not based on any fact."

Fiona shook her head. "I wouldn't put too much stock in what the couple said in here. There were only one or two other customers at the time and they were with me; I was showing them a model train set I picked up in Germany years ago. But if I hear anything else, I'll be sure to let you know."

Elaine nodded, trying to take Fiona's soothing words to heart. It wasn't easy. "I'm just concerned that people will think it was something we did—Jan, Rose, and I—but we would never knowingly serve something that might cause a customer to become ill."

"The locals know that, Elaine. We all love Tea for Two and want to see it succeed."

"Thank you. That means a lot."

Fiona smiled. "It's just the truth."

Elaine set her shoulders back and glanced around the shop, remembering why she'd come in the first place. Christmas was just around the corner and she hadn't yet found the right thing for Jan. Her cousin had many interests and was easy to shop for, but this year Elaine wanted to give her something special as a thank-you for the time they'd spent together getting Tea for Two up and running, for her hard work, and for bringing her such comfort in the wake of Ben's passing.

"If you don't mind, Fiona, I'd like to look around for a bit."

"By all means, take your time. If you get a chance, take a look at the new tea collection over there with the other porcelain. There's something over there I think you'll enjoy, and I know you'll find it without me even pointing it out." Fiona winked.

Elaine couldn't help but feel a little giddy at the mention of a new treasure. "That will just make it more fun to look," she said, rubbing her hands together as she set off in the direction Fiona had pointed.

The shop owner had been correct. Only a minute after she arrived at the shelf, she spotted it: a beautiful Meissen pink rose sugar bowl. A little gasp escaped her throat as she reached out to run her fingers along the finely glazed glass. The bowl was bright white, with roses the color of cherry blossoms, a gauzy shade somewhere between cream and pink. Tiny jade-colored leaves branched out from each bud and flower, all in different sizes, and the icing on the cake was the handle—a gently sculpted rose rising out of the top of the bowl's lid.

The piece was far too delicate to actually use, but Elaine knew it would look wonderful in the parlor, in the cabinet they kept full of pretty things just for customers to enjoy looking at while they waited for their tea. And she knew instantly that it was just the thing for Jan. Her cousin would love it.

But something's missing, she thought, searching the shelves for the sugar bowl's mate.

"Fiona?" she called over her shoulder.

"Yes?" Fiona answered, quickly making her way over.

"Does this sugar bowl have a matching creamer?"

Fiona studied the bowl still sitting on the shelf, as Elaine didn't want to risk picking it up just yet. "It does."

"Oh, that's good to hear. I'll take the set," Elaine said, excited.

Fiona's face fell. "It does have a matching creamer," she said softly, as though choosing each word carefully, "but I'm not in possession of one."

"Oh," Elaine said, her shoulders drooping. She'd so looked forward to wrapping up the gifts for Jan. The sugar bowl was pricey, but it would be worth it to see her cousin's face when she opened her Christmas gift. "Oh, I see."

Fiona made a soft noise. "Don't get too disappointed just yet, Elaine. I'm sure if you give me a little time, I can find one for you."

Elaine perked up. "It's a lot to ask, but would it be possible to have one in by Christmas Eve?"

Fiona bit her lower lip, considering. "It'll be close, but I think I might be able to. I won't make you a promise I can't keep, but I'll do my very best."

"That would be just wonderful, Fiona," Elaine said. "Thank you so much."

Fiona offered an encouraging smile. "After the morning you've had, it's the least I can do for a friend."

Elaine was about to ask Fiona to set the sugar bowl aside for her when her phone buzzed from inside her purse. Taking a deep breath, she fished it out and saw Jan's name on the screen. Then she signaled her departure to Fiona as she answered the phone, equal parts eager and wary to see what news the call might bring.

CHAPTER FIVE

On their way home from visiting Clara in the hospital, Jan and Rose stopped at Daniel Benson's home to give their statements.

Jan glanced over at Rose as she turned into Trooper Benson's driveway. "Are you okay to do this?" she asked. "We can wait until tomorrow if you'd rather."

Rose shook her head, loosening a few strands of hair from her long braid. "No," she responded resolutely. "I think I'd rather get it out of the way."

Jan nodded in agreement, keeping her eyes straight ahead as she pulled her blue Camry into the drive. She'd called Elaine to give her an update before leaving the hospital, knowing she'd be worried about Clara. "I feel the same way. Even though we don't know anything, I think I'll feel a little better once we've talked it through with a law enforcement officer, and there may be something important that we didn't notice because we were all working."

"That's true," Rose answered. "I hadn't thought of that. Also, maybe going through the story again out loud will spark a memory."

"You just do the best you can—that's all anyone can ask."

Jan parked the Toyota and turned to Rose, who gave her a half smile.

"It will be okay," Jan said. "There's nothing to be afraid of. All you have to do is tell them the truth. Everything else will sort itself out in due time."

"That's easy enough. I just wish I knew what happened to poor Clara. I wish there was some way to help."

Jan pulled in a breath. "I know exactly what you mean. Yes, it's terrible that something happened to her at Tea for Two, and yes, it could harm the business once word gets out, but none of that compares to how badly I feel about what happened to Clara."

"At least we know she's in good hands, and she'll be okay within a couple of hours."

After asking Clara if it was all right to share, Dr. Ross at the hospital had reassured Rose and Jan more times than Jan could count that the patient would most likely make a full recovery. It did little to calm Jan's nerves, but she was very glad the journalist would not suffer any real harm. Clara felt better, although still very concerned about what had caused her reaction. That's why Jan wasn't ready to give up yet. She had to know what had happened in order to make sure that it never happened again to another customer.

They wouldn't reopen until they were certain all of their goods were safe. The tearoom was Jan's livelihood and she needed it, but, more importantly, it was her home. She couldn't stand to think about what might happen if they had to shut down for very long, or if people started to think their food and drinks could be toxic.

"Now it's my turn to ask," Rose said, chuckling softly. "Are you okay?"

"Yes," Jan said. "I will be." She unbuckled her seat belt and Rose did the same. "Come on, let's go inside. It's no use sitting out here worrying all day."

The words of comfort were as much for herself as they were for Rose. It would do Jan good to think about one of her favorite Bible verses of all time: "Be anxious for nothing, but in everything by prayer and supplication, with thanksgiving, let your requests be made known to God; and the peace of God, which surpasses all understanding, will guard your hearts and minds through Jesus Christ."

"All right," Rose said. "In we go."

The two women were welcomed into Trooper Benson's home by his wife, Charlotte, a kind woman with lively green eyes and chocolate-colored hair. Once they'd moved beyond the greetings and their reason for being there, Charlotte offered hot chocolate to Jan and Rose. They happily accepted, and their hostess led them to a comfortable dining room.

A few toys were strewn along the hallway; it made Jan smile to see Charlotte casually kick them out of the way as she walked, reminding Jan of her kids' homes full of her grandchildren's favorite dolls, trucks, and action figures. She made a note to call Brian, Amy, and Tara when things calmed down at the tearoom. She needed to speak with them about finalizing Christmas plans anyway, and it would do her good to hear their voices.

Charlotte got Jan and Rose settled at the table and came back a few moments later carrying steaming mugs of thick, sweet cocoa topped generously with whipped cream.

"Give me just a minute and I'll get Daniel. He's in his office, but I thought you two would be more comfortable in here." Charlotte giggled. "It's a mess in there. I keep trying to sneak in there to tidy things up, but he likes things in disarray for reasons I can't fathom. I couldn't find anything in there if my life depended on it, but my husband assures me there's organization to that chaos."

Jan and Rose laughed as Charlotte hurried off back down the hallway.

"I know the feeling," Jan said. "When I finally decided to sell the house where Peter and I had lived for so many wonderful years, I couldn't believe how much stuff we'd accumulated. I suppose that's just what happens when you live in one place for a long time, but I wouldn't have it any other way."

Rose's eyes softened at the mention of Jan's late husband, then they both quietly sipped at their drinks. The hot chocolate was delicious, and it really helped to put Jan in the mood for Christmas, which was her favorite time of year. She couldn't wait for Elaine to see the surprise she'd been planning. If they could just get past that morning's incident, and find a way to prove to their community that the tearoom was a trustworthy establishment despite the setback, she knew the Christmas celebration would be extra special this year.

"Thank you, ladies, for coming by."

Jan and Rose turned from their beverages at the same time to find Trooper Benson standing in the doorway, Charlotte at his side.

"Is there anything else I can get you before you get started?"

"No, thank you," Jan said. "Again, we're sorry about the intrusion."

"Oh, it's no problem at all," Charlotte reassured them. "It was so nice to see you both."

"Same to you," Rose said, smiling.

"Stop by sometime, Charlotte, and we'll serve you breakfast—on the house of course," Jan added.

Charlotte beamed and left the room as Trooper Benson pulled out a chair to join the two women at the table. "I'm glad you came by," he said. "It would have been perfectly okay for you to wait until it was more convenient for you to drive out to the office, but, in my experience, it's best if people have a chance to give statements as close to the incident as possible. Keeps things fresh in your mind."

"We just want to help figure out what happened. As you might imagine, we're worried about what our regular customers might think," Jan said.

Daniel nodded. "We'll do all we can to clear this up as quickly as possible, starting with a toxicology screen."

Though they'd done nothing wrong intentionally, the phrase made Jan a little nervous. What if some toxic substance had somehow gotten into one of their teas, or into some of the ingredients for the baked goods? She, Elaine, and Rose were always so careful to keep their stock up to date, doing weekly and monthly inventory just to check that everything was fresh. Was it possible they'd missed something and unintentionally allowed a product to spoil, causing Clara to become sick?

Surely not. Oh, but she hoped not.

"Now, we'll just go over the basics, since you've both had a little time to process what happened and to recover a bit from the initial shock."

"All right," Rose said, with a nod.

Jan reached over and briefly patted the young woman's hand, hoping to offer some encouragement, however minimal. She feared Rose blamed herself, but the truth was, if something of theirs had caused Clara's illness, she and Elaine were responsible.

"Do either of you remember any of the baked good ingredients smelling odd or looking strange? As in, possibly contaminated?"

Rose and Jan shook their heads simultaneously. "No, not at all," Rose said.

Jan relayed their process of going through their stock on a regular basis. "I'd be happy to provide the documents we keep when we take inventory, if that would help."

Daniel wrote something in a pocket-size notebook with a stubby pencil. "Yes, that would be great."

"Of course," Jan said. "I'll get that to you as soon as possible."

"There's no rush," Daniel said, his voice low and calm. "No one's pressing any charges and we don't have any suspects at this time. We're in the same position as you are—we just want to make sure everybody's safe, including you, and to rule out any criminal intent."

Jan swallowed. She and Elaine had lent a hand in solving a few local mysteries since they'd moved back to Lancaster, but the personal stakes were so high now. It was unnerving to say the least.

Trooper Benson asked several more questions about their morning routine, a rundown of the list of customers, and the various food items and teas they'd used to prepare breakfast that day. Even though Jan knew he was just doing his job—very kindly at that—and as much as she and Rose wanted to help, it was an exhausting procedure. By the time he reached his last question, she was ready to be doing something else, and she could tell from the fatigue on Rose's face that the younger woman was experiencing some of the same emotions.

Daniel closed his notebook and shoved it back into a pocket. "One last question, and then I'll let you ladies get on with your day."

Rose let go an audible sigh of relief.

"I can't imagine that there would be, of course, but can either of you think of anyone who might want to harm you, your business, or Clara Hill?"

It shouldn't have, but the question surprised Jan a little. She and the other two women had no enemies that she could think of. It was hard to envision anyone in Lancaster having the goal of bringing malice to their tearoom, to them personally, or to Clara, though of course they didn't know her well.

Now that the considered it though, something did tickle at the back of her mind. She wasn't sure if anything would come of it, but she decided to try to voice her thoughts anyway.

"I don't know if this is related in any way, but Clara Hill's reason for being at Tea for Two this morning was to write a review for her paper. She's well known and well respected as a food critic and, well, I guess it's possible someone may not have wanted her to write about us." Jan shrugged. "I really don't know if that's relevant or not, but I thought you should have that information."

"Thank you for letting me know. Everything helps, and sometimes we don't know how the puzzle pieces will fit together, or even if they will at all, until they're all out on the table to be sorted."

He stood up from his chair and she and Rose followed suit.

"I certainly don't mean to rush you out of here, but I can imagine you'd like to get on with your day," Daniel said, waving an arm toward the dining room entrance.

He led them to the front door and thanked them again for their time before promising to keep them updated on any new developments in the case. Jan and Rose said they would do the same.

By the time they were back out to Jan's aging Camry, snowflakes were falling much faster and the temperature had noticeably dropped a few degrees.

"I'm sure you're ready to get home," Rose said as Jan opened the driver's side door and quickly got in. They buckled their seat belts and Jan made fast work of turning up the heat.

"Actually," Jan said, rubbing her hands together before removing her mittens, "If you don't mind, I'd like to stop at Sugar Plum and get us a little snack. My treat."

Rose's eyes widened and Jan was pleased to see that she looked a little less peaked. "I could go for some peanut butter fudge."

"We've definitely earned it today, haven't we?" Jan grinned, and when the window wipers had cleared off the thin layer of snow that had fallen during their interview, she pulled the car out of the drive and headed back toward Main Street.

"I JUST LOVE this store," Rose said, smiling as she and Jan strolled up and down the aisles at Sugar Plum.

"I do too," Jan agreed, nibbling her second piece of cinnamon fudge from its paper wrapping as they passed by the Victorian-themed Christmas tree. Sugar Plum had lots of different trees that the owner kept decorated in all sorts of styles. There was a country tree, a patriotic one, and lots more. The store sold anything and everything related to Jan's favorite season, but it wasn't any secret that one of the things she loved most about it was the selection of homemade fudge, fancy chocolates, and old-fashioned ribbon candy. Just the thing for a gloomy winter's day, especially when her snow forecast had been on the nose.

And she'd been right in thinking that a little retail therapy would help them manage the events of that morning. It wasn't her intention to minimize what had happened to Clara, but knowing that the food critic was feeling better and on the road to recovery had done a great deal to settle her mind. There was nothing more they could do at the hospital except get in the way, she and Rose had given their statements as best they could, and she'd touched base with Elaine.

With the tearoom closed indefinitely, there wasn't much she could do except mope around, and that just wouldn't do. It was good for Rose to have something to take her mind off the situation, and anyway, the two women both had some Christmas shopping left to do. Jan still hadn't found anything right for Elaine.

She had an idea.

"What do you think of heading next door to Oldies But Goodies to check things out?"

Rose swallowed the big bite of peanut butter fudge she'd been munching. "Sounds like a plan."

Deciding to leave the car since it was so close, they headed to the antique store, shielding their faces as the wind picked up and whipped against their coats.

"The weather's getting worse, so I promise we won't stay long," Jan said, having to raise her voice for Rose to hear. The younger woman nodded.

The inside of Oldies But Goodies was warm and welcome after the rush of cold air, and Jan took a deep breath, pulling in the delightful scents of cinnamon, cloves, and very old treasures. She glanced around for Fiona Latimore but, not seeing the owner, said hello to the girl running the shop. Jan tried jogging her memory but, though she'd seen her before, couldn't remember the young woman's name. She was a college student who helped Fiona during her breaks.

The girl, smiling sweetly, came over to join Jan and Rose. "Is there anything I can help you with today?" she asked. When she looked over at Rose, Jan swiftly checked her name tag, not wanting to appear rude. Yes, that was it—Bree.

Rose looked at Jan.

"I think we're just looking," Jan answered.

Bree gave them another kind smile. "Enjoy yourselves, and be sure to let me know if there's anything you need."

Jan and Rose thanked her and wandered off in separate directions—Rose toward the large collection of books, and Jan toward the glass and ceramics. She and Elaine didn't have any official plan, but it was sort of their unwritten rule to look at tea things whenever they had a chance, just in case they found something to add to their growing selection of serving items, or for lovely pieces to display in the parlors. Jan found it both comforting and challenging to keep an eye out for such objects wherever she went that stocked antiques. It had become quite an entertaining pastime since she'd started Tea for Two with Elaine.

She looked over the shelves, not seeing any new arrivals since she'd last visited the shop, until, suddenly, something out of the corner of her eye caught her attention.

She turned to spot a beautiful sugar bowl—a Meissen if her guess was correct. She picked it up and found it without flaw, admiring the dainty hand-painted soft-pink roses and the rose-shaped handle.

That was it! She'd found the perfect Christmas gift for Elaine. With Christmas just around the corner, it was a relief to know she'd be able to give her cousin something special, as a thank-you for asking Jan to go into business with her and for opening up the chance for a new chapter in her life. The sugar bowl was stunning. There was only one problem.

She put down the delicate piece and went in search of Bree. "Excuse me," she said, tapping the young woman on the shoulder to get her attention. "I don't mean to bother you."

"Oh no, it's no bother at all," Bree said, putting down the price tags and felt marker she'd been holding. "What can I do for you?"

"I found a lovely sugar bowl that I'd like to take home with me, but the thing is, I didn't see a matching creamer anywhere near. I'm wondering if you might have it in the back...?" Jan's voice sounded hopeful to her own ears and she realized even more how much she wanted to give the set to Elaine.

Bree bit her lip. "The Meissen?"

Jan nodded.

"I'm not sure. Give me just a moment and I'll check."

"Oh yes, of course."

Jan waited with anticipation and felt a little twinge of disappointment when Bree returned empty-handed.

"I'm so sorry," she said, "but it doesn't look like we have the set."

Jan tried not to look too let down, but evidently she was not successful.

"Oh, goodness," Bree said. "I'll tell you what. Let me run a search this afternoon and check in with Fiona when she gets back from her errands. I'm sure we can find what you're looking for. And, if we hurry, we may even be able to do so in time for Christmas."

"That would be wonderful," Jan said. "In the meantime, I'd like to go ahead and purchase the sugar bowl."

"Absolutely," Bree said, heading toward the cash register.

Jan couldn't help beaming as Rose came to join her.

She just knew Elaine would be thrilled with the set.

CHAPTER SIX

What began as a fairly gloomy day had turned into a beautiful winter's evening by the time Nathan arrived to pick up Elaine for their dinner. When she heard the crunch of his tires slowing to a halt, Elaine began winding a scarf around her neck.

"Nathan's here," she called out to Jan, who was preparing a grilled cheese sandwich to eat in front of the fireplace. Elaine had asked if her cousin would like to join them, but she wasn't surprised when Jan politely declined, saying she'd had a long couple of days and would like a quiet evening to rest at home.

In all honesty, though she did truly enjoy her old friend's company, Elaine would have preferred the same. She and Jan had spent the morning cleaning the basement, including all the small, narrow windows and the storage areas where they kept wood and canned goods. They both agreed over an afternoon cup of gingerbread tea that the work had helped to clear their heads and help them relax a little. A text from Clara letting the two of them know that she'd been released from the hospital, and felt much better, made things seem a little more like normal.

But it wasn't over yet. Elaine and Jan had both begun to have a growing hunch that whatever made Clara sick had not been an accident related to preparation or ingredients, but had been deliberate and intentional. Even Trooper Benson had suggested it was possible.

Elaine did her best to put all of that out of her mind so she could concentrate instead on the evening ahead of her. For their dinner, she'd chosen to wear an elegant but not too formal cream-colored sweater and a pair of black slacks, unsure of where Nathan was taking her.

Nathan rang the doorbell and gave Elaine a broad smile when she opened it to greet him. He came in and chatted with Jan for a few moments before leading Elaine out to his black Cadillac. He helped her into the vehicle. Tucked behind the front seats on the floor in the back, Elaine caught a glimpse of Nathan's gym bag and racquetball gear. Her friend liked to stay active, and Elaine grinned to herself, thinking about the fact that a person could tell what sport he'd gotten up to that day by the type of stuff he had back there. She would never call it junk...at least not in his presence.

They settled into the car and Nathan turned on the heated seats to warm them up, then they were off.

"Where are we going?" Elaine asked.

Nathan turned to her and grinned before shifting his eyes back to the powdery road ahead.

Streetlights glinted off the freshly fallen snow, casting little sparkles everywhere. Sometimes she thought she might prefer to live somewhere warm again, like any number of the tropical climates where she and Ben had resided temporarily, but on an evening like this, when the snow made everything so fresh and lovely looking, she was glad to call Lancaster her home.

"I thought we'd take a walk down by the marina and stop in at the art gallery before having dinner." He glanced over again quickly to check her expression. "If that sounds all right with you."

"Yes, that sounds nice," she said. She wouldn't say so out loud, but it actually sounded a bit romantic, which made her more nervous than she wanted to admit. She'd been thinking a lot about this evening, but now that it had arrived, she felt a bit like a schoolgirl, unsure of herself. In her heart, though, she still missed Ben—probably always would—and she just wasn't ready for a relationship to be anything more than friends. Surely Nathan would understand. She just hoped that if she was open with him, he wouldn't shy away from spending time with her. She would not like to lose the company of her dear old friend.

Nathan pulled to a stop outside the marina, got out of the car, and went over to open Elaine's door for her. He offered a hand to help her out.

The scene was magical.

It seemed that every year around this time, staff from the library and town office took a day away from their posts to decorate, and that year was no different. They'd strung lights everywhere—from plain, tiny white ones to some shaped like angels and wreaths—and the whole town twinkled delightfully. Even several docked boats shone with strings in various shades of color.

"It's so pretty," Elaine said.

"It is, isn't it?" Nathan agreed.

The two strolled down the sidewalk toward the art gallery, enjoying the peaceful evening. A few tourists milled about here and there, but, for the most part, things were calm. In the summer, when the weather turned warm again and the sky shifted from gray to the shade of a robin's egg, Lancaster would be booming with activity. But for now, Elaine was thankful for the serenity.

She and Nathan reached the art gallery and gazed in through the windows at the Christmas-themed displays, including a particular Norman Rockwell print that Elaine had always admired. She almost said something about it to Nathan just then, but did not. Knowing how generous her friend could be, the print might become her Christmas gift from him, and it would simply be too much.

She decided right then and there that, no matter how anxious it might make her, she would be completely honest if he asked her if she'd like to date him. It would do no good to have him thinking they could be more than friends if her heart wasn't in the right place.

Could it be, someday? She couldn't have answered that question without a caveat, but somewhere deep inside her heart she thought maybe it could be yes. Someday. But, looking out over the wide lake, all she could think was that she still missed Ben. So very much. She owed it to Nathan to be truthful about that.

"Hungry?" he asked.

"Very," Elaine answered, and Nathan held out an arm to lead her back past the marina.

He'd reserved a table at the Pine Tree Grill, not because of formality, but because the restaurant was usually so busy that, unless a person did so, there was no guarantee of finding an open seat.

Bianca Stadler, part owner of the grill with her brother, Mel, hurried over to greet Jan and Nathan. Bianca was a hoot. Elaine had rarely seen the fiftyish woman in any footwear other than her cowboy boots, and a person could tell if she was coming by the sound of her gold jangly bracelets. That night, her long brown hair was held back by a sparkly purple headband that caught light from the ceiling's fixtures.

"So glad to see you two," Bianca said, leading them to an empty table near a window that overlooked the lake. The three of them chatted happily for a good while—Bianca was an expert in the art of talking—then she took their orders, not needing to write them down, and promised she'd be right back.

Elaine was bursting to ask Nathan what he wanted to talk about, but she didn't want to push the subject, so she asked after his family instead, and then he did the same.

"I'm sure you miss them," Nathan said softly, his brown eyes full of warmth, "especially at this time of year."

Elaine took a sip of the water a busboy set in front of her. "Yes, I do. They're just so far away."

Nathan nodded sympathetically.

"Jared and Corinne are doing well, busy as ever with work and the two kiddos. Lucy just had a birthday and Micah's will be just after New Year's. And I keep trying to convince Sasha to move closer." She grinned. "It's not as though Colorado is the only place with snow, after all. We've got plenty around here."

"That's the truth," Nathan said, chuckling. "She doesn't want to move?"

Elaine shook her head, a little sadly. "Not at this time. And I wouldn't want her to if it would make her unhappy. She loves her job, and the gym where she works is popular with Olympic hopefuls, so I think she enjoys being around other people with similar goals. They have a common ground."

"That makes sense," Nathan said.

He and her daughter had some common interests, actually, in that they were both very athletic and loved to spend time outdoors. Nathan and Sasha would almost certainly get along well should they happen to spend much time together, if, for instance, Elaine and Nathan's friendship went further.

This thought, having come to the forefront, made her clear her throat.

"Nathan," she said, hesitantly, "yesterday when you invited me out to dinner, you mentioned that there was something you'd like to talk about."

The end of her statement came out as a question, and Nathan nodded *yes*.

"There is." He fiddled with his silverware bundle and Elaine could tell he was a little nervous.

It made her heart ache. The last thing she wanted was to wound a friend's feelings. She breathed a sigh of relief when their food came and they tucked into their meals, probably both glad for the respite from what was bound to be an uneasy conversation.

Elaine put all her concentration into thoroughly enjoying her mushroom and swiss burger, and Nathan made quick work of clearing his plate of the Reuben sandwich he'd ordered. But when they'd both swallowed the last of their fries, nothing else stood in the way.

"Elaine," he said quietly, "we've known each other for a very long time now."

She folded her napkin in her lap and tried very hard not to twist it into knots. "Yes, we have, since we were kids. I'm so glad we resumed our friendship when I moved back here."

"Me too." He nodded, then looked straight into her eyes. "And you know I truly enjoy your friendship and value your company."

"Likewise," she responded.

He gave her a warm smile and her heart melted ever so slightly.

"I don't want to dance around the subject, so I'll just get right down to it. The thing is, Elaine—while I wouldn't trade your friendship for anything…I'd really like it if it could be something more."

As much as she'd been ready for it, the admission still caused Elaine's breath to catch in her throat. She was quiet for several long seconds, carefully arranging the array of thoughts and emotions swirling around in her mind and heart.

"I think, Nathan, that I would like that too," she said, and paused before she added, "someday."

She caught a hint of disappointment in his expression before he composed his features. "I completely understand," he said, his voice betraying a touch of sadness.

Elaine gave him a soft smile. "I know we're not getting any younger, but I'm just…I'm not quite ready to move on yet."

Nathan nodded and genuine care shone in his eyes; Elaine was thankful for that beyond measure. They'd spoken about it, and had both survived. And, most importantly, their friendship would remain intact.

"That's absolutely, one hundred percent okay," Nathan said. "But if you change your mind, I'll be right here waiting."

Elaine's heart swelled with a mix of missing Ben and Nathan's kind heart opening up to her.

"You're worth the wait," he added.

CHAPTER SEVEN

I can't believe how close it is to Christmas," Jan said the next morning, folding her hands together in front of her.

Elaine stared at the cup of espresso in front of her, appearing lost in her thoughts.

"Earth to Elaine," Jan teased, leaning closer to her.

Elaine blinked and then looked up at her with a sheepish smile. "Oh my. You caught me daydreaming."

"I hope it was a good daydream."

Her smiled widened. "Well, more like an intriguing one. I was thinking about the day we found the sapphire ring."

Jan nodded, remembering the hustle and bustle surrounding the days after they'd bought the house, preparing to live together and open the tearoom. They'd had to do some renovations, and had been pleased with the work of their hired contractor, a local man named Bill Bridges. He'd showed them the sapphire ring, nestled in a lovely, carved rosewood box, that had been found behind a wall by the electrician, Roland Nance.

"That was our first mystery here," Jan reminded her. "And one we haven't solved yet."

"Well, here's what we do know," Elaine began, ticking the clues off with her fingers. "The ring was attached to a string at one time, likely hanging inside the wall from a flue cover placed over an old stove pipe hole."

Jan smiled. "That's when Bill gave us an education about old chimneys and flue covers and how they used to heat houses like this before there were furnaces to keep us warm."

Elaine nodded. "And we're still learning things about this wonderful old house. You know, I loved traveling around the world with Ben during his years in the military. It was a great opportunity to meet new people and learn about different cultures. But I didn't realize there was so much to learn right here at Chickadee Lake."

Jan smiled at her cousin, aware that Elaine's memories of her late husband gave her solace in the rare moment when she missed him most.

Elaine took a sip of her coffee, a curious gleam in her eyes. "I keep thinking of that carved rosewood box with the crest and the motto that was etched inside it in Morse code and Latin—the same crest on the flue cover after the wallpaper was scraped off."

"For love and blood," Jan said, reciting the words that Bob had helped her translate.

More digging had revealed that both crest and motto belonged to the rich and influential Wood family who had settled in the Lancaster area in the late 1700s and owned a woolen mill nearby.

They'd also learned that the sapphire was natural and somewhat rare, making it quite valuable. Given the age of the setting, they assumed that the ring had been behind the wall about seventy years.

But they still didn't know how it got there.

Jan took a sip of her tea, noticing that Elaine had gone quiet again. She wondered if it had anything to do with her outing with Nathan last evening, but didn't want to push for a reason. So instead she suggested that they pull their Christmas supplies out of the craft room, and see what they had to work with. Since they now shared a living space, it only made sense to think about consolidating all of their personal decorations and to cull out anything they didn't need to give to charity.

"We probably should have done this sooner," Elaine said. "The time's gotten away from me this year and now Christmas is just around the corner."

ALREADY ALMOST THE second week of December, it was past time to add some Christmas cheer to the upstairs. A week ago, Bob and Nathan had strung up some outdoor lights for customers to enjoy, and Rose had helped to hang twinkle light strings and decorate the parlors, but the two women hadn't yet had a chance to deck out their personal living space. Neither Jan nor Elaine was accustomed to waiting so long to put up a tree or holly, as they shared a deep love for everything about the Christmas season, but with business going well, decorating had simply fallen by the wayside. Jan was excited to pull out what they had and start transforming the Victorian house into a winter wonderland, and she hoped that doing so might cheer up Elaine.

"Elaine?" she asked.

"*Hmm?*" Elaine mumbled, her attention occupied by a box of glass jewel-toned ornaments.

Jan set down the wreath she'd picked up to examine for damage. "Is there something bothering you?"

Elaine turned to face her. "Me?"

Jan nodded, catching a glimpse of something shadowy at the back of her cousin's eyes.

"Oh no, no. I'm fine."

Jan felt her eyes narrow in doubt.

"Really, I am," Elaine reassured. "I'm still a little shaken up about Clara, but I'll be okay in due time."

"All right. But promise that if you need to talk about it, you'll let me know," Jan offered.

"I will."

"Good," Jan said. "I'll feel better too once we've heard back from Trooper Benson regarding that tox screen."

"Me too," Elaine agreed. "Somehow, even though Clara is doing better and she's out of the hospital, I can't stop thinking about what Trooper Benson said to you—that somebody may have hurt her intentionally. Could it be possible someone was trying to make it look like *we* were the masterminds behind their plan?"

"I've been thinking that exact same thing," Jan said, "though the idea is just ridiculous. Why would we want to hurt anyone who came into our tearoom?"

"We wouldn't," Elaine said. "And, besides, I don't know about you, but I've never been the mastermind behind anything nefarious."

Jan laughed, and when she looked over, Elaine's eyes were smiling, and she was glad to hear her cousin make a joke. They both went back to rifling through the craft room and Jan found the box she'd been looking for. She opened it and pulled out an angel tree topper, holding it up to admire. The angel held such sentimental value, having graced the top of the tree in her home each Christmas for over three decades.

Looking at it that moment brought back so many memories. She'd bought it when she and Peter first got married. A young wife with hardly any money to spare, she'd been unable to resist purchasing it for a dollar at a yard sale in the neighborhood she and her then-new husband had just moved into. The angel was still lovely, with wings of finely woven gold-colored lace and a ceramic face, the eyes, lips, nose, and rosy cheeks hand-painted with obvious care.

It touched her heart to see such a reminder of so many happy Christmases with her family, and she thought of the plan she'd hatched, months ago, to surprise Elaine by inviting all of her cousin's family members for Christmas Day. Jan had spent a great deal of time organizing for Sasha and Jared to travel from Colorado and Ohio. Jared was bringing his wife, Corrie, and his kids, Lucy and Micah, and Jan knew that Elaine would be thrilled to see their kids and grandkids all at one time, and to have the rare opportunity to spend the holiday with them.

Jan said a silent prayer then, thanking the Lord that all of her children still lived in Maine and she could see them regularly. It truly was a blessing to have so many family members close by, and she wanted to gift Elaine with that feeling.

Just then, Rose appeared in the doorway. As she didn't usually come upstairs into the cousins' private living area, she knocked tentatively on the door frame. "I think I've got everything we need on this list for you," she said, holding up a slim piece of paper. "Trooper Benson sure did take a lot of our inventory, so the list is long."

"That's not a problem," Jan said, noticing that Rose's face was a little pale. She hoped the young woman was not still blaming herself for what happened to Clara. "It was to be expected. He had to take almost everything we touched that morning, just in case. Besides, it's not as though there is much to be done around here until we're given the okay to open up again."

Rose handed the list to Jan, then hid a yawn behind her hand.

Jan gave her a pat on the shoulder and a soft smile. "We've got everything under control here, Rose. Why don't you go on home early?"

"Are you sure?" Rose asked.

Jan nodded. "Yes, of course. Have lunch with your dad. Do something fun this afternoon, and just rest and relax. It'll do you some good."

"That sounds wonderful," Rose said with a smile. "Thank you. I'll see you both on Monday."

"Enjoy your afternoon," Elaine said, waving.

When Rose left the room, Jan and Elaine tidied up the boxes.

"This will have to wait," Elaine said, sighing. Jan could tell her cousin was disappointed about not having their private quarters of the house looking seasonal yet, but the list Rose had made was indeed long, and it would take the two women most of the afternoon to pick up all the items on it.

They went to their rooms and changed out of their dusty clothes before donning coats, gloves, and scarves and heading out to the car. It looked like only a few flakes of additional snow had fallen overnight, so the drive would not need to be shoveled again. *Thank goodness for small mercies*, Jan thought as she slid into the driver's seat of her Camry. It made more sense to take her older car out to the dairy, the first stop on their list of errands. Jan didn't want Elaine's new Malibu suffering any damage on the rural road.

As she drove, a few rays of sun slid halfheartedly through the clouds, adding a hint of brightness to an otherwise gray day.

"I stopped at Oldies But Goodies yesterday with Rose," Jan said.

"Did you find anything interesting?"

Jan swallowed, thinking of how to answer the question without giving away her sugar bowl discovery.

"We were just browsing," she said. "Mostly, I wanted to take our minds off of yesterday morning."

"Ah, I see," Elaine said. "It's funny—I had the same idea and stopped there myself yesterday. Fiona said something interesting to me while I was there."

Jan glanced over at her cousin just as Elaine's brows knit. "Oh?"

"I asked her if she'd heard anything about what happened at Tea for Two. I wanted to find out if any word had spread around town by then, and she mentioned that a couple in their midthirties had stopped in, and were making something of a show of talking about how a customer had fallen ill while they were having breakfast at the tearoom."

Jan kept her eyes on the road as her hands tightened on the steering wheel. "Did she describe them? That sounds like the couple you mentioned that morning—the pair from out of town who weren't all that interested in making small talk."

"Yes, she did. Their names were Irene and Scott, and I don't know what their relationship is, but they didn't strike me as a married or dating couple. The way they talked to each other was more...formal. As if they were in business together."

"Didn't they order the green tea?" Jan asked.

"I believe so."

When Jan turned quickly to look at her cousin, Elaine had a finger to her lips, thinking.

"*Hmm.* So they didn't have the same thing that Clara had. She ordered the cinnamon spice tea, didn't she?"

"That's right," Jan answered, carefully steering the car off Main and on to the rural road leading to the Richardsons' property. She bit her lip in concentration as details flooded her mind. "And River also had the cinnamon spice tea, and a bite of a white maple brownie. Rose and I ran into him at the hospital when we went to visit with Clara—he mentioned that he'd felt queasy as well. Now whether that was true or an overactive imagination, I'm not sure. Or he might have been there sniffing out the story."

Elaine released a little puff of air. "That sounds like River, all right."

"So if River wasn't feeling well, and he and Clara had the same thing, it might have been something to do with the brownie or cinnamon spice tea."

It hadn't seemed obvious before—perhaps because of all the distracting commotion at the time—but now Jan could connect the maple brownie and cinnamon spice tea with River as well as Clara.

"I suppose so," Elaine said. "Did you see any other of our customers from that morning while you were at the hospital?"

Jan shook her head, concentrating on the road ahead. The plows hadn't made it out that far and the road to the dairy wasn't as clear as the ones in town. "No, I didn't."

"But," Elaine said, holding up a finger, "that doesn't necessarily mean much. If River said he only had a stomachache and he didn't have any more severe symptoms than that, we can't be sure that other customers didn't feel ill as well."

"If I felt queasy at a restaurant and saw someone else pass out," Jan said, following her cousin's train of thought, "I'd want to get checked out, just to be on the safe side."

"Me too," Elaine said. "And maybe some of our customers did just that, even if we haven't heard about it." She sighed. "But there's no need to worry ourselves over it too much. The toxicity report hasn't come back yet from the police lab, and until we know what it shows, we can't jump to any conclusions."

Jan nodded again, but she wasn't ready to let go of the idea just yet. Something seemed to have gone wrong with the cinnamon spice tea. Was it spoiled? Was there something in there that didn't agree with some folks' digestive systems? That seemed more likely than a problem with the maple brownies, but they couldn't rule anything out yet.

Especially when River and Clara had ordered and consumed the exact same tea and brownies, with very, very different reactions. There was a long distance between a simple tummy ache and passing out, and Jan needed to know what that was.

THE RICHARDSONS' DAIRY spanned dozens of acres, and the private road leading up to its entrance was banked on either side by rows of trees. During the spring and summer, they were breathtakingly beautiful—green and full of tiny white flowers, but in winter, they made for a stark appearance. As Jan drove down the slender road, she and Elaine watched the matchstick trunks pass outside the car windows, snow covering the ground more completely than it had in town. As they neared the main part of the property, Jan saw a red barn in the distance, adding a much-needed touch of color to the white-blanketed landscape.

When they pulled up to the house, Annie Richardson must have heard the car. She came out of the front door in the process of pulling on a thick parka, a purple scarf already wrapped around her neck. Jan smiled as she shifted into park and put on the parking brake, while Annie closed the door behind her.

Jan and Elaine got out and made their way to the porch as Annie waved.

"Hi there, Annie!" Jan called.

"So good to see you," Annie answered.

"We hope we didn't come at a bad time," Elaine said. She had used her cell phone to call on their way out, fairly certain that it would be okay to stop by, knowing that the Richardson family would be glad for the business at such a slow time of the year.

"Not at all," Annie said. "Gavin's on the phone with a feed salesman, so I'm all yours." Annie gave a broad smile. Despite the slightly weathered appearance that was par for the course with an outdoor job, Annie was very pretty. She had shoulder-length wavy auburn hair that always looked like it had gotten away from its owner, intent on doing its own thing. Annie had hazel eyes and her cheeks were always flushed from the pleasant but constant work of being a mom to three active young ones.

The three women shared small talk for a few moments before Annie led them out to the dairy, where there was a little shop with a walk-in refrigerator. "What all do you need today?" she asked, still wearing her outdoor jacket.

Jan glanced at Elaine. "It's probably best if we just hand you the list."

Annie smiled. "Business must be good, then?" she asked, taking the piece of paper. She ran a finger down to the section where Rose had written the amounts of eggs, butter, milk, cream, and half-and-half she estimated they'd need for the next two weeks or so at the tearoom. "Looks like eggs are popular."

"Baked goods are popular," Jan said, grinning.

"Ah yes," Annie said. "Your maple brownies are something special, that's for sure."

Jan felt the temperature rise in her cheeks. "Well, thank you."

"I'll just get this stuff together for you." Annie disappeared into the fridge, closing the door behind her.

Jan opened it a few seconds later. "We'll also take a couple gallons of chocolate milk, if you've got some," she said, poking her head into the chilly metal room. "It's a hit with kiddos."

Annie gave a thumbs-up.

"And plenty of big kids too," Jan added, grinning.

She shut the door and turned to chat with Elaine while they waited. Annie popped out from time to time to hand them several items, which they loaded into the cardboard boxes the Richardsons kept just outside the fridge. Soon they had all they needed and were just about to head out when Gavin entered.

"Hi, ladies. How are you two doing?" he asked, rubbing his hands together for warmth after being outside. "I could use a cup of coffee if you'd like to join us in the house. Would you care to catch up a little? We haven't seen you in forever, it seems, since Rose is usually the one to stop by." He looked at his wife.

"That sounds like a great idea, honey," Annie said. "I'll go make a fresh pot while you load up the car."

Gavin nodded and picked up several boxes at once. Elaine opened the door for him. "Car's unlocked," she called.

"That's very nice of him," Jan said.

Annie waved a hand. "It's nothing. The milking's finished for the morning and I'll make his lunch here soon. You came at a great time. I think it actually causes him pain to sit still for too long."

The three women laughed. She and Elaine could certainly relate. Peter had been a welder and had loved the constant busy work, and Ben, of course, had taken a lot of joy in traveling the world for his job. They knew what it was like to be married to men who couldn't slow down, but they wouldn't have traded them for the world.

Once Gavin had loaded their car, which, in that weather, would be plenty cold enough to keep their goods until they were done with their errands for the day, the four of them sat down for a quick cup of coffee. Jan didn't usually prefer the stronger beverage over tea, but she could tell from the way Elaine's face perked up that her cousin was enjoying "the hard stuff," as they'd jokingly called it since Jan's discovery a few months back that Elaine had a closet love for espresso.

"How are the kids?" Jan asked.

Annie swallowed a sip of coffee. "They're doing great."

Gavin nodded. "We're looking forward to their being out of school on Christmas break," he said, "I just hope we have enough to do to keep them occupied."

Annie smiled. "It will be a challenge to keep up the books with them home, but I'll enjoy the company. We've only got Dori here for a year and a half more, and I'm starting to miss her already."

Jan and Elaine nodded, both knowing what it was like when that first child moved away from home, and then the empty nest that followed closely behind.

Jan took a small sip of her drink, then added another splash of cream. "It's great when your kids spread their wings and go off to make their own way in the world, but it can be hard too," she said.

Annie nodded and Gavin touched a finger to his wife's hand. "It's really starting to become real," she said, a hint of wistfulness touching the words. "Dori's already been looking into colleges, and before long, I think she'll have her mind made up."

"Yeah," Gavin added. "She wants to go out of state, which we fully support, but the tuition won't come cheap. Dori started beekeeping last spring to raise money selling honey, but college is so expensive."

He and Annie shared a look.

"We even recently sold off an acre of land." She swallowed. "We weren't using it, but it felt like a big step all the same."

"It's been in the family for years," Gavin said. "But we agreed that it was the right thing to do. Dori's such a good kid. We want her to be able to fulfill her dreams."

"Well," Jan said softly, "she's certainly blessed to have two very supportive parents."

Elaine nodded her agreement, and Jan could tell she was thinking of asking the same question but had decided against it.

Annie went ahead and told them anyway. "I guess we should probably tell you this before you hear it from someone else."

The words, so similar to what Jan had been thinking about the incident with Clara recently, caught her attention.

Gavin cleared his throat as husband and wife shared a look. "We were approached by a company called Gram's Victorian...Tea Company." He looked down at the black liquid in his mug. "They want to open a tearoom on the land, and they gave us an offer we couldn't refuse, not in light of Dori's college plans."

Annie breathed out a sigh. "I don't think it will be too close in competition with your business," she said, glancing nervously between Jan and Elaine. "It's way out here, so not physically near your tearoom, and their shops have a little different feel to them."

Jan raised her eyebrows, curious, so Annie went on.

"They're a chain, for one thing. I've been to one on a trip I took to visit my parents a few months back. They're designed to replicate small-town, old-fashioned tea parlors, 'just like Gram's,' as the saying goes, but instead they come off a tad forced. I get the feeling they're trying a little too hard."

Elaine looked at Jan.

"I admit, the news is a little jarring, but it's nothing we can't handle," Jan said.

Elaine nodded her head. "A little competition might do us good," she added. "It'll keep us on our toes."

"So you're not upset?" Annie asked.

"No, of course not." Jan smiled. "We can't keep change from happening, and it would do no good to get in a tizzy over something like that. Besides, as you said, it's not on Main Street, and your farm is on the way out of town with not much around. It'll be somewhere people can stop as they're leaving Lancaster."

"I'm so relieved to hear you say that," Annie said. "I was going to call you and let you know, but then you said you were coming by."

"The question is," Jan said, "how do you feel about it? Will it bother you to have a public place so close to your property?"

"It's not ideal," Gavin said, "but it was something we felt we had to do."

"Maybe Gram's will give you some business as well," Elaine suggested with a hopeful note.

"I'm not so sure," Annie mused, gripping her coffee cup tightly. "It doesn't really seem like that kind of place."

"Oh," Jan said, her eyes falling to her still-full mug. She took a long sip. The strong java was better with the extra cream she'd added, but it still wasn't the tea she preferred. Though she would never even think of saying such a thing to her hostess.

"They probably get their dairy from a giant company," Gavin said.

There was no bitterness in his tone, but Jan could imagine it hadn't been easy to sell a chunk of their land to a chain store. She understood the need for money to pay tuition, and college was so much more expensive now than it had been when Amy applied for business school. Her heart went out to the Richardson family, and she wished there was something she could do.

"I got the impression they weren't really into the local business thing," Annie said. "The company's representatives were decent enough in their dealings with us, but I wouldn't describe them as particularly friendly."

"They met us here to sign the closing paperwork after school had let out one day, and they weren't too keen on the kids being around."

"That sounds unpleasant," Elaine said. "I'm so sorry to hear that."

"It's over now," Annie said, "and we're ready to let it go and just move on."

An idea began to take shape in Jan's mind, shoving its way into her thoughts until she couldn't help but asking, "Do you mind if I ask their names?"

"Oh, sure, not at all," Annie said.

"We'll never forget them," Gavin added. "Irene Kelly and Scott Landon."

CHAPTER EIGHT

Elaine sat in her office later that afternoon, updating the books and listening to a delightful baking lesson in the kitchen between Jan and her two granddaughters.

"Careful how much sugar you add now, Avery," Jan said to the eleven-year-old. "We don't want the cookies to give us a toothache."

Avery laughed, the sound carrying like jingling bells into Elaine's office and signaling that she'd done enough work for the day. She smiled as she closed the books in front of her and then made her way into the kitchen in time to see Avery shaking excess sugar from a measuring cup back into its canister.

Avery was the oldest daughter of Jan's son, Brian, and his wife, Paula, and she was quite the budding little baker. She loved to help Jan in the kitchen whenever she had the chance. Jan liked to believe it was her favorite thing to do besides gymnastics and playing cello, and she took every opportunity to spend time with the preteen, doing what they both enjoyed.

After their errands earlier, and following the karate class of Paula and Brian's other daughter, Kelly, Paula had brought the girls by so that they could all make cookies together. Now Jan and the girls were making quite a mess of the kitchen while Paula watched with amusement. It was a delightful sight.

"Oh my," Elaine said, joining Jan and Avery at the counter, reaching to hug the girl from behind. "Are those what I think they are?"

"Yep!" Avery sang out with excitement. "Snickerdoodles."

"Snickerdoodles," echoed Kelly, as she danced her way over to the counter near her sister.

"You just like saying the name, don't you, Kel?" Paula asked, ruffling her daughter's hair.

"I do," Kelly said, raising her hands in the air. "Snickerdoodles, snickerdoodles, snickerdoodles!"

All three women burst into laughter. But Avery, in all her preteen coolness, ignored her little sister and concentrated on the task at hand.

After another hour, when a few batches of cookies were cooling on the counter, they all made their way up to Elaine and her cousin's private sitting room to decorate the tree. Before, Jan had worried that it was too late to put it up, but it had actually worked out really well with her daughter-in-law and granddaughters stopping by. It would be a much more fun experience with the young people there, especially with the holiday drawing closer and Elaine missing her own Lucy and Micah.

Paula helped Jan and Elaine carry a few boxes of ornaments from the guest room closet into the sitting room where they'd put up the tree, and Kelly opened them as fast as she could.

"I made this one when I was little," Kelly said. "Oh, and this one has a picture of Avery with funny-looking hair."

Kelly giggled and Avery playfully stuck out her tongue at her sister. Paula walked over to see the old keepsakes and Jan quickly joined them.

Elaine took the opportunity to head downstairs to make some hot chocolate, and was surprised to hear rustling in the pantry. She fumbled around and quietly pulled a frying pan out of a cabinet. "Who's there?" she called, lifting the heavy cookware when a shadow grew larger in the doorway. Her pulse thudded in her ears as her heartbeat raced.

"Rose!" she gasped, holding her free hand to her heart as she set the pan down on a countertop. "You scared me. I wasn't expecting you back this afternoon."

"I'm so sorry, Elaine," Rose said, holding up her hands and looking a bit guilty. "I just couldn't relax at home, so I thought I'd come back and get some work done here. You know, organize all the groceries you two bought earlier. The back door was open."

"Oh, I wish you'd have told me," Elaine said as Jan joined them in the kitchen. "We've already done all of that. Jan and I meant it when we said you should take the afternoon away from work."

"We sure did," Jan agreed, worry furrowing her brow.

"I know," Rose said, "but after a nice lunch with my dad, I kept thinking about what happened to Clara. I thought I'd come back here and try to retrace my steps from that morning— just to see if I'd missed anything."

"Oh, Rose," Jan said, sighing, "it wasn't your fault."

Rose didn't look convinced. "I hope not, but something caused her to collapse. And her doctor couldn't really explain it. Now the tearoom is closed—and people might think it *is* my fault."

Elaine brushed off the comment. "Not at all." She couldn't promise that Rose's fear wasn't founded on anything real, but she did know the locals, and she knew they wouldn't think Rose would do something like that. "Look, Rose, even if some people are thinking that, and they're probably not, the tox screen will come back soon and this will all blow over."

"I hope so," Rose said, squaring her shoulders. "I really don't think I did anything wrong. I just want to find out what happened."

"So do we—and we're not going to stop investigating until we solve this mystery," Elaine promised, meaning every word.

"Actually," Jan said slowly, "we found out something at the Richardsons' that might help to figure out what happened to Clara."

Rose perked up, pushing herself forward. "Oh?"

Jan and Elaine exchanged a glance.

"It seems that two of the new people who were here that morning—Irene and Scott—are business partners," Elaine said.

Rose's mouth formed a thin line.

"As it turns out, they work for a company called Gram's Victorian Tea Company, a chain of tea establishments that is looking to expand in the Northeast," Elaine explained.

"That's right," Jan said, "and evidently, Irene and Scott have been in town for a few days. They've purchased a parcel of land from the Richardsons for their newest branch."

A hand flew to Rose's mouth and her forehead lined in concentration. "I had no idea," she said.

"Neither did we," Elaine concurred.

"So they would potentially be in competition with Tea for Two?"

"It seems so," Jan said.

"Are you concerned?" Rose asked.

Jan and Elaine looked at each other again. "I don't think there's a reason to be. We will continue to run this place the very best that we can, and to remain a place where locals can bring their families and friends to chat and enjoy some wonderful tea and pastries," Jan said, her voice confident.

"This is a dream come true," Elaine said, "and nothing will change that. I'm certainly not afraid of a little friendly competition," she said, grinning at Rose.

"If it is indeed friendly," Rose replied.

"Yes, there is that," Jan said. "The Richardsons told us that they sold the land to boost Dori's college fund—she'll be a senior next year and she's very bright—but I could tell they felt bad about it."

Elaine nodded in agreement. "I got the same impression. They certainly shouldn't feel bad—what they do with their land is their business."

"There may be a connection here though," Jan said. "Scott and Irene purchased the land to build a competing tearoom and then, after they were here the other morning, something terrible happened to Clara in *our* tearoom." Jan shook her head. "It's probably just a coincidence, but it's strange."

"It is," Elaine agreed, "and it's definitely piqued my curiosity. Trooper Benson said the toxicity report would be finished soon, and I'm hoping that will give us more information to go on."

Suddenly, they heard a crash upstairs, followed by a burst of giggles.

"What in the world is going on up there?" Rose asked, looking up at the ceiling.

"Paula and the girls are here," Jan said with a smile.

A corner of Rose's mouth turned up, and Elaine was glad to see a little cheer.

"That explains everything," Rose said, chuckling.

"Yes, it does," Elaine said. "Would you like to come up and join us? There's nothing to do down here, and we don't want you moping around all afternoon."

Rose hesitated.

"Don't argue, now. Come on, help us make up the hot chocolate and we'll head upstairs," Elaine urged. "The girls will be glad to see you."

Rose gave her a full smile—finally—and began pulling ceramic mugs from a cabinet. Elaine got out the cocoa powder, sugar, and whipped cream, and they all set to work. When they were almost done preparing all six hot drinks, Paula appeared in the kitchen doorway.

"Well, hello there, Rose," Paula said with a smile. "I was wondering what happened to Jan and Elaine."

"We sent Rose home with strict orders not to work this afternoon," Elaine teased. "But I'm happy to say she didn't listen to us."

"Me too," Rose said, setting mugs on to a bamboo tray, along with several of the freshly baked cookies.

"There's always room for one more," Jan added, "especially when it comes to decorating for Christmas. The grandkids are a blast, but I can't say we've accomplished much in the way of actually putting things on to the tree. They're having much more fun laughing at old pictures and the ornaments they made when they were smaller."

Elaine was so happy that Jan had her family nearby—she truly was—but a piece of her heart ached to see Jan having such a wonderful time with them. What a joy it would be if her own children lived closer. She would love to have them all—her kids and Jan's and their grandkids—gathered around the tree and the table for Christmas dinner. She didn't want to press her kids to visit; they had their own lives and she would never try to stand in the way of that. But it didn't stop a mother from wishing, especially at Christmastime.

Back upstairs, when they'd all finished their hot cocoa and a fair number of cookies, Rose joined Jan and Elaine as they sprinkled tinsel on the tree. Paula and the girls had settled in with a holiday movie and appeared to be dozing off, their energy expended after a full day of fun. Brian was away for the weekend at a work convention, so they would all spend the night before returning home in the morning. Elaine and Jan had told Rose again that, while she was very welcome, she didn't have to stay, but Rose hadn't seemed particularly eager to get home.

Elaine thought that maybe it was because Christmas was just around the corner, and Rose had just lost her mother. It was only Rose and her father at home, and Elaine could understand how things might get a little lonely from time to time. Aside from his regular work as an orthodontist, Rose's father, Clifton Young, was one of the town's selectmen and thus was often busy conducting town business after office hours. It made sense that Rose might want to be in the company of older women.

Jan talked to Rose about some of the new recipes she wanted them to try now that they'd restocked the pantry after their visit to the dairy.

Soon the conversation slowed and Elaine looked around the room, reveling in the peaceful scene. The Christmas tree was now full of red and green glass orbs, silvery tinsel, and an assortment of sentimental family ornaments. The couch they were sitting on had a couple of red and green throws to curl up in, and last rays of afternoon light were streaming through the window, casting a golden glow over everything. Even though her own family couldn't be with her, Elaine thought, she was so blessed to be surrounded by people she cared for.

"Oh, I just remembered something," Rose said, sitting up straight. "I didn't think anything of it at the time because it didn't seem important, but now, with all of these details coming together, I'm starting to reconsider what it might mean."

"What is it?" Elaine asked.

"I'm all ears," Jan said.

"So the day before the incident—after the tearoom closed for the day, I was cleaning up and Archie was helping me."

"Yes, that's right," Jan said. "Elaine and I were out running errands."

"Well, we were almost done," Rose continued, "and before Archie left he offered to refill all of the tea canisters that were low."

Jan and Elaine nodded.

"Anyway, while I was out in the parlor, I heard Archie shouting. I went to check on him—he was making a pretty big commotion—and the door to the porch was open." Rose grinned and put a hand over her mouth. "Archie said Earl Grey had snuck in somehow and he had to shoo the cat out before either of you saw the old fur ball in the kitchen."

Jan shook her head. "Earl Grey has never done that before."

"Maybe he caught a sniff of something tempting in the kitchen," Elaine said, "and couldn't resist."

"I asked Archie if he needed any help," Rose continued, "but you know how he is."

Elaine felt the corners of her lips turn up. None of them would ever say a harsh word about Archie, a world traveler with multiple degrees and a thick, posh British accent. He was also one of the sweetest and most charming men they'd ever met. She very much enjoyed his company and both she and Jan had been thrilled when they'd hired him to work part-time at the tearoom.

Rose went on. "Archie said he had things under control, so I went back to cleaning up the parlor. But the next day, before Clara collapsed, I noticed that a couple of the tea canisters were out of their usual order. I just rearranged them back to the way we normally have them. It occurs to me now that Archie probably knocked them over in his haste to get Earl Grey out the kitchen door." Rose smiled. "I don't think he would have enjoyed admitting that the cat had gotten the better of him before he was able to get Earl back out of the house."

Elaine and Jan couldn't help but chuckle.

"I can just imagine that scene," Jan said. "I don't think I would have been able to keep a straight face."

"It wasn't easy. You should have seen Archie. I didn't know skin could turn that shade of red," Rose said, grinning. "I don't think that has anything to do with what happened. I just wanted you to know that some of the canisters had been knocked down as far as I could tell, just in case I'm not here to mention it when Trooper Benson comes by."

"Thank you for telling us, Rose," Elaine said. "Maybe it won't amount to anything more than a funny story, but you're right to share that detail."

Jan nodded. "It's like Dan said the other day when Rose and I went to give our statements. You never know what could be important."

Rose looked at the slim silver watch on her wrist. "Goodness, it's getting late. I'd better get on home before Dad starts to worry."

"And before it snows again," Jan said, glancing past them at the waning light in the window.

"That too," Rose said.

Jan and Elaine stood up from the couch and Elaine pulled two of the throws from the back, then headed over to cover Paula and the girls. Avery stirred a little and opened an eye, smiling softly when she saw Elaine putting the blanket over her and her sister. The girl's smile touched her heart.

After seeing to Paula and the girls' warmth, she followed Jan downstairs to walk Rose out. They saw her off and then went to the kitchen for a quick cup of tea. Soon it would be time for dinner, but they were all feeling tired and Elaine thought it would be best to just order a pizza. It would be dark early, but it hadn't yet begun snowing, so the roads were safe enough for delivery.

Elaine set out two cups and soon the kettle whistled on the stove. "I'm in the mood for something light and fresh," she said to Jan. "What do you think about chocolate mint?"

"That sounds great," Jan said, turning off the burner. The whistled died down to a whisper and then stopped as the heat dissipated.

Elaine pulled the chocolate mint canister from the pantry and spooned leaves into two infusers—one for each cup. Jan poured the steaming water over them and set a timer for five minutes so the tea could steep. She set the kettle back down on the stove.

"I haven't gotten a chance to ask you about it yet," Jan said. "But how was your date with Nathan yesterday evening?"

"Oh, it wasn't a date," Elaine said, a little unsure that was true. She hadn't thought too much about that evening, what with their busy morning full of errands and Paula and the girls stopping by. "It was just dinner."

"Ah, I see," Jan said. "So then, how did dinner go?"

Elaine smiled. "We had a lovely time. We always do." She hesitated. "Only, Nathan asked me..."

"To be more than friends?" Jan interjected, her eyes soft and knowing. "Did he ask if you'd like to begin dating?"

Elaine looked up in surprise. "How did you know?"

Jan's mouth curved into a little smile. "I just did. It's in the little things: how he looks at you with such admiration, the way he's so careful about helping you with your coat and holding doors and all of that. And he has been looking for any excuse to stop by lately, if you haven't noticed. The outdoor lights, for example."

Elaine gave a small nod. "I've been telling myself that he was just being a gentleman."

"I can understand that completely," Jan said. "You've known him for so long that it must be strange to think of him in another light."

"A little strange," Elaine said, her cheeks warm. "Although I've been wondering what it might be like to have something more...someday."

"Do you mind if I ask what you told him?" Jan asked.

"Not at all. You can always ask me anything," Elaine answered. "I told him the truth—that I'm attracted to him too, but I'm not ready to be anything beyond friends. It was hard to do that, and I could tell he was disappointed."

"Well, it was the right choice for the time being," Jan encouraged her.

The timer buzzed. They removed the infusers from their teacups and moved to the table. "You still miss Ben, and that is definitely okay."

Elaine nodded, thankful for the support. They took sips of their tea. The chocolate was mild and smooth and the mint tingled on her taste buds; the tea was just what she'd wanted. If only everything in life were that simple.

"That's just it though," she said. "Now that he's got me thinking about it, I'm not so sure it was the right choice."

CHAPTER NINE

M y flight will be in at 5:00 p.m. on the twenty-fourth" Sasha told Jan on the phone Sunday before church. "And Mom doesn't know, right? It's still a surprise?"

"Yes," Jan whispered into the mouthpiece, looking over her shoulder to make sure Elaine hadn't heard anything. Planning around her cousin, when they lived together and spent so much time in each other's company, was proving to be a challenge. Jan reminded herself that it would all be worth it when Elaine saw her kids' and grandkids' faces on Christmas Eve. In the meantime, she did not enjoy sneaking around behind Elaine's back, even if it was for a good cause.

"Okay, good to know," Sasha said. "It's getting harder and harder to keep a secret from her."

"I know the feeling," Jan said, rubbing her forehead. "It's not easy on this end either."

"I'm sure it's not," Sasha laughed.

Jan heard noise in the background.

"Listen, I've got to get going, but I won't forget to sync up with Jared. He and Corinne and the kids come in at five thirty, so we should all be ready with our bags and stuff for you or Brian to pick us up at six or so."

Jan nodded, even though Sasha couldn't see her through the line. She wrote all the information on the notepad in front of her, then tore off the sheet of paper and stuffed it into a pocket. If Elaine saw flight times, she would get suspicious and the whole plan would fall through.

"All right," Jan said. "Got it. We'll see you then. Make sure you call me if something pops up or if you need anything."

"Sure thing, Jan," Sasha said, her voice warm. "See you soon."

"And be careful," Jan said into the phone.

"I will. Looking forward to it."

Jan and Sasha said their good-byes, and once more, Jan peeked out of her bedroom door to make sure Elaine hadn't heard from the hallway. She would be very glad when all of this culminated in a happy family at their table on Christmas. She certainly wasn't cut out for a life of hiding things.

Jan put the phone back into its charger and went to her dresser. She checked her hair and put in lavender earrings to match her cardigan.

"Is everything okay?"

Jan nearly jumped out of her skin at the sound of her cousin's voice. "Oh my," she said, a lavender necklace sliding out of her hand. "You startled me."

Lines of worry creased Elaine's forehead. "You seem awfully jumpy this morning," she said. "Are you okay?"

"Yes, I'm fine," Jan said.

"I heard you talking to someone on the phone."

Jan's stomach fell to her toes. If Elaine asked to whom she'd been speaking, she would not lie. "It's nothing to worry about. Just making some arrangements."

Elaine looked puzzled but she didn't ask after it any further. Jan breathed a sigh of relief. "I'm headed down to Green Glade after church," she said. "I want to ask Macy if Clara Hill is still there. I'd like to know how she's doing."

"I'd like to know if she still plans to review Tea for Two," Elaine said. "Honestly, I'm surprised she didn't hightail it out of town after what happened to her."

"She may have left already." Jan pulled on a dark purple scarf. "Although when Rose and I saw her at the hospital, she said that she'd originally planned to stay for a long weekend and was looking forward to it."

Elaine pursed her lips. "I suppose that's understandable. After all, people get food poisoning all the time, especially on vacation, and they don't necessarily call off the whole trip."

"That's true. She seems like a very nice woman. The whole thing is just really unfortunate. I was looking forward to an honest review so we could learn what we're doing well and what needs work, but really, at this point, I don't know what to expect. Whatever she's going to write, it hasn't run in the paper yet—I've been keeping an eye out—so there's a chance she's decided against doing the review at all."

Elaine shook her head. "That's a shame. I was looking forward to reading the article too. There was the potential to learn a lot from it."

Jan finished getting ready and checked her appearance in the full-length mirror. "Are you sure you don't want to come with me?" she asked. "I confess I could use the moral support. Macy can be a little…grating sometimes."

Of the two cousins, Jan was the less naturally social. Elaine was generally more confident and could have a conversation with anyone about anything, seemingly without effort. An introvert, Jan didn't always find it so easy.

"You'll be just fine," Elaine said, patting her shoulder. "Don't let her make you feel uncomfortable."

Jan nodded and smiled, thankful for the encouragement. She had a feeling she would need it.

"What are you up to this afternoon?" she asked Elaine.

"Oh, this and that. I'm going to run a few errands and finish up some last-minute Christmas shopping."

"I'm surprised you haven't been done for months already," she teased her cousin. "You've usually finished your list by July, and I always wish I could be like that."

"I'm not that bad," Elaine said humbly. But she couldn't hide her grin.

Jan could tell she was pleased with the compliment. Elaine loved to pick out just the perfect thing for everyone on her list each year; it was something she truly enjoyed and she had a real talent for choosing something special and on the mark for her loved ones. Jan wasn't kidding when she'd said she envied her cousin's skill.

It was just one of the reasons she'd been so happy to find that Meissen sugar bowl at Oldies But Goodies. And she couldn't wait to give it to Elaine for Christmas, along with, hopefully, the matching creamer. She just knew her cousin was going to love them.

JAN HUMMED QUIETLY to herself as she turned the Camry's steering wheel to the right, pulling on to Cottage Road later that afternoon. Macy Atherton, along with her son and daughter-in-law, ran a string of rental cottages on the lake, most of which were usually vacant during the winter months.

Macy could be a little trying at times. She and her friends were regular visitors at Tea for Two, and, unless she was in a particularly good mood, Macy almost always found something to complain about. Though none of the other customers ever said anything, and though she, Rose, and Elaine were diligent about taste-testing anything they served, Macy seemed determined to nitpick. Either her tea was too hot or too cold, the pastries were too tough, or there was something about the décor of one of the parlors that she didn't find favorable.

Jan knew the younger woman meant no harm. Macy was a pillar in the Lancaster community; she ran the cottages with care year-round, including Maine's snowy winter, she was active in a multitude of organizations, including the Bookworm book club and raising funds for the Fire Department Auxiliary and the Forrest High alumni, among countless others. She was always eager to offer her opinion on things—especially when it was unsolicited. Despite all of that, though, Macy was one of the tearoom's most avid supporters. She sent her cottage renters to Tea for Two on a frequent basis, so Jan and Elaine easily tolerated the times when she could be unpleasant, knowing that, at the end of the day, Macy was kindhearted.

Jan pulled to a stop in the curved gravel drive outside of Green Glade Cottages. Most of the units were empty, but Jan noticed a car parked outside the cottage two doors down from the clubhouse.

She took one last deep breath and opened the door, relishing the bracing cold air as it hit her lungs, giving her energy. Jan headed toward the large, cream-colored clubhouse, only half hoping Macy would be out running errands or something. The other half of Jan, genuinely concerned with Clara's well-being and wanting to follow up on the food critic's health, did truly hope Macy was there.

The door opened before she could knock, and Jan sensed Macy had been watching her from the front window near the desk.

"Hello there, Macy," Jan said, waving.

Macy raised a hand in greeting. "I wasn't expecting any visitors this afternoon," she said, cutting right to the chase.

Jan grinned to herself. Macy was nothing if not direct. It was a quality Jan sometimes admired; at any rate, she wished it was easier to speak her mind on occasion. She knew about herself that she could be timid to a fault sometimes, though living with Elaine had started to rub off on her a bit.

"Come on in, then," Macy said. "It's mighty cold out."

Once inside the clubhouse, Jan took a look around, admiring the buttery yellow walls, high ceiling, and cozy atmosphere. Red embers glowed in the stone fireplace, warming the entire room. She removed her coat and hung it on the rack near the door before Macy motioned for Jan to sit in one of the two sand-colored club chairs that flanked either side of the fireplace.

"Would you like something to drink?" Macy asked. "I have coffee."

Jan shook her head. "Thank you so much, Macy, but that's okay. I don't want to take up much of your time."

"What brings you by?" Macy asked, taking a seat in the other club chair.

Jan had the sudden feeling that she was a young child at school, having been sent to the principal's office, though nothing of the sort had ever actually happened to her in real life. Macy simply had an air of authority.

Jan fiddled nervously with a string that had come loose on the sleeve of her sweater. "I wanted to ask you about your guest," Jan said. "Clara Hill?"

"Oh yes," Macy said, reaching over to brush a tiny piece of lint off the coffee table between them. "Miss Hill has been here since Wednesday." She studied Jan's face. "She called ahead and, well, when I heard that she was a food critic from Portland here to write an article about your tearoom, I offered her my best cottage at a reduced rate."

"That's very kind of you," Jan said. "I'm sure she appreciates it."

Macy gave a small shrug, but Jan could see she was pleased with the compliment.

Until then, she hadn't really considered that the reporter might stay in town. Macy would demur if Jan came outright and thanked her for accommodating Clara while she visited the tearoom to write her review; but it didn't stop her from feeling warmed by the gesture. "All the same," she said instead, knowing the sometimes difficult but loyal businesswoman would understand her gratitude.

Macy nodded, and that was that. "Now," she said, picking up a pen to fiddle with, "you know I won't disclose anything private about my guest, so what is it you wanted to talk about?"

"I understand and respect that," Jan said, meaning her words. "I just wanted to check on Miss Hill after something that happened to her at Tea for Two on Thursday morning."

"I see," Macy said, clearly trying not to sound too interested. "What was that?"

"Well," Jan said, meeting Macy's curious eyes, "after drinking one of our newest tea flavors and having a maple brownie, Miss Hill collapsed and we had to call for an ambulance."

Macy's eyes grew wide, and a look of concern played across her sharp features. "I'm so sorry to hear that," she said, her voice full of genuine-sounding worry.

"Yes, it was an unpleasant morning," Jan said, resisting the urge to blurt out everything. She knew that, when it came down to it, she could trust Macy, but it probably wasn't a good idea to expand too much on what happened, especially considering she herself didn't really know for certain yet. "There are still a lot of things that are unclear, but the police are working on it."

"The police?" Macy raised a single eyebrow.

Oops. Well, now the cat was out of the bag. This was why she preferred it when Elaine was with her; it was why they made such a great team, and why the townspeople trusted the two of them so much. Next time, she would insist that her cousin join her.

"They're investigating the possibility that someone tampered with Clara's food or tea. The intent may have been to harm us; or the reputation of our tearoom, using Clara as a vehicle. Or someone may have been targeting her personally."

Macy's brow furrowed. "That's terrible, Jan. I'm so sorry to hear that."

"Thank you, Macy. I appreciate that."

Macy blinked. "Well, even though your brownies are dry, and you don't carry that honey butter that I like...is there anything I can do to help out?"

Jan stifled a grin. She could always count on Macy to be consistent. "For now, we know that the police are running a toxicity screen, and in the meantime, Elaine and I are trying to figure out who might have been motivated to do such a thing, and why."

"*Hmm,*" Macy said. "You know, I didn't think anything of it at the time, but I got a call from someone a little less than a week ago—a man who wanted to make a reservation. He said he and his business partner were coming to town to buy some land; he wanted to book two cabins."

Jan sat forward in her chair. "Do you remember their names by any chance?" She had a hunch how Macy would respond, but she didn't want to say it out loud in case Macy didn't recall them and Jan's suggestion influenced her.

Macy shook her head, looking disappointed. "I'm sorry, but no, I don't. I really wish I did."

Jan sat back, deflated. "It's okay." She had a thought. "But did you rent them the cabins?"

Macy looked at Jan as though she might be dense. "No, I did not. I didn't like the way he sounded."

Ah, Jan thought but didn't say.

"Miss Hill was extremely polite and has been nothing but a joy to put up. She's very tidy and is hardly a burden to me at all." Macy made a face Jan couldn't decipher. "Besides, I didn't appreciate the man's tone when he called. I know we're a small town and we do things a little differently than they do in the big cities, but when I refused to offer him the cottages, he implied that I didn't know what was best for my business."

She hated to think it, but that fit right in with the picture she was beginning to form in her mind of Scott Landon. There was nothing wrong with running a chain of tearooms, but treating small-town people like they were somehow less savvy than city business owners…well, that was unkind.

"My only consolation," Macy went on, "was that he wouldn't get very far in Lancaster with that attitude." She gave a little huff. "So whatever his business is, I hope he takes it elsewhere."

"Somehow, I don't think we'll be so fortunate," Jan said, sighing. "If it's the person I'm thinking of, and I have a feeling it is, he and his business partner have already purchased land just outside of town."

Macy's eyes widened.

"And I have a hunch that we'll be seeing plenty more of both of them."

Jan relayed what she knew about the Richardsons' sale of land to Scott Landon and Irene Kelly, and Macy grew more and more determined to help as Jan shared.

They chatted for a bit and Jan eventually accepted a glass of water to wet her throat. "I hate to ask, Macy, but since Clara has been staying here for a few days, is there any chance that something in her cabin may have given Clara an adverse reaction?"

Macy looked appalled and Jan wished she could backtrack and find a gentler way of asking the same thing.

"Absolutely not." Macy put a hand to her lapel. "My cottages are pristine, and of course I'm shocked that you would even ask such a thing."

Jan held out a hand. "I didn't mean it like that, Macy. I'm just trying to find out if maybe there's a cleaning substance that doesn't agree with her, or if there was something else in the air that made her so sick." She gave Macy a pleading look. "I didn't intend to imply that you had anything to do with this—not by any means—I'm just trying to sort through every little detail so I don't miss anything."

Macy's coloring went back to its normal shade and, after looking Jan up and down, she seemed adequately placated. The last thing Jan wanted to do was to alienate her; the woman could be a fierce ally.

"It would be against my policy to allow you to go into Clara's cabin," Macy said.

Jan shook her head. "I would never ask that of you, and I don't need to go in there anyway. I was just hoping you could tell me if she's mentioned anything about getting sick on

Thursday and, most important, if she's doing all right. Rose and I visited her in the hospital on Thursday and Clara told us she planned to stay here a few days. I mostly came by to see to it that she's fully recovered."

Macy narrowed her eyes. "She hasn't made me privy to any details, and she never actually told me that she'd been sick that day," she said, pausing. "She did, however, tell me something else that you might be interested in hearing."

CHAPTER TEN

Jan's ears pricked up. Given Macy's involvement in many clubs and community events, the woman could be a font of information. And now it sounded like Macy possessed some new information about Clara.

She took a deep breath, eager to hear what Macy had to say. "I'm very interested. What did Clara tell you?"

A hint of reluctance showed itself in the thin line of Macy's mouth. "I just thought you'd like to know that Miss Hill isn't leaving this evening like she'd planned. She's staying here—indefinitely."

Macy sat back in her chair, looking like the cat that got the cream. She definitely had Jan's attention then.

"Indefinitely?" Jan echoed, both intrigued and perplexed by that tidbit. "Did she say why?"

Macy scowled. "Unlike some people around here, I'm not the nosy type. I didn't ask Miss Hill for the reason and she didn't tell me. So I guess you'll have to ask her yourself."

Jan wasn't ready to do that. Not yet, anyway. First, she wanted some time to think about her next move and consult Elaine about the latest wrinkle in this mystery.

"MY, MY," ELAINE said late Monday afternoon, clasping her hands together. "Don't you look wonderful!"

"Oh, thank you." Jan glanced at the full-length mirror on the back of her closet door. "You don't think it's a bit too much, do you? I mean, we're just going out for dinner and then the concert."

Elaine put a hand in the air, then twirled her forefinger in a little circle. "Give me one more spin," she said.

Jan complied, as much for her own enjoyment as for her cousin's. The dress she wore had been hanging, neglected, at the back of her closet for far too long. It was the right length to be warm enough for the winter weather and the fabric was the most beautiful emerald green, perfect for an early-December outing. Plus—the very best part—it had a subtle gossamer detailing that made it sparkle when she spun around.

"Nope. I have not changed my mind," Elaine said, her eyes gleaming. "It's still just perfect on you."

"Well, thank you again," Jan said. "That's enough twirling then." She'd tried to inject a serious tone in her voice, but it was impossible. She was having too much fun getting dressed up for an evening out on the town with Bob.

When she looked up again though, despite Elaine's wide grin, she could detect a hint of wistfulness in her cousin's eyes.

Suddenly, Jan realized she'd been parading around in her emerald dress while Elaine was still thinking about her recent conversation with Nathan. Jan went to her.

"Elaine, look, if you'd rather I stay in..."

Elaine shook her head vehemently. "Absolutely not. You'll do no such thing."

Jan's eyes softened. "If you're having a difficult time after what happened with Nathan, I just want to let you know that I understand, and I'm here for you."

Elaine shook her head. "That's not it at all. Actually, I'm rather flattered that Nathan wants to be more than friends."

"Are you sure?"

"Positive," Elaine said with a soft sigh. "I just hope I don't lose him as a friend. Maybe I handled it wrong—although we parted on good terms."

Jan reached out to give her cousin a hug. She understood the frustration that came with second-guessing yourself. "If he cares about you, and I believe he does, then he'll stick around." She smiled. "Besides, he adores Earl Grey."

Elaine laughed, reaching out to brush a loose thread off Jan's shoulder. "You're right, our cat is quite the charmer. And I'm just being silly. I have to follow my heart, no matter where it leads." Then she changed the subject. "And this evening, my heart is leading me to a good book and a nice hot bubble bath."

"That sounds lovely. What are you reading?"

"It's a mystery by a new author. I've just started it, but it looks intriguing." She narrowed her gaze as Jan checked her makeup in the mirror. "Almost as intriguing as Clara Hill. I'm still trying to figure out why she's staying so long."

Jan had relayed her conversation with Macy, including that fact that Clara had extended her stay at Green Glade indefinitely. "Maybe she just needs a vacation." Jan leaned toward the mirror as she touched a dab of lipstick to her mouth. "A sudden illness can make a person take stock of her life—and think about what's really important."

"That's very true," Elaine said, walking over to pick up a towel off the bed. "It's strange though. Most people are more comfortable in their own home. I hope she's all right."

"Me too." She turned from the mirror and met Elaine's gaze. "Perhaps we're reading too much into it. I'll admit, I was surprised when I heard she was staying on at Green Glade. Is there something we're missing here?"

"It's possible," Elaine said, folding the towel. "But we don't know much about her. Perhaps she does this kind of thing all the time."

"It could be that simple, couldn't it?" Jan smiled.

A flash of headlights through the window made Jan's smile widen. "He's here." She slipped on a pair of black pumps that shared the same gossamer shine as her dress.

"Have a great time." Elaine opened the bedroom door. "You're going to knock Bob's socks off."

Jan laughed. "I'll settle for a making it to his car without slipping in these heels."

Elaine looked down at Jan's feet with a frown. "You're right. You might slip on the slick pavement in this weather. Why not wear your boots until you get to the restaurant? The wet snow might damage your shoes anyway. Better to keep them nice and dry."

"Good plan," Jan said, walking over to her closet to pick out a pair of black ankle-length boots. She held up the sturdy fur-lined leather boots. "These don't exactly go with my outfit, but they'll do."

Elaine reached out to take the boots from Jan's hands. "Let me carry them until Bob gets a look at you in that outfit. Then you can change into the boots."

Jan laughed, giving a reluctant nod as the doorbell rang. They headed out of her bedroom and down the stairs to the first floor, where Elaine hurried to the back door.

Jan stood a few feet behind her, catching the frigid breeze that drifted in when Elaine opened the door leading to the screened porch. Bob stood on the other side, wearing a black wool overcoat with a cobalt-blue scarf and dark-gray slacks. The cold had reddened his cheeks a bit and Earl Grey was doing his part to help keep Bob warm by slowly winding around his ankles.

"Good evening," Elaine said with a cheerful smile, opening the door wider to usher Bob inside.

"Hello, Elaine," Bob said, smiling as he gently untangled himself from the cat. He walked through the open door, leaving Earl Grey behind on the porch as his gaze fell on Jan. "I hope I'm not late."

Jan's cheeks warmed when she noticed the flash of appreciation in Bob's chocolate-brown eyes as he looked at her. "You're right on time."

Jan admired Bob's punctuality and his attention to detail. There was a silent strength that emanated from him, making her believe he could handle almost any situation.

"You look…" Bob's gaze lingered on her for a long moment. "Lovely."

Her blush deepened. "Thank you. You're quite handsome yourself."

Elaine looked between them, a gleam of amusement shining in her blue eyes. "I agree with both of you." Then she handed the boots to Jan. "Now you two better scoot if you don't want to be late for dinner."

Jan made a fast change into the boots and then slipped her pumps into a small tote bag that Elaine handed her. After giving both her cousin and Earl Grey a quick good-bye, she took Bob's outstretched arm, and they left the house and made their way over the snow-dusted sidewalk to his silver Acura purring in the driveway.

"Oh, it's nice and toasty in here," Jan said, sliding into the passenger seat before Bob closed the door. She unspooled the seat belt and clicked it into place as he rounded the car and joined her in the driver's seat.

"I wanted to keep the heater running on a cold night like this." Bob shifted the car into gear.

"I decided to carry my shoes with me so they don't get wet," Jan explained, holding up the bag in her hands.

"Smart," he said, turning on the radio to a classical music station playing Christmas songs.

Jan beamed when she recognized a favorite. "'Winter Wonderland'! That's a perfect way to describe this evening."

"It sure is," Bob agreed as the car moved easily over the road.

Snow glistened all around them, hanging heavily on the tree branches and frosting the rooftops and every square inch of the ground.

Jan hummed along to the carol on the radio, moving her feet in rhythm to the music.

"If you don't mind," Bob said, glancing over at Jan. "I thought we might take a little detour before dinner."

"Oh?" Jan smiled at the mischievous gleam she saw in his eyes. "Do we have time?"

He nodded, turning the car on to a back road and heading east. "I factored in some extra time when I made our dinner reservations. There's something I want to show you."

Jan leaned back in the car seat, curious. *Leave it to Bob to plan something special,* she thought to herself. Stars sparkled in the night sky like a glittering canopy above them.

They chatted easily together as Bob's car moved smoothly along the road, passing lone farmhouses along the way, with the Christmas songs on the radio providing cheerful background music to their conversation.

Before Jan knew it, they were parked near the top of a bluff. The narrow gravel road was hugged by thick fir trees and she could hear an owl hoot in the distance.

"We'll have to brave the cold for the best view," he told her.

"I'm game," Jan said, smiling as she unbuckled her seat belt. Bob had her curious now. She hadn't been keeping track of their journey during the drive, too distracted by Bob's interesting stories about his work as a busy attorney.

Bob switched off the engine and climbed out of the car first, quickly rounding to Jan's side to open the passenger door for her. She left her purse inside, and clasped the top button of her coat as she joined him on the path, glad to be wearing her boots as the snow crunched under her feet.

"This way," he said with a smile, holding out a gloved hand.

She took his hand, the fingers of their black leather gloves entwining around each other as they started walking. The snow was deeper on the bluff, reaching almost to the top of her boots, and she was glad for the extra support of Bob walking beside her. The crisp, cold air felt refreshing after the warmth of the car.

"Here we are," Bob said, coming to a standstill at the top edge of the bluff.

Jan gasped in delight at the sight before her. The town of Lancaster brightly dotted the landscape below with colorful Christmas lights twinkling in the dark. "Oh, Bob! This is breathtaking."

"I thought you'd like it," he replied, a note of pride in his voice.

"I love it," she breathed, her gaze moving over the gorgeous view below the bluff. Beyond the town, she could see Christmas lights on the cabins around Lake Chickadee, their colors reflected on the icy lake.

Then Jan shivered as a sudden gust of frigid air blew over them.

"*Brr,*" Bob said, rubbing his hands together. "I think that's our cue to go."

"I second that motion, counselor," Jan said, laughing as they both turned and hurried back to his car.

Bob reached for the passenger door handle, but it wouldn't open. "Oh no."

"What's wrong?" Jan asked, seeing a shadow of dread pass over his face.

He dug his hands into the pockets of his wool overcoat. "I think I locked the keys in the car."

"Oh no!" Jan stared at him as he continued searching all of his pockets for the elusive keys, her toes inside her boots beginning to tingle from the cold.

"To be honest, I didn't know that was even possible with these newfangled keys." Bob cupped one hand over his eyes as he leaned close to the passenger door window to peer inside, then he groaned. "Yes, they're still in the ignition. I must have hit the lock button accidentally." He turned around, his eyes full of regret. "Jan, I'm so sorry. I can't believe I forgot them. I guess I was too eager to show you the view."

"You don't need to apologize," she assured him, trying not to shiver. "I could have been the one to bump the lock when I was getting out of the car. But I'm sure we can call someone and..." Too late Jan remembered that she'd left her purse in the car with the cell phone inside. "Do you have your phone?"

He shook his head, his mouth pressed into a firm line. "No, it's in the console, so we can't call anyone." He rubbed one hand over his jaw. "I saw a farmhouse about a quarter of a mile from here. I'll head down there as fast as I can and..."

"I'm coming with you," Jan insisted. "A brisk walk will warm me right up. Besides, we're on a date, remember?" she said cheerfully, trying to inject a little levity into the situation. "I don't want you running out on me."

A reluctant smile tipped up one corner of his mouth as they began walking down the bluff. "This isn't the date I had planned," he told her, allowing Jan to walk in the snow-packed tire track while he trudged through the deeper, softer snow beside her. "I hope you're not too cold."

She could hear the concern in his voice and tried with all her might to keep her teeth from chattering. "No, I'm...good." The wind had picked up again and she was freezing, but she didn't want to make Bob feel worse than he already did.

When they reached the bottom of the bluff, Jan could see the glow of a tall yard light just down the road. "I have an idea," she said, doing her best to keep up with Bob's long stride. "Let's start singing a Christmas carol and see if we can reach the farmhouse before we've reached the end of the last verse."

He chuckled. "Leave it to you to make a game of it."

A rustle in a nearby bush told Jan they were disturbing the local wildlife on this peaceful bluff, most likely a rabbit on the way to its burrow. At this moment, she wished she could burrow someplace nice and warm, but the long walk ahead of them promised no such comfort.

"So what song do you want to sing?" Jan asked, determined to think about something other than the cold breeze chapping her lips.

"It's the lady's choice," he said, looking resigned to the idea. He slowed for a moment, offering his arm to help her over a fallen branch in their path.

They'd veered off from the tire tracks to take a more direct path to the main road. The snow was deeper now, so Jan held on to Bob's arm to keep her balance. She breathed a prayer of thanks that Elaine had suggested she bring her boots along, certain she wouldn't have made it this far in her heels.

"Okay, let me think a moment," she said, mentally running through a list of her favorite Christmas carols. She decided to choose one with a peppy beat to match their pace. Then she began to sing, her voice breaking the silence around them. *"Deck the halls with boughs of holly, Fa la la la la, la la, la la."*

Bob laughed and then joined in, his voice loud and deep. *"'Tis the season to be jolly, Fa la la la la, la la, la la."*

They sang together, walking as fast as their legs could carry them. The farmhouse yard light seemed so far away that Jan wondered if they'd ever get there. When they finally reached the road, she kept singing, grateful for the snowplow that had gone through earlier which made their snowy trek a little easier.

"See the blazing Yule before us, Fa la la la la, la la, la la." At that moment, Jan would give almost anything to be near a blazing Yule log. She was so cold that her toes felt like popsicles in her boots. But she wasn't about to give up or let Bob think she was too weak to make it.

Soon she could see all three stories of the colonial-style farmhouse instead of just the rooftop. It was made of mortar and stone, with a curl of white smoke drifting out of the chimney. *Keep singing*, she told herself.

As they left the road and turned into the driveway, they reached the last verse of the song. *"Sing we joyous all together, Fa la la la la, la la, la la. Heedless of the wind and weather, Fa la la la la, la la, la la!"*

Then they started laughing together through their chattering teeth. The moon cast an ethereal glow over the farmyard, revealing a red barn in the distance and a small chicken coop just behind the house.

At that moment, Jan's legs felt so numb with cold she wasn't certain she could make it the last few steps to the house. But she plodded forward, trying to keep pace with Bob.

"I'm not sure who lives here," Jan said as they approached the screened-in porch at the front of the house. "Do you know?"

"Not a clue." Bob opened the door, allowing Jan to enter first, then he followed close behind her, rubbing both of his gloved hands up and down his arms.

To Jan's surprise, she suddenly felt warmer. "This is wonderful," she breathed, her body beginning to thaw.

Bob pointed to the small, box-style heater affixed to the rafters of the porch ceiling. "Now that's what I call a great idea. It's an infrared heater. They heat people and objects in the room, but not the air itself."

They both moved closer to the heater, relishing the reprieve from the cold air outside. Jan's toes ached as they began to thaw and she silently thanked God for bringing them safely to shelter.

"We should think about getting one of those heaters for Earl Grey," Jan said, appreciating the warmth and thinking of their own screened porch.

A sudden movement in the dark corner of the porch made Jan gasp.

"Baaaaa." A shaggy white goat pranced toward them and began nibbling on the toes of Bob's boots.

"Oh my," Jan said, laughing. "This is a surprise." She bent down to pet the goat's fuzzy white head. "Hello there, cutie."

The front door suddenly opened and an older man stepped outside. He looked about seventy and wore faded denim overalls over his red-and-black flannel shirt. His thin silver hair was combed over from one side of his head and barely covered his bald pate. A pair of silver wire-rimmed glasses sat precariously on the tip of his nose.

But the thing that really got Jan's attention was the shotgun he held in his hands. It was an old-fashioned double-barrel, just like Jan's grandpa used to own. She just hoped it wasn't in full working order.

Bob moved protectively in front of Jan as the man's grip tightened on the shotgun and he raised it higher.

CHAPTER ELEVEN

H ey, what's going on out here?" the older man asked, his voice gruff as he looked between Bob and Jan. "Are you folks trying to steal my goat?"

"No sir," Bob said, slowly approaching the man with an outstretched hand and keeping himself positioned between Jan and the shotgun. "I'm Bob Claybrook and this is my friend, Jan Blake. And you are?"

"Harley Ferrell," he said with a scowl, taking a step back, his shotgun at the ready. "I own this place and I own that goat," he said, pointing to the goat now chewing on the hem of Jan's coat.

"We're sorry to intrude on you like this, Mr. Ferrell," Bob continued, as Jan tried to distract the goat from making a meal of her wool coat, "but I accidentally locked my keys in my car about a quarter mile back and I was wondering if we could use your phone to call a locksmith."

"Oh, is that all?" Harley lowered the gun with a sheepish smile. "I thought you were goat rustlers." He set the shotgun down in the corner.

"Are there goat rustlers in the area?" Jan asked. She'd never heard of such a thing.

"Haven't come across one yet," Harley told her. "But I keep ole Rusty here just in case. It's not loaded, but it'll scare 'em away."

"It sure will," Bob said, glancing at Jan with a relieved smile. "Now, about that phone call…"

"No need for you to call a locksmith," Harley said, waving them inside the house. "I've got one of those tools that will unlock your car door in a jiffy."

Jan gave the goat one last pat before following Bob and Harley inside the house. She inhaled the scent of fresh-baked bread the moment she walked over the threshold and found a cozy, spacious living room inside. She was hungry enough to eat an entire loaf of bread after their long, cold walk from the bluff.

"Come on in and warm up," Harley said, a little less brusque now that he knew they weren't goat thieves. He pointed to the large stone fireplace in the living room, where a cheerful fire blazed.

Jan and Bob didn't hesitate, both of them still half-frozen from their walk. They walked straight to the hearth, each pulling off their gloves and holding their hands out to warm them. That gave Jan a chance to look around, admiring the high-beamed wood ceiling of the classic New England farmhouse.

She imagined it had looked much the same a century ago, although the place was immaculate and the hardwood floor polished to a high shine.

There were two sofas on either side of the hearth with a long oak coffee table in between them. The green sofa fabric looked reminiscent of the '50s, but it was spotlessly clean and adorned with lovely embroidered pillows, similar to those one could find in a designer showroom.

"Dottie?" Harley called out, disappearing down a hallway. "We've got company."

"I'm finally warming up," Bob said, loosening the scarf around his neck and unbuttoning his coat. "How about you?"

Jan smiled as she removed her coat. "I'm fully defrosted, although my toes are still tingling a bit."

"So are mine," he said with a sigh, then turned to face her. "Jan, I'm so sorry our date turned out this way. I'm sure you weren't planning a nature hike on a night like this. I still can't believe I locked the keys in my car. And my phone as well." He shook his head. "What in the world was I was thinking?"

"It was an accident," she said, not wanting him to feel bad. "And I think we handled the situation quite well." She flashed a smile. "Now we're warm and toasty again, and ready for the next adventure."

He stared at her for a long moment, then cracked a smile. "You're something else, Jan Blake."

"I'll take that as a compliment," she said as they moved toward the nearest sofa. She was eager to take a closer look at the embroidered pillows and pulled one on her lap after sitting down.

She admired the neat, even stitches and the colorful image of a plant embroidered on it. The name of the plant, *sorrel*, was embroidered underneath a vibrant green leaf. She saw other herb names on the pillows as well, including *burdock* and *yarrow*, all found in Maine.

"Looks like whoever made these pillows really likes flowers," Bob said, moving a red rose-embroidered pillow aside to sit next to Jan.

"Flowers and herbs," Jan said, her gaze moving over the other pillows. Then she looked down at the hardwood oak floor and realized the rug beneath the coffee table had been hand-stitched too, depicting a farmstead full of goats.

"Uh-oh," Jan said, wincing as she stared down at the teeth marks in Bob's boots. "Looks like the goat got more than a nibble."

"It's a banner night," Bob said wryly.

Harley returned, bringing a petite woman along with him. "This is my wife, Dottie," he said.

"Nice to meet you, folks," Dottie said, beaming at them. Her smile lit up the room and Harley seemed to bask in it. She had silver hair like her husband, but hers was thick and swept up into a bun on the top of her head. She wore a black tunic top and slacks under a red apron.

Jan recognized one of her favorite Bible verses stitched in white on the front of the apron: "Man shall not live by bread alone; but man lives by every word that proceeds from the mouth of the Lord (Deuteronomy 8:3)."

"We haven't had much company lately," Dottie said, folding her hands over her slender waist, "so we're glad to have you." Dottie walked over to the sofa opposite them and took a seat while Harley remained standing.

"I thought I heard singing earlier when I was at the stove. Was that you two?"

Jan smiled, hoping their voices hadn't been off-key. "I'm afraid so. We decided to sing while we walked to keep our minds off the cold."

"Well, that's a wonderful idea. And you two have lovely voices." She glanced over at her husband. "Harley and I used to sing in our church choir back home. He sounds just like Elvis Presley."

"Now, Dot," Harley said, a flush on his grizzled cheeks, "that's going a bit too far. We don't want to give these folks the wrong idea."

Jan smiled, glancing over at Bob and thoroughly enjoying herself. He looked more relaxed now too. "Where is back home?"

"Buffalo, New York," Dottie told her. "We lived there for thirty years, but decided we wanted to try farm life and have always loved Maine."

"Once Dottie sets her mind on something, there's no changing it," Harley said, trying to sound gruff but unable to hide the affection in his voice.

"So how long have you lived here?" Bob asked them.

"Oh, about six months." Dottie smiled. "So this is our first Christmas in our new home. Our kids and grandkids are all coming to visit for the holiday so we've been busy fixing up the second- and third-floor bedrooms."

They chatted together for a while longer, then Dottie rose to her feet. "Well, supper should be ready by now and you arrived just in time to join us."

"Thank you for the invitation," Bob said, glancing at Jan, "but we don't want to be any bother. If we could just get my car unlocked..."

"It's no bother at all," Dottie countered with a wide smile. "Besides, if Harley heads outside now, his dinner will be cold by the time he gets back."

"Don't bother arguing with her," Harley told them with a cheerful grin. "Like I said, once she sets her mind to something, there's no stopping her."

Jan gave Bob an encouraging smile, acknowledging that Dottie Ferrell's cheerful hospitality was too infectious to resist. And, as a cross-stitch enthusiast, she'd love to find out if Dottie had made those gorgeous pillows herself.

Bob glanced at his watch. "Well, we've already missed our dinner reservation, so if you'll have us, we'd be honored to join you."

Two hours later, Bob pulled his car into Jan's driveway. "I don't think I'll be able to eat another bite for three or four days."

She laughed. "It must have been that third piece of pumpkin pie."

It turned out that Dottie was not only an expert in embroidery but cooking as well. They'd feasted on roast chicken, twice-baked potatoes, strawberry salad, home-canned succotash, and fresh baked bread. The conversation had been as good as the food, with Bob recommending local eateries, including Tea for Two, and Jan inviting them to Lancaster Community Church, where they would be more than welcome to join the choir.

Bob walked Jan to the back of the house, where Earl Grey greeted them at the door. He took one tentative sniff at Bob's chewed boot and then scurried away. "I guess he doesn't like the scent of goat."

"Thank you for the lovely evening, Bob," Jan said, smiling up at him.

"So you're not too disappointed?" he asked, his brown eyes searching her face. "To say this date didn't turn out like I planned would be a huge understatement."

"You're right," she said, her smile widening. "It went even better than planned. I saw a beautiful view of Lancaster, went Christmas caroling during a snowy hike, met a friendly goat, and had a delicious dinner with its kind owners."

He laughed, shaking his head. "You sure know how to put a positive spin on it."

"I mean it," she told him. "Best of all, I can't believe Dottie offered to embroider custom-made pillows for my daughters and daughter-in-law for Christmas. So my shopping is almost done for them."

He smiled. "I don't think I could have had nearly as much fun with anyone else." He gave her a long, lingering look before leaning over to kiss her cheek. "Good night, Jan."

"Good night, Bob," she breathed, his words touching her heart as he turned around to walk out the door.

Jan began humming to herself, the same Christmas tune they'd sang together on their long, cold walk to the Ferrell house, their voices blending in perfect harmony.

She knew how much pride Bob took in managing all aspects of his life, so seeing how well he'd handled this evening when everything seemed to go wrong—including his run-in with a hungry goat—made her like him even more.

CHAPTER TWELVE

Y ou're doing it again," Elaine said, watching Jan stand near the oven in their cozy, sunlit kitchen. Her cousin wore a pair of blue jeans and a light-pink sweatshirt, but her feet were still clad in her pink slippers.

Jan started at the sound of Elaine's voice, almost as if she'd forgotten that someone was in the room with her. She turned from the kitchen counter, where she'd been transferring fresh-baked cookies from the cookie sheet to a cooling rack. "Doing what?"

"Smiling to yourself," Elaine teased, folding her hands on top of the kitchen table. Clad in a thick, furry robe and slippers, Elaine took a sip of her tea, feeling much too lazy for a Tuesday morning. "That must have been some date with Bob last night."

Jan's smile widened. "You wouldn't believe it if I told you."

"Try me," Elaine said, as Jan carried a plate of spiced pumpkin raisin cookies over to the table and sat down.

"Let's just say it involved a goat."

Elaine blinked, never expecting those words to come out of Jan's mouth. Then she burst out laughing. "Okay, now you *have* to tell me everything!"

Jan chuckled, reaching for a cookie as Elaine poured her a cup of English breakfast tea from the yellow ceramic teapot setting on the table between them. "Where do I begin?"

Elaine helped herself to two warm cookies, placing them on the dainty china plate in front of her, then settled back in her chair as Jan began telling her about her date with Bob.

As she listened, Elaine took a bite of her cookie, enjoying the spicy pumpkin flavor and chewy raisins and feeling so snug in the warm kitchen as frost sparkled on the windowpanes.

By the time Jan got to the part about Harley Ferrell accusing Bob and Jan of trying to steal his goat, Elaine was doubled over with laughter.

"Oh my," Elaine said, gasping to catch her breath. "Bob was so brave—facing down a shotgun like that! And it sounds like he had such a romantic evening planned for the two of you."

"But that's the best part," Jan said, leaning forward in her chair, her blue eyes sparkling. "It *was* romantic. Maybe the most romantic date we've ever had. Singing a Christmas carol to keep us from freezing during our walk, the supper with two complete strangers who we now consider friends, and of course, that adorable, hungry goat." She drew in a deep breath, her face slightly flushed. "I know it sounds crazy, but it was just…the most wonderful evening."

Elaine's throat tightened at the glow of happiness she saw on her cousin's face. Jan looked so in love. Her mind harkened back to dating her late husband, Ben, and the certainty of knowing that she wanted to spend the rest of her life with him—no matter what that life might bring. And their life together had been better than she'd ever imagined—and given them two wonderful children and two adorable grandkids.

Plus so many wonderful memories.

"Elaine?"

She looked up to see Jan looking quizzically at her. "Oh, I'm sorry, you caught me daydreaming. Did you say something?"

"I asked if you liked the cookies."

Elaine smiled. "They're delicious—and the perfect treat on a cold morning." She reached for a third cookie. "Are you trying out a new recipe?"

"Yes, and trying to get back into the groove of making a cookie of the day." Jan gave a small sigh. "We've been closed for too many days in a row now. I'm starting to get restless."

"Me too," Elaine admitted. "If only that toxicology report would come back, we could finally move forward. I feel as stuck as a car on a bluff with the keys locked inside." Then she grinned. "That was an amazing story, by the way. Sometimes the best moments are the ones we don't plan."

"They sure are," Jan said wistfully.

Elaine sipped her tea, remembering some romantic, unplanned moments with Ben. Those memories would always be precious to her, but what about making new memories? She thought about Nathan, wondering once more if she'd made the right decision to wait.

"So what should we do today?" Jan asked, refilling her empty teacup and then topping off Elaine's cup. "I really miss the hustle and bustle of the tearoom. I've been feeling a bit lazy, to be blunt about it."

"Me too," Elaine replied. "That's why I told Rose to take the day off to do some Christmas shopping. I know she wants to practice her baking, but without any customers to serve all the pastries, our freezer is filling up with dough."

"Yes, we're well stocked on pastries—especially sugar cookies." She grinned. "That's never a bad thing, is it?"

Elaine chuckled as she reached for another cookie. "No, not bad at all." Then she looked up at Jan. "Say, why don't we have all your grandkids over after they get out of school to decorate some of those cookies?"

"That's a great idea. I'll call their parents later and set it up."

Elaine nibbled on her cookie, wondering what to do with the morning that stretched ahead of them. "What do you say to good old-fashioned deep-cleaning day?"

Jan looked up at her. "You mean like a Grandma Willard cleaning day?" She smiled. "With our sleeves rolled up and a scrub brush and bucket in our hands?"

"Exactly." Elaine grinned. "The tearoom and kitchen are clean, but my office has some dirt and dust settled in the grooves of the floorboards."

"So does my bedroom," Jan said, perking up at the idea. "If we get started now, we can be done by noon and treat ourselves to lunch somewhere."

"Perfect." Elaine stood up, gathering the empty plates and teacups in her hands and carrying them over to the sink.

"I'll wash those," Jan said, rising from the table, "while you get started on the office. The first one done cleaning this morning gets to pick the restaurant for lunch."

Elaine grinned as she turned around and hurried up the stairs to her bedroom to change out of her pajamas, already looking forward to the day ahead.

Three hours later, she knelt on the floor of her office, digging at a stubborn spot in the corner. Every inch of the office sparkled, from ceiling to floor, except for this one small spot. She smiled to herself as she gently rubbed at the stain with a damp rag, remembering Grandma Willard saying she always liked to pray while she was on her knees scrubbing the floor, cleaning away debris on both the outside and the inside.

She'd turned the radio up in her office before beginning her cleaning spree and was now humming along to "O Come, All Ye Faithful" as she removed the last of the spot, then sat back on her heels with a happy sigh. The floor looked perfect. All she had left to do was run a damp rag over the baseboard and she'd be done.

The roar of a vacuum cleaner overhead told her that Jan was vacuuming the area rug in her bedroom. That probably meant she was almost done too. She smiled to herself, moving into action so she would win their fun little game and choose their lunch spot. A grilled cheese sandwich and a cup of soup at Kate's Diner sounded mighty good to her right now.

Starting at the door to the office, Elaine ran the cleaning rag around the eight-inch-tall baseboard separating the floor from the walls. The dings and scratches on the original baseboard just gave it more character, along with the intricate, decorative carvings near the top edge, no doubt crafted by hand over a century ago.

When she reached the corner of the wall, she turned to start down the next strip of baseboard. That's when she saw a tiny slip of paper trapped behind the baseboard, near her desk. Using the tip of her thumbnail, Elaine worked for several minutes to wiggle it loose, assuming it was an old receipt that had fallen though the tiny gap that separated the wall from the baseboard.

But when the paper finally slid free from the baseboard and she was able to pull it out, she saw that it wasn't a receipt at all. It was a photograph.

Surprised, she set down her cleaning rag and stared at the old black-and-white photo in her hand. It was a picture of a three young men, perhaps in their early twenties, and judging from the way they were dressed and the Model T car in the background, the photograph had been taken sometime in the late 1920s or early 1930s.

Elaine flipped the photograph over and saw three names scrawled on the back: Hawkins, Kershaw, and Murphy. The first two surnames she didn't recognize, but the last one was very familiar.

Forgetting about the contest to see who could finish cleaning first, Elaine bounded to her feet and hurried out of her office. She met Jan walking into the kitchen.

"Looks like it's a tie," Jan said, smiling as she untied her cleaning apron.

"No, you win," Elaine said cheerfully. "I didn't quite finish the job because I got distracted by this." She held out the photograph. "I found it behind the baseboard."

Jan's eyes widened as she took the photograph from Elaine's hand. "Well, this is interesting. Who are these men?"

"I have no idea," Elaine told her. "But one of them is named Murphy, so it's possible he's related to Des Murphy. Maybe I'll stop by Murphy's General Store sometime soon and ask him about it."

Jan smiled, handing the photograph back to Elaine. "I love it when we find these little surprises around the house. Who knows what other treasures might be buried here?"

Elaine set the photograph on the kitchen table, then took off her cleaning apron. "If you're ready to go to lunch, I can finish the rest of my cleaning afterward. Do you have a place in mind?"

Before Jan could answer, the front doorbell rang.

"Who could that be?" Elaine asked as she and Jan headed toward the door. When she opened it, she saw Trooper Daniel Benson standing on the other side.

His large frame filled the doorway as he held up a sizable brown envelope. "I have the toxicology results."

IT TOOK ALL of Elaine's willpower to hold off asking Trooper Benson for the results until they had him seated at a table in the tearoom with a cup of English breakfast tea and platter of cookies in front of him.

"This hits the spot," the trooper said, finishing his first cookie in two bites. Then he sat back in his chair with a contented sigh. "I wish all my official visits were like this."

"We're just happy to finally get the results," Jan told him.

Elaine's gaze fell on the unopened brown envelope in front of him. Would the information inside that envelope help them or hurt them? As anxious as she'd been for the results to arrive, now Elaine's heart was racing in her chest. She took a deep breath and tried to relax. Then she glanced over at Jan, seated at the opposite side of the table. Jan looked calm, but both of her hands tightly cradled her teacup and one finger nervously traced the outline of a blue rose on the china.

The trooper placed his cup back in the saucer and then reached for the envelope. He opened it, pulled out a couple sheets of typewritten paper, then cleared his throat. "So it looks like you're in the clear."

Elaine blinked, taking a moment to let the words sink in. "You mean, they didn't find anything suspicious in the maple brownies or the tea?"

Daniel shook his head. "Nope. No foreign substances or toxins of any kind. Nothing you wouldn't expect to find in loose tea leaves, according to the lab."

Elaine breathed a silent prayer of thanks, so happy to hear the good news and knowing Rose would be relieved as well. It still didn't explain what had happened to Clara, but at least she hadn't actually been poisoned.

Jan smiled. "Well, that's a relief." Then her smile faded. "Although we still have a mystery on our hands. What in the world caused Clara to collapse like that?"

"Maybe it *was* just a food allergy," Elaine said. "I agree, it's strange, but there doesn't seem to be any other explanation."

"I made a copy of the report for each of you," Daniel said, handing one page to Elaine and the other to Jan. "But there's no reason for the tearoom to remain closed. The lab did a careful analysis of all the food and equipment gathered here and found nothing suspicious."

Elaine studied the report, uncertain what some of the lab values meant. She scanned down to the summary paragraph at the bottom of the report and began to read it out loud. *"After careful laboratory testing and analysis, no toxins or other dangerous substances were found in the submitted products."*

"Wait a minute," Jan said, her forehead creasing as she studied the report. "It says senna is one of the ingredients found in the cinnamon spice tea leaves."

"That's an herb, isn't it?" Elaine asked, looking at the report once more. "Used in medicinal teas?"

"Yes, it is." Jan leaned forward. "But the cinnamon spice tea we served to Clara wasn't a medicinal tea."

The trooper looked between the two of them. "What are you saying? Is senna poisonous?"

"No, not at all," Jan said, shaking her head. "But it is a natural herbal laxative—which could explain River's queasy stomach if he ingested too much of it."

Elaine nodded, as one of the pieces to this puzzle suddenly clicked into place. She checked the report again. "Yes, senna is listed as an ingredient for the cinnamon spice tea that was analyzed—but only that tea."

"So this senna herb," Daniel asked, reaching for another cookie, "would it cause the kind of symptoms that sent Clara Hill to the hospital?"

Jan shook her head. "I don't know. That's the part that doesn't make sense. I'm no expert, of course, but I think, at most, she just would have had an uncomfortable digestive disturbance."

Daniel shrugged. "Then maybe her passing out had nothing to do with the food or drink she consumed here."

Elaine looked over at Jan, wondering what it all meant. One thing was apparent though—the toxicology report proved that there was nothing poisonous in their tearoom that had caused Clara's illness.

Which meant they could open again.

A thrill shot through Elaine at the thought of opening the doors to their tearoom and, judging by the hopeful expression on Jan's face, her cousin felt the same.

Elaine turned back to Daniel. "Thank you so much for coming here today. We've been on pins and needles waiting for this report."

He smiled. "It was my pleasure. I honestly didn't expect the lab would find anything nefarious." He paused for a long moment before adding, "This place is a real asset to our community."

"Thank you," Jan said, smiling as she rose to her feet. "Now I'm going to box up some of these cookies for you to take with you."

He stood up, reaching for his hat. "You really shouldn't . . . "

"Oh, I insist," Jan told him, picking up the platter and carrying it into the kitchen.

Daniel glanced over at Elaine, a smile tugging up one corner of his mouth. "Guess I didn't put up too much of a fight, did I?"

Elaine chuckled. "Not really, but Jan's cookies are hard to resist. I'm just so happy that she and Rose can start baking for our guests again."

A few minutes later, Jan returned with a covered cookie box and handed it to the trooper. "These should last you awhile."

"Don't count on it," he said with a grin, heading toward the door.

Elaine and Jan followed him outside, waving as he walked out to his patrol car.

Then Jan turned to her. "So are you as confused as I am by the presence of senna in that canister?"

"It is strange," Elaine mused as they stepped inside again. "I think I'll call the tea company and ask them if they include senna in those specific tea leaves."

"It's not listed on the label, so perhaps it's some kind of cross-contamination on their end. If so, they need to know. And I'll be interested in what they have to say." Then she looked at her watch. "Let's head out to lunch after your phone call."

"Sounds good," Elaine said, as they walked back toward the kitchen. "Where are we going to eat?"

"Let's go to Lucia's, that fancy Italian restaurant in Bangor."

"Bangor?" Elaine echoed in surprise.

"Why not?" Jan asked, amusement dancing in her eyes. "Since the toxicology report cleared us, I'm in the mood to celebrate. We can do a little Christmas shopping after lunch and still be home in plenty of time for cookie decorating."

"I like the way you think," Elaine said with a smile, looking forward to a fun afternoon. "I'll make that phone call right now. I want to know if there are any secret ingredients hidden in the tea we serve."

LATER THAT DAY, Elaine stood at the kitchen table, helping Avery fill a pastry bag with green frosting.

"Look, Grandma," Kelly said to Jan. "I put a belly button on the snowman!"

Elaine looked over to see a red cinnamon candy placed in the center of a snowman cookie. Nine-year-old Kelly and eleven-year-old Avery, along with Jan's five-year-old twin grandsons, were having so much fun—almost as much fun as she and Jan were.

"Here you go, sweetie," Elaine said, handing the pastry bag to Avery. "Start frosting."

Avery eagerly took the bag and began carefully squeezing green frosting on to the Christmas tree–shaped cookie in front of her.

Elaine stepped back to watch, wiping her floured hands on her apron. Christmas music played in the background and all the kids were half-covered in flour. It was the perfect way to end a productive day.

She and Jan had enjoyed a delicious lunch at Lucia's followed by shopping in some of the specialty shops around Bangor, where they'd both made great progress in whittling down their Christmas gift lists.

Elaine glanced at her cell phone, still awaiting a call back from the tea supply company. Her earlier call before lunch had gone to the company's voice mail and Elaine had left a message explaining her question and urging them to contact her as soon as possible.

"Earl Grey needs more pink frosting," Max announced. The five-year-old sat at the kitchen table holding up his empty pastry bag. A cookie shaped like a cat sat on parchment paper in front of him, although it looked as if most of the frosting had found its way to Max's mouth, judging by the circle of pink frosting around his lips.

His twin brother, Riley, sat next to him, frosting his own cat cookie. Jan had thought the grandkids might get a kick out of decorating the cookies to look like Earl Grey, and she'd been right. Elaine had never seen such creative—and colorful— cat cookies.

Elaine's phone began to ring, distracting her from the fun. She saw Jan look at her and nod as Elaine quickly made her way into the office to answer the phone.

"Hello?"

"Yes, this is Gloria Hanes from the tea supply company. Is this Elaine Cook?"

"Yes, it is. Thank you for returning my call." Elaine gently closed the office door. "As I said in my message, I need to know if senna is one of the ingredients in any of the tea leaves we order from you."

"I've looked into it," Gloria began, "and I can tell you unequivocally that there is no senna present in any of your orders for the last three months. Because of its herbal properties, we reserve senna for only a few of our medicinal herbal teas and they are clearly labeled."

"That's good to know," Elaine replied. "We mix our own special tea blends, including a cinnamon spice that's popular with our customers—specifically using three types of black tea leaves with essences of nutmeg, cinnamon, orange peel, and cloves."

"I can assure you that there is no senna present in any of our black tea leaves."

Elaine was happy to hear it, but wanted to be certain that their supplier wasn't to blame. "So there's no chance of cross-contamination with your herbal teas?"

"Absolutely none," Gloria replied. "We're very serious about quality control with our products. We even tested some samples in our bulk tea leaves here after we received your message and found no trace of senna in any of them."

That confirmed what Jan and Elaine had thought. She thanked the company representative and ended the call.

When she opened the office door, Jan was standing near the doorway. "Was that the tea supply company?"

"Yes. And we were right. They don't add senna in any of the tea leaves we order from them. Which means someone added it to the tea canister after it got to our house."

Jan frowned in confusion. "But who would do such a thing? And why?"

Elaine met her gaze. "I don't know. But we're dumping out all our tea canisters and starting with fresh tea leaves. Then we'll reopen the tearoom for business tomorrow and keep our eyes open for anything suspicious."

CHAPTER THIRTEEN

W hy am I so nervous?" Jan asked, rubbing her hands together.

Elaine stood with her cousin in the spacious entryway between the two parlors of the tearoom, both watching the antique clock on the wall. They'd awakened earlier this morning than usual, eager to start the day off right.

"Because we'll see today if anyone shows up," Elaine replied. "We both know rumors about what happened to Clara and River here have spread around Lancaster. The question is how much damage did they do?"

"Well, at least the folks I spoke to last night seemed excited about our reopening," Jan said, her face brightening. "That has to be a good sign."

Elaine nodded, hoping she was right. "And it's a beautiful, clear day, so the weather shouldn't keep anyone away."

They'd both called regular guests of the tearoom last evening to let them know it would be open today and asked them to spread the word. Elaine also planned to post some signs around Lancaster later today, advertising upcoming Christmas specials at Tea for Two.

The clock began to chime ten times, the sound tightening the nervous knot in Elaine's stomach. She hadn't even been tempted by the delicious blueberry scones that Rose had baked today, or any of the other luscious pastries filling up trays in the kitchen.

Jan tipped up her chin. "Well, this is it. We're officially open for business again."

Elaine smoothed down the skirt of her crimson Victorian-style gown and then straightened her white lace apron. They'd decided to make today extra special by dressing in their Victorian clothes. She'd chosen the damask crimson silk while Jan wore a sapphire blue satin gown that matched her eyes.

Rose appeared in the entryway, wearing a gold taffeta gown embroidered with tiny red flowers. Her wheat-colored hair was swept up into an elegant French roll, but the worried frown creasing her forehead made her look younger than her twenty-six years. "Nobody's here yet?"

"Not yet," Elaine told her. "But it's only ten. I'm sure someone will show up."

"I hope so," Rose said, adjusting a curl drooping from her simple up-do. "Because we have enough pastries to feed an army."

Elaine glanced over at Jan as Rose returned to the kitchen. "We should know better than anyone that a watched teapot never boils."

Jan's face relaxed into a smile. "You're right. Let's pour ourselves a cup of tea and relax. We can talk about our plans for Christmas."

"Great idea," Elaine said as they both turned around to head toward the kitchen. Then she heard the sound of a car outside the house and stopped in her tracks. "We may have a customer!"

Jan hurried over to the window and parted the lace curtain. "It's Macy! And she looks like she brought a friend."

Elaine smiled, thinking she'd never been so glad to see Macy Atherton.

"And I see two more cars pulling up," Jan said excitedly, standing up on her toes as she peered through the window. "And there's another one coming down the road!"

Elaine's smile widened. "We're back in business."

The next few hours passed by quickly as the tearoom did a steady business, serving tea and pastries to their cheerful clientele. Elaine and Jan made it a point to stop by each table and thank the guests for coming.

As closing time neared, Elaine and Jan found a moment alone in the kitchen as Rose was out tending to the last table of guests.

"I'm thrilled with how today turned out," Jan said with a wide smile. "No one mentioned a word to me about what happened to Clara. Did you hear anything?"

"No, nothing," Elaine replied. "That's a good sign, isn't it?"

"I'd say so." Jan carried an empty serving tray over to the counter, setting it near the sink. "And I didn't notice anything suspicious—or more specifically, anyone."

"Neither did I," Elaine said, untying her apron and slipping it off. "Everyone seemed happy with their food and tea."

"No complaints about stomachaches either," Jan said. "Or guests passing out."

Elaine smiled. "Maybe we really are in the clear and can finally put this behind us."

"Maybe." Jan didn't sound convinced. "I'm so glad our guests came back after the incident. But if another one like it occurs..."

A cold chill swept over Elaine. Jan was right—their customers were loyal, but if anyone else became ill at their tearoom, they might not risk ever coming back. "All we can do is continue to be watchful," she said at last. "And trust that God will lead us in the right direction."

"Amen," Jan said softly. Then the kitchen door swung open and Rose walked inside, a wide smile on her face.

"Everyone loved the blueberry scones," Rose exclaimed. "As well as your lemon cookie of the day, Jan. It was a big hit. I like how you used powdered sugar to create a snowflake pattern on the top."

"That was easy and fun," Jan told. "I just used a snowflake cut-out and sprinkled the powdered sugar on top. Now, we might want to try the same technique tomorrow with a colored sugar..."

As Rose and Jan continued to talk about baking, Elaine slipped out of the kitchen and walked upstairs to her bedroom to change clothes. Their day had been a success, but she still intended to pass out the flyers. And maybe solve a small mystery along the way.

An hour later, Elaine walked into Oldies But Goodies, eager to look around and see the latest additions to shelves. She peeled off her gloves, her fingers tingling from the cold, and blew on her hands.

"Good afternoon, Elaine," Fiona greeted her, wearing a green turtleneck sweater and black slacks beneath her red-and-white checked apron. "Are you looking for anything special?"

"Actually," Elaine said with a smile, "I'd like to purchase that sugar bowl you set aside for me."

Fiona blinked. "What?"

"The Meissen rose," Elaine reminded her. Judging by the crowd of people in the antique shop, Fiona probably had orders coming in left and right. "Remember when I was in here the other day and asked you to set it aside for me?"

"I remember you asking me to look for the matching creamer," Fiona said slowly, her brow furrowed, "which I'm sorry to say I haven't been able to find yet. But you didn't say anything about saving the sugar bowl for you."

Elaine opened her mouth to disagree, then suddenly remembered the phone call from Jan that had sent her hurrying out of the shop. "You're right," she admitted. "I got a call and forgot to tell you I wanted to buy it."

"Oh, I'm so sorry," Fiona said, looking crestfallen. "I should have followed up with you. We've just been so busy around here."

Elaine smiled, placing a gentle hand on Fiona's shoulder. "It's not your fault. With everything going on at the tearoom, I was a bit of a scatterbrain that day. But if you wouldn't mind wrapping it up for me now, that would be great."

"Of course," Fiona said, with an eager smile. "Just give me a few minutes to locate it. Items move around a lot this time of year, with customers picking things up and then setting them down—sometimes they end up in the strangest places."

"That's fine, take your time," Elaine told her. "I'd love to browse for a while."

Fiona smiled. "Perfect. And I'll still keep an eye out for that matching creamer and give you a call if I locate one."

Elaine watched Fiona walk away, then headed for the nearest curio cabinet. There was a miniature tea set inside that she thought her granddaughter, Lucy, would love. It was blue and white and matched a similar antique set that Jan owned.

A tap on her shoulder made Elaine turn around.

Nathan smiled. "Hello there."

Her heart skipped a beat—she had not expected to see him. She smiled, realizing they hadn't talked since their awkward dinner together. "This is a nice surprise."

"I just came in to...do some Christmas shopping," Nathan explained. "My mother collects vintage costume jewelry and I've heard they have some unique pieces here."

"I believe Fiona has some right over here," Elaine replied, walking a few feet to a nearby display case. The jewelry inside the case was nestled in black velvet beneath a glass countertop.

"Ah, yes," Nathan said, moving beside her. "They've got quite a collection."

"Are you looking for a particular piece?" Elaine asked. "A brooch? A bracelet?"

"I hadn't really thought about it," he said, staring down at the jewelry.

Elaine saw several pretty pieces. "That gold filigree bracelet is lovely," she said, pointing it out. "I like all the colorful rhinestones."

"Yes, it's nice."

"Or maybe she'd like something simpler. Like that cameo necklace." Elaine glanced up at him, surprised to see Nathan now looking at her instead of the jewelry.

He smiled. "I have no idea. I guess I should ask her before I make a purchase."

"Maybe so," Elaine said, returning the smile and turning from the display case to face him. "Unless you want to surprise her?"

"Well, I'm just browsing today. But you've given me a couple of good choices to think about." Then he cleared his throat. "So how have you been?"

"Just fine," she said cheerfully. "And you?"

"Busy." He took off his gloves and placed them in the pockets of his dark overcoat. "I was glad to hear that Tea for Two is open again."

"Yes, we are." Elaine pulled out a sheaf of flyers from her purse, feeling a little awkward at seeing him again but trying not to show it. "I'm handing these out to businesses in town to do a little promotion."

Nathan held out his hand. "I'll be happy to put some up at the auction house."

"That would be wonderful." She handed the flyers to him, their fingers touching briefly until he placed the flyers into the large front pocket of his coat.

Elaine sensed a strange tension between them. They'd parted on good terms after their dinner together, but how could they go back to being just friends when they both knew he wanted more?

"Are you ready for Christmas?" Nathan asked her.

"Getting there," she said, smiling. "I just have a few gifts left to buy, but I love to shop, especially in places like this."

His gaze moved around the store. "Yes, I don't come here often, because I see so many antiques at the auction house. Things like that old record player over there, always bring back memories." He met her gaze, an amused gleam in his eyes. "Does that make me an antique?"

She laughed. "If you are, then so am I. But I think I prefer the phrase *one of a kind.*"

"One of a kind," he echoed, his gaze lingering on his face. "That sounds about right." Then he cleared his throat. "Elaine, I was wondering..."

Before he could continue, Fiona walked up to them. "I hope I'm not interrupting."

"Not at all," Nathan told her, pulling his gloves out of his pocket and slipping them back on his hands. "I just wanted to stop in and take a look around, but I need to get back to the office." He nodded toward Elaine. "Nice to see you again."

"You too," she replied, then watched him walk out of the shop. The cold breeze that drifted through the open door made her shiver.

"Elaine?"

She turned her attention to Fiona, feeling rude for almost forgetting she was here. "Yes, did you have any luck finding the sugar bowl?"

"I'm afraid not," Fiona said with a frown. "It's been sold."

"Oh no!" Disappointment washed over her and Elaine mentally kicked herself for not coming in sooner.

"I'm so sorry about the mix-up. But I promise to keep my eyes open for another Meissen rose sugar bowl and creamer set. I'll contact you as soon as I find one."

Elaine swallowed a sigh, knowing it was the best she could do. "Thank you, Fiona. And the mix-up wasn't your fault. I should have bought the sugar bowl the day I saw it."

"Don't give up yet," Fiona said with a smile. "I have some great sources and will be in touch with you soon."

Her words buoyed Elaine as she said her good-bye and left the shop. Then she stood on the sidewalk, her gaze scanning the street for Nathan, but he was nowhere to be seen.

As her gaze fell on her red Chevy Malibu parked in front of the antique store, Elaine realized that Nathan must have recognized her vehicle and assumed she'd be inside.

"Well, at least he's not avoiding me," Elaine said to herself. She wondered what he'd been about to ask her—and why he'd left so abruptly.

Elaine sighed, thinking about her unexpected meeting with Nathan as she turned to walk toward Murphy's General

Store. She took comfort in the fact that he'd sought her out at Oldies But Goodies. She valued his friendship and though their meeting had been a little awkward, she sensed that he wanted to remain friends too.

She walked into the general store, adjusting the strap of her purse higher on her shoulder before grabbing one of the hand-held plastic shopping baskets stacked by the entrance. Then she looked around for the owner, Des Murphy, but only saw one of his clerks manning the cash register.

The high shelves lining the aisles in the grocery section of the store made it difficult to see anyone else, so she began slowly walking down each aisle, keeping an eye out for any specials that appealed to her. The store had a little of everything, from clothes to tools to ice cream bars in the grocery freezer. Des was the third-generation owner here in Lancaster and took great pride in his merchandise, making sure it was good quality for his customers.

She paused near a seasonal display of Christmas ornaments and decorative gift boxes. Elaine loved wrapping presents, keeping an array of bows and ribbons among her rolls of wrapping paper. But one gift box on the display table caught her eye. It was a square box, about eleven inches on each side and eight inches deep, with a lovely red Christmas rose on the top cover, surrounded by delicate green-and-white holly and ivy. She picked it up, liking the light but sturdy feel of the box, and knowing it would be perfect for the Meissen sugar bowl and creamer set she wanted to give Jan.

Elaine placed it in her shopping basket, deciding to be optimistic that Fiona would locate the set for her before Christmas.

Then she rounded the corner of one aisle and saw Bethany Elderberry, the store manager, arranging boxes of Christmas lights into a pyramid on another display table. Bethany wore a pine-green apron over a crisp white blouse and navy-blue slacks, her blonde hair pulled back into a high ponytail.

"Hello, Bethany," Elaine said, walking toward her. "Looks like you're keeping busy."

Bethany looked up and smiled. "We always are during the Christmas season." She placed the last box of lights on top of the pyramid and then turned to face Elaine, her gaze dropping to the basket in Elaine's hand. "I see you're buying my favorite Christmas gift box."

Elaine smiled. "I am. It's perfect for the gift I plan to put in it."

"I love those boxes. They're so easy—and can be used year after year." Bethany brushed back an errant curl that had come loose from her ponytail. "Is there anything else I can help you find?"

"Well, actually, I'm looking for Des. Is he here?"

"No, I'm afraid he just left," Bethany said with an apologetic smile. "But Jo is still here if you'd like to talk to her. She's in the back room."

"That would be great," Elaine replied, hoping Jo Murphy, Des's wife, might be able to identify the man in the photograph.

"Follow me," Bethany said cheerfully.

Elaine walked with Bethany to the back of the store and through a swinging door. Pallets full of packaged store goods were lined up on the left side of the large room and a small nook with an office desk sat on the right. That's where she saw Jo.

Jo looked up from the computer, a smile lighting her green eyes when she saw Elaine. "Hello there."

"I'm sorry to bother you while you're working," Elaine said, as Bethany gave them a quick wave and headed back into the main part of the store. "I found..."

"Oh, it's no bother," Jo interjected, rising from the office chair. "I've been looking at numbers for so long that my eyes were beginning to cross."

Elaine smiled. "Well, I won't keep you long." She dug into her purse and pulled out the photograph. "I found this at my house and when I saw the name on the back, I thought Des might know something about it."

Jo leaned closer, her expression curious. "An old picture?"

"Yes, it has the word *Murphy* written on the back, along with two other names." She handed it to Jo. "Do you think one of those men could be related to Des?"

"I'm not sure, although..." Jo's voice trailed off as she tapped the middle of the photograph. "This man looks somewhat familiar. He's got the Murphy smile, don't you think?"

"He just might." Elaine studied the photo. "Maybe you could show it to Des and let me know what he says. I'm quite curious how it ended up in my house."

"Let's go ask him right now." Jo turned around and reached for the coat hanging on a hook by the door. "He left earlier to do some work on a project in his woodshop, and now you've got me curious as well."

"If you're sure it's no bother," Elaine said, eager to find out the answer.

"Not at all. Des will be tickled if this is one of his relatives. And a little mystery in life is always fun, isn't it?"

"It sure is," Elaine agreed, happily following Jo out of the store after quickly paying for her purchase. She couldn't wait to hear what Des had to say and just wished the mystery of who put the senna in the tea canister could be this easy to solve.

CHAPTER FOURTEEN

The fragrant scent of freshly sawed wood surrounded Elaine as she and Jo walked into Des Murphy's heated workshop. It was located in a small, metal-clad outbuilding in the Murphys' backyard and had been outfitted with a variety of saws and other woodworking tools.

On one side of the workshop stood long planks of wood in various lengths and widths. On the other side was a long, wide table with a shelf above it lined with cans of paint and stain.

Des stood next to a large table saw in the center of the room and looked up as the two women walked through the door. He lifted the plastic safety glasses he wore, propping them onto his forehead.

"Well, this is a surprise," he said, looking between Jo and Elaine. "What brings you to Santa's workshop?"

Elaine laughed as she looked around at some of the toys he'd built. She saw a couple of wooden airplanes, a rocking horse, and a half-finished doll cradle on the table beside him. "You have been busy, Des. These toys look wonderful."

"He sure has," Jo agreed, moving closer to her husband. "I just wish he had a few elves to help him finish in time."

Des grinned. "Don't worry, Mrs. Claus, I'll have them done in time for Christmas."

Jo turned to Elaine. "We have so many nieces and nephews, and we wanted to give them something handcrafted for Christmas."

"That's a wonderful idea," Elaine said. "I still have a lovely doll quilt that my grandmother made for me when I was six. It's one of my special treasures."

"And speaking of treasures," Jo said with a smile as she turned to her husband, "Elaine may have found one for you."

"Oh?" Des replied, looking intrigued as his gaze moved to Elaine.

"Well, I'm not sure if it will mean anything to you," Elaine said as she dug into her purse and retrieved the photograph, "but I found this tucked away in my house."

Des brushed the sawdust off his hands and moved closer to Elaine and Jo. "A picture?"

Elaine held it out to him. "I don't recognize the three men in the picture, but the name Murphy is written on the back."

Des just stared at the photograph, not saying a word.

Jo took a step closer to him. "Des, are you all right?"

Des looked up to meet his wife's gaze, his eyes shining with joy. "I've never seen a picture of my grandpa as a young man before."

Jo's eyes widened in surprise. "You mean your grandpa Murphy?"

Des nodded, a smile wreathing his face. "That's right. Arthur Desmond Murphy. My folks gave me his middle name."

"And you don't have any pictures of him?" Elaine asked, surprised. The proliferation of cell phones and the ability to take a digital photograph at a moment's notice had changed the way people documented their lives, but most folks she knew had at least a few family photographs from the early twentieth century.

Des turned to look at her. "A house fire destroyed all of our old family pictures back in 1941—so we don't have any pictures of Grandpa Murphy before then." He breathed a happy sigh. "I'm so happy you found this one."

"This calls for a celebration," Jo announced. "Let's go inside and enjoy some cookies and apple cider."

Elaine followed Des and Jo into their house, thrilled that she'd brought a family treasure to the Murphys. But she still wanted to know why that photograph had been tucked behind a baseboard in her house.

She was about to ask Des that question when they entered the front parlor, but the sight of the old-fashioned Christmas décor took her breath away. Handcrafted vintage Christmas stockings hung from the mantel above the stone fireplace. A gorgeous Christmas garland made of fresh balsam fir branches sat on the mantel, filling the air with its festive scent.

More fresh garland branches were wrapped around the carved banister of the staircase, adorned with red ribbon and holly.

"This is lovely," Elaine exclaimed, taking in the antique train set circling the Christmas tree in the corner, and the hand-painted nativity set displayed on a walnut table near the front entrance. "Your home should be on a Christmas tour!"

Jo laughed. "Don't give Des any ideas," she said on her way to the kitchen. "He's the mastermind behind all of this and we've got plenty to keep us busy this season."

Elaine laughed as she took a seat in a wing chair, still marveling at the beautiful spirit of Christmas the room evoked.

Des walked over to an antique bureau and opened the bottom drawer.

"I have a picture of my grandpa in an old album here somewhere," he said, kneeling by the drawer. "Ah, here it is."

She watched him carry a thick photo album over to the chair next to her and take a seat. Then he began flipping through the pages.

"Here we go," he said, handing the album to Elaine. "That's him in the top right hand corner, taken in 1942."

Elaine studied the old photograph of a man in uniform. "So he served in World War II?"

"He sure did," Des said proudly. "Enlisted right after Pearl Harbor. He was twenty-five years old at the time and had just gotten engaged to my grandma, but he said it was his duty to fight for our country." He smiled as he looked up at Elaine. "My, the stories he told. After he retired, he spent almost every day in the store while I was growing up. He'd sit on a stool with a cup of coffee and spin stories for the customers all afternoon. Some of the stories were about the war, some about his early years on the farm growing up, and almost all of them kept his listeners on the edge of their seat—me included."

Jo entered the parlor carrying a tray with three mugs on it and passed them around. "Your mom always regretted not writing down his stories. She told me once that he was a better storyteller than most of the old radio shows."

"That he was," Des said wistfully. "But I've still got most of them up here." He tapped his forehead. "Grandpa Murphy was unique."

Elaine smiled, hearing both love and admiration in Des's voice. "Sounds like you two were close."

"We sure were," Des replied. "When I was eighteen, he even lived with us a short time before his death. Those were some of the best times we had together."

Elaine set the photograph she'd found behind the baseboard next to the photo of Des's grandfather in the album. "He looks like he could be a teenager in this picture. Do you think it was taken in the 1930s?"

"That sounds about right." He smiled down at the picture. "Even in that old photo, you can still see the ornery twinkle in his eye. It must have been taken when he was about seventeen. That's around the time he left Augusta and hitchhiked his way to Lancaster."

Elaine looked up in surprise. "You mean he wasn't from here originally?"

"Your grandpa Murphy was born here, right, Des?" Jo asked.

Des nodded. "Yes, but his folks moved around 1920 and settled on a farm near Augusta. The Great Depression sent him back this way, looking for a job."

"And he found one here?" Elaine asked, starting to put the pieces together.

"Yes, he worked at the local woolen mill for a short time—in 1933, I believe. He became the owner's right-hand man, until he was falsely accused of stealing from the mill. He was exonerated by an airtight alibi." Des picked up the photograph Elaine had brought him. "I'm sure that's why you found this picture at your house."

Elaine stared at him, confused. "What do you mean?"

"Grandpa Murphy boarded at your house for a few months—a lot of the mill workers did back then. Maybe the other two men in the picture boarded there too."

Her mouth gaped. She knew the sapphire ring had originally belonged to the Wood family, who had owned the mill before it was burned and the land was later sold to a banker. And she had recently learned that the former owners of their house, the Gardeners, had taken in boarders. But this was the first time she'd heard mill workers had boarded there.

"What else can you tell me?" Elaine asked, a flutter of excitement in her throat.

He smiled. "What else do you want to know?"

CHAPTER FIFTEEN

"Did your grandpa Murphy ever mention the Wood family?" Elaine asked him. "They originally owned the woolen mill before it was sold to pay off debts."

Des nodded. "He always said they were good people— honest and hardworking. Said they got a raw deal too, although he never elaborated on that."

"Anything else?" Elaine asked, eager for more. "Anything about a sapphire ring?"

His brow furrowed. "A ring?"

"It's a long story," she said with a smile.

He thought for a long moment, then shook his head. "Sorry, Elaine, but I don't remember anything else about the Wood family and no stories about a sapphire ring. Frankly, most of his tales from that time in his life were about his escapades around town—all just harmless hijinks."

Elaine took a sip of apple cider from her mug, her mind working furiously. "Do you recognize the other two names on the back of the photograph? Kershaw or Hawkins?"

Des shook his head. "No, and I can't remember my grandpa ever mentioning those names." Then he snapped his fingers together. "Wait a minute—I do remember something. That car in the photo is a Model T, right? Is it a Tudor sedan?"

"That's exactly right," Elaine said, surprised at his vintage car acumen. "I looked it up. And judging by the picture, it was probably made in 1925."

"That was the first car Grandpa Murphy ever owned." Des grinned. "He used to tell stories about that car. He'd named it Wally—in honor of the guy who sold it to him. Both Wallys— the man and the car—used to get Grandpa Murphy in all kinds of trouble." Des arched a brow. "Maybe one of these men in the photo is *that* Wally."

"Wally," Elaine echoed, both intrigued and determined to do some follow-up research. "Thank you so much, that helps. This is one of those little mysteries that I love to solve."

Jo grinned. "We're just happy you found the picture. May we have a copy?"

"You can have the original," Elaine said with a grateful smile. "I scanned that photo and have a copy on my computer, so I don't need this one anymore."

"You don't know how much this means to me," Des said wistfully. "There's got to be something I can give you in return."

Elaine shook her head, touched by the offer. "You've already given me more than you know," she told him. Then another thought occurred to her, sparked by the dazzle of Christmas lights on the tree. "But I am in the market for some homemade toys for my grandchildren and Jan's—if you have time to make them."

Des chuckled, rubbing his hands together with delight. "I can't think of anything I'd rather do. Let me get a paper and pencil so I can write down the specifications."

Elaine sat up in her chair, taking another sip of the warm cider and feeling the joy of the season surrounding her. A joy heightened by the newest piece of the puzzle she'd discovered, thanks to Grandpa Murphy. He might have even known who hid the sapphire ring in the wall—although he surely would have told *that* story.

But someone knew. And now that she had discovered that workers from the woolen mill had been among the boarders at her house in the 1930s, that someone might be one of them.

Her instincts told her there were more secrets connected to that photograph—and she couldn't wait to uncover them.

THE NEXT DAY, Jan spotted an open parking spot directly in front of Kate's Diner. "Perfect timing," she said to herself, smiling as she pulled into the spot.

Christmas lights outlined the plate glass window of the diner, blinking a bright red and green. Her stomach growled as she switched off the engine and opened the car door, a reminder that she'd skimped on breakfast in anticipation of lunch out with her son, Brian.

Brian had called her last night, surprising her with an invitation for lunch. She suspected he wanted her to help him shop for a Christmas gift for his wife, Paula, who shared Jan's taste in jewelry. And Jan was thrilled at the thought of spending some one-on-one time with her busy son.

She headed toward the front entrance of the diner, her boots crunching on the snow. The busy sidewalk was full of people out and about on their lunch hour, their arms full of bags and packages.

The inside of the diner was bustling too, with only one empty table in sight. When Jan realized that Brian hadn't arrived yet, she hurried over to it, unwrapping the blue knit scarf around her neck and then unbuttoning the black wool coat she wore before slipping it off.

"Merry Christmas, Jan!" Pastor Mike called out to her from a few tables away.

"Merry Christmas," Jan replied, smiling and waving at her pastor from Lancaster Community Church and his wife, Sarah, a nurse at the clinic.

She hung her coat on the back of the chair, then took a seat, enjoying the cozy warmth surrounding her and the mouth-watering aromas emanating from the kitchen.

Jan looked around as Bing Crosby crooned "Silver Bells" over the diner's sound system, then saw a waitress walking toward her.

"Hello," the waitress greeted her with a smile. She placed a menu on the table. "Just one today?"

"Actually, I'm meeting my son, so we'll need two menus."

"May I get you something to drink while you wait?" the waitress asked, placing a second menu on the table.

"A hot tea would be lovely," Jan told her. "Black, please."

"Coming right up."

A cheerful voice behind her said, "You must really love tea, Jan, since you drink it away from home."

Jan turned to see Sharon Reddick, the real estate agent who'd sold her and Elaine their house, seated at the table behind her with an older woman whom Jan didn't recognize. "Hello, Sharon. This is a nice surprise. And I do love tea— that's why I have the perfect job."

Sharon laughed. "Jan, this is my mother, Doris Lam. She's visiting from Chicago for Christmas. Mom, this is Jan Blake, one of the owners of Tea for Two."

"It's so nice to meet you," Sharon's mother said. "I've heard wonderful things about your tearoom."

"Thank you," Jan replied. "I hope you can stop by before you leave town."

"Oh, we will," Sharon promised.

Jan chatted with the women for a few minutes longer before turning back around in time to see Brian walk through the door of the diner.

He was dressed in dark slacks and black leather bomber jacket, his cheeks red from the cold. "Hey, Mom," he said, approaching the table. "Looks like you beat me here."

"Just by a few minutes," she said, rising up to give him a hug.

As they both sat down, the waitress arrived with Jan's tea, setting it in front of her. Then she turned to Brian. "May I get you something to drink, sir?"

"Coffee is good for me," Brian said, leaning his forearms on the table. "What's your special today?"

"Crab linguine alfredo," she said, pulling her notepad and pencil from the pocket of her apron. "And today's soup is split pea."

Brian looked over at Jan. "Shall we order two specials?"

She nodded. "Sounds good to me."

After the waitress left, Jan leaned back in her chair and gazed at her son. "You look good today."

He grinned. "You always say that."

"It's always true," she said, chuckling. "How's work?"

"Busy, as usual. But I've decided to play hooky for the rest of the day."

"I suspected as much," Jan said with a smile. "Are we shopping for Paula's Christmas gift after lunch?"

"No, I bought that a week ago. I have something else in mind for us."

Jan recognized the mischievous twinkle in Brian's eyes and wondered what he had up his sleeve. "I'm almost afraid to ask."

Brian reached into his jacket and pulled out a white envelope, handing it to Jan. She could see the words *Merry Christmas* written on the front in his handwriting.

Jan opened the envelope and pulled out two slips of paper inside. "Movie tickets?"

He smiled. "There's a matinee at the Pine," he said, referring to Lancaster's historic theater. It had been built in the early twentieth century and at one time had featured vaudeville acts, musical comedies, and silent movies. After falling into disrepair in the 1960s, it had recently been restored to its former glory.

"They're showing *It's a Wonderful Life* this afternoon," Brian continued. "I thought we could go together."

She stared at her son, tears welling in her eyes that he'd remembered their old family tradition. Every Christmas Eve when Brian, Amy, and Tara were growing up, they'd gone to the candlelight service at church and then returned home for a pajama party, complete with popcorn and an annual viewing of *It's a Wonderful Life*.

"Brian," she breathed, so touched by his thoughtfulness, "this is perfect."

He smiled. "Merry Christmas, Mom."

The waitress arrived with their food and both Jan and Brian dug into their crab linguine alfredo and the basket of warm, buttery breadsticks. As they enjoyed the delicious food, they caught up with each other on the week's events.

"So the tearoom is back in business," Brian said, taking the last bite of his linguine.

"It sure is, and doing well, considering." Jan took a sip of her tea, feeling full and satisfied. She usually couldn't resist the aroma of popcorn at the movie theatre, but this time it might be easier than usual.

"And what about the review from the food critic?" he asked. "Is it out yet?"

Jan put down her cup, the question unsettling her. "No, and I'm not sure what's going on. Clara was going to spend a long weekend at a Green Glade cottage before heading back to Portland, but now it sounds like she plans to stay there awhile."

Brian arched a brow. "Well, with her job, she can work from anywhere. Perhaps she's combining business with pleasure for a Christmas vacation."

"Maybe," Jan said, before taking another bite of her linguine.

"As long as she gives Tea for Two a good review, I guess it doesn't matter where she stays. Do you know when it will be published?"

"I don't know when, or even if there will be a review. Clara didn't say anything about it when Rose and I saw her in the hospital and I didn't think that was the right time to ask her about it."

He frowned. "Maybe that's for the best—after what happened to her. A bad review would be worse than no review."

"I suppose you're right," Jan said. "I just wish we know *why* it happened."

"Mom, you'd tell me if you need any money, right?" Brian asked, his gaze intent on her face. "I know the tearoom was closed for several days and..."

"I'm fine," Jan said with a smile, holding up one hand to stop him. "You don't need to worry about me. The tearoom is still a dream come true for me—in every way."

Relief flashed on his face. "Well, that's good to hear." Then he checked his watch. "We'd better get going if we want to make the movie."

"Well, I'm ready," she said, pushing away her empty plate. "That was delicious. Now bring on Jimmy Stewart!"

TWENTY MINUTES LATER, they walked into the Pine Theater. Even though Jan had been there since the restoration, she still marveled at the tiled, domed entryway and the stained-glass windows. There were two theaters available: the original large auditorium and a smaller theater that had been added in the late 1940s.

Since Brian had purchased the movie tickets in advance, they were able to skip the ticket line and go directly to the concession stand.

"You're sure you don't want any popcorn?" Brian asked her again as they approached the counter.

"Positive," she told him. "I'll just have an iced tea."

He nodded, then placed his order, asking for a large popcorn with extra butter. Then he turned to Jan. "I'll have plenty of popcorn in case you change your mind."

She laughed, patting his arm. "You know me too well."

Then she stepped away from the counter to make room for the other customers and to give herself time to admire the marble columns, decorative moldings, and the three original crystal chandeliers hanging from the ceiling.

One of her fondest memories as a child was watching a John Wayne western at the Pine with her father, and sharing a bucket of popcorn between them.

She smiled to herself, so happy to now be making another precious memory with her son. With a contented sigh, she turned around to look for him.

That's when she saw River White approaching her.

"Hello, Jan," he said. "This is a nice surprise."

"Hello, River. Are you here for a newspaper story or a movie?" Jan asked him.

"Both, I hope." He moved a step closer to her. "Tell me, has that food critic, Clara Hill, caused any more trouble at your tearoom lately?"

His question perplexed her. "Trouble? The woman suffered a bad reaction and passed out. That's hardly her fault."

He sniffed. "Maybe. Maybe not."

Something about his tone made Jan suspicious. "Is there something you're not telling me?"

River breathed a long sigh, then leaned closer to her, his voice low. "Let's just say that Clara Hill isn't as sweet and innocent as she pretends to be. I've done a little digging and there's something you should know about her."

CHAPTER SIXTEEN

Jan stared up at River. "What is it?"

A muscle flexed in his jaw. "Clara Hill is using you and Elaine."

Jan blinked in surprise. "What makes you say that?"

"Because I talked to a friend of mine who works for a newspaper in Massachusetts. They've offered Clara a job." River said, moving a step closer to Jan. "From what I've gathered, they've even dangled the possibility of a syndication deal for her column."

So far, Jan wasn't impressed with River's investigative skills. "So she got a job offer? Is that it?"

"My friend says she's waiting for the *Pelican* to make a counter-offer. And who knows what that woman might pull to get an upper hand in negotiations?" He stared intently at Jan. "She was the talk of the town a few days ago."

Jan stared at him for a long moment. "Wait, are you saying she faked her illness as a publicity stunt?"

"Stranger things have happened in the news business." He shrugged. "And the story of a food critic getting poisoned at an establishment she was reviewing would really sell papers. In fact, it would probably end up on the wire service and be reported all over the country." River frowned at her expression. "Maybe that sounds crazy to you, but I've heard that Clara is holed up in one of the cottages at Green Glade, so who knows what she's got up her sleeve."

Jan glanced over at Brian, who still waited at the concession stand. Then she turned back to River. "Her illness was quite real. I was at the hospital, remember? You were there too."

She remembered now that he'd seemed a little nervous or preoccupied at the time, and wondered if he'd been suspicious about Clara even then.

He placed a hand over his stomach, as if reliving the moment. "It's true. I didn't feel well after my visit to your tearoom, but Clara's reaction was extreme." He gave her a skeptical smile. "Certainly more than a stomachache."

Jan didn't know what to say. She'd never doubted Clara's sudden illness. You couldn't fake pale skin or the clammy perspiration that had beaded her brow. The paramedics had noted her low blood pressure and the doctor had obviously taken it seriously too.

No, Clara hadn't been faking her illness. But Jan and Elaine had both wondered why Clara was spending so much time staying at a lake cottage in the middle of winter when she didn't know anyone in Lancaster.

"Here's another wrinkle," River continued. "She hasn't written a review for your tearoom yet, has she?"

"No," Jan replied, "she hasn't." That fact *did* bother her—especially since Clara had been so kind about the incident. She hadn't threatened to sue them and had even balked when Jan insisted that she and Elaine would pay her medical expenses.

"I think Miss Hill is holding out," River surmised, "to see which newspaper makes her the best offer. And she's using her illness as an excuse to hide away at Green Glade."

Jan shook her head. "I just don't believe she would purposely make herself sick."

He shrugged. "People do all kinds of things for money—or fame."

Before Jan could reply, Brian walked up to them, holding a big bucket of popcorn in one arm and a drink tray with two cups in the other. "Ready, Mom? The movie is about to start." Then he nodded at River. "Hello, River. I'm surprised to see you here in the middle of the afternoon. Are you taking the day off?"

"I'm reviewing one of the new Christmas movies," River said, then muttered, "while I still can." Then he gave them both a wave and walked toward the ticket counter.

Brian looked at Jan. "What was that all about?"

"It's just River being River," she said, planning to go into more detail later. She reached over and picked a buttery kernel of popcorn off the top of the bucket and then popped it into her mouth. "Yum."

He grinned. "Good thing I got the large size. I knew you wouldn't be able to resist."

She linked her arm loosely through his as they made their way to the theater section of the movie house. "I just hope the large popcorn is big enough," she teased, putting aside all thoughts of Clara, River, and any possible schemes so she could enjoy a Christmas matinee with her son.

Two HOURS LATER, Jan parted ways with Brian and headed toward her car. The classic Christmas movie had transported her to days gone past and she still felt the glow of cozy nostalgia as she climbed into the driver's seat and started the engine.

The temperature had dropped since lunchtime and her breath came in frosty puffs of air as she adjusted the heater and waited for the car to warm up. She'd planned to head straight home, but the longer she sat there, the more she thought about River's accusation against Clara.

Had Clara Hill come to the tearoom with an ulterior motive? And if so, had her bad reaction helped or hindered her plan?

Jan shook that thought from her head as warm air finally blew from the vents, easing the chill in the car. She pulled out of the theater parking lot, telling herself that River was acting on rumors and innuendo. The only way she could find out the truth was to go to the source.

No doubt Clara would be surprised to see her show up at Green Glade this afternoon. And Jan intended to use the element of surprise to her advantage.

By the time she arrived at the cottage where Clara was staying, a flurry of tiny snowflakes fell like silver glitter from the sky. Jan stepped out of her car, taking a moment to appreciate the beauty of the snow-covered fir trees and the winter wonderland that surrounded her.

When she reached the front door of the cabin, she took a deep breath before knocking three times, then heard the gobble of a wild turkey roosting somewhere in the distance.

As she waited on the front stoop, her ears picked up the sound of footsteps on the other side of the door. There was a long moment where Jan sensed that Clara was looking at her through the peephole.

She knocked again, hoping that Clara wouldn't ignore her. Although, if she did, that might be reason enough to give some credence to River's suspicions about the woman.

Jan was about to give up when the door opened. Clara stood on the other side, wearing a baggy black sweatshirt and a pair of blue jeans.

"Hello," Clara greeted her, a tentative smile on her face. "This is a nice surprise."

"I hope you don't mind my popping in like this," Jan said. "I heard you were still in town so I wanted to stop by and ask how you're doing."

"It's freezing out there," Clara said, opening the door wider. "Please come in."

"Thank you." Jan walked inside, where a fading fire burned in the stone hearth. A game show played on the television in the corner, but the sound had been muted.

"As you can see, I'm doing just fine," Clara said, motioning toward the living room.

Other than the glow of the TV screen and the fire, the rest of the room was completely dark. All the blinds were closed and none of the lamps in the room were turned on.

After walking in from the white snow-covered landscape, it took a moment for Jan's eyesight to adjust to the sudden dimness. When it did, her gaze scanned the rest of the room, which was neat and tidy. The only sign that Clara was staying there was a wool blanket half draped over a loveseat and a laptop computer open on the coffee table.

"I hope I didn't wake you," Jan said, assuming Clara had been napping on the sofa.

"Oh, not at all," Clara assured her. "I had a slight headache earlier, and reducing the light seemed to help." Then she walked over to the nearest end table and switched on a lamp. "There, that's better."

Jan stared at Clara, concerned. "Are you sure you're all right? You're not still feeling the effects of what happened at the tearoom, I hope."

"Not at all," Clara replied, quick to reassure her. "It's probably just eye strain from staring at my computer screen too long. I'm supposed to be on vacation, but I just can't stop writing."

Jan smiled. "Then it must be your true calling."

"I think so." She walked to the other end of the loveseat and switched on another lamp. "It's nice to be able to relax for a few days—especially during the busy Christmas season."

"I'm sure it is," Jan said, moving farther into the room. Now that she was inside, she began to have second thoughts about her purpose for coming here.

She watched Clara walk over to the coffee table and quickly close the laptop before carrying it over to the desk.

Then Clara turned around to face Jan. "I'm sorry I don't have anything to offer you—except water, of course. Would you like a glass?"

"No, thank you. I'm not staying long," Jan promised her. "It's just that I heard something..." She let her words trail off, willing to let Clara wonder where the conversation was going.

All the color drained from Clara's cheeks. "Heard what?"

Jan gave a small shrug. "That you might go to work for a paper in Massachusetts."

The relief on Clara's face was almost palpable. "Oh yes. That is a real possibility, although I'm not letting myself get my hopes up too high."

It was obvious from Clara's reaction that she'd feared Jan knew something *other* than a rumored career move. Something worse. The woman *was* hiding something. But what?

"So do you have family back in Portland?" Jan asked her, trying to stretch out the conversation. "Will you be spending Christmas there?"

"Yes, I have two sisters—both older than I am." Clara smiled. "We always have Christmas dinner together and, as the youngest, I'm usually put in charge of bringing the relish tray."

Jan chuckled. "So your sisters must like to do all the cooking."

"Yes, and that's fine with me. I love reviewing other people's food, but I'm a disaster in the kitchen myself."

Jan saw her opening. "Speaking of reviews..."

"Oh yes," Clara interjected, "you must be wondering about my review of Tea for Two. It's on my to-do list, but I just haven't gotten around to it yet."

"Well, you are supposed to be on vacation," Jan said, hoping Clara might give a hint about what she intended to write in the review, but the woman just smiled at her.

"Yes, the lake area is so peaceful. I'm taking plenty of time to rest and relax."

That was Jan's cue to leave. "Well, take care of yourself," she said, moving to the door. "And if I don't see you again before you leave, good luck with that relish tray."

"Thanks," Clara said, walking her to the door. "I'll probably need it."

Jan gave her a smile and a small wave as she walked outside and headed to her car. Clara was a nice woman, but there was something under the surface that made Jan uneasy. Clara Hill had a secret—one she was definitely trying to hide.

THAT EVENING, JAN stood in front of her dresser mirror and ran a comb through her wet hair. She wore her white terry cloth bathrobe and matching slippers, her skin still a rosy pink from her hot bath.

She opened a jar of face cream and scooped up a generous dollop with two fingers, then began to spread it evenly over her face and neck. When she'd covered that area, she rubbed the excess cream over both arms, enjoying the light rose-milk scent.

The bath had relaxed her and Jan knew she'd have no trouble falling asleep tonight. The hot water had eased the chill from her trek out to Green Glade—a chill that had touched her inside and out after realizing that Clara might not be quite what she'd seemed.

Elaine had been busy in her office when Jan had returned home, so she hadn't spoken to her about it yet. She padded over to the door and switched off the light before heading downstairs, the savory aroma of chicken soup drifting up the staircase.

"Something smells good," Jan said as she walked into the kitchen.

Elaine stood by the stove, slowly stirring a soup in the deep kettle on the burner. She wore her robe too, a long red flannel that tied at the waist, both of them enjoying a lazy evening. "It's just about ready. I see you've had your bath."

"I couldn't resist," Jan said with a contented sigh as she took a seat at the table. Elaine had already set it for supper, including a basket of fresh-baked rolls and creamy butter from the Richardsons' dairy. "Since you made supper, I'll do the dishes."

"Deal." Elaine smiled as she carried the soup pot over to the table and set it on a trivet. Then she picked up the ladle and filled her soup bowl. "I made a big batch so we'll have plenty to freeze for later."

"Good," Jan said as she filled her own bowl, "because I love your chicken soup."

Elaine smiled. "I can't compete with your cooking skills, but I have my moments."

Her words made Jan remember her conversation with Clara earlier and she told Elaine all about it.

"So you think she has a secret?" Elaine asked after Jan had finished her story.

"She was visibly spooked when I mentioned that I'd heard something about her." Jan reached for a second roll and slathered it with butter. "And even more visibly relieved when she realized I was talking about her possibly working for another newspaper."

"So what is she trying to hide?"

Jan sighed. "I have no idea. Or why anything that I might hear would scare her. Unless it has to do with what happened to her here."

Elaine arched a brow. "Do you think River is right about her overplaying what happened here?"

Jan put down her spoon. "No, we both know she wasn't faking. She passed out. The doctor definitely took it seriously."

"But?" Elaine prodded.

Jan shook her head, feeling like the answer was just out of her reach. "But something is *off* with her. She's sweet and funny and hiding something."

Elaine didn't say anything for a long moment, the only sound in the kitchen her spoon hitting the side of her bowl. Then she looked over at Jan. "Is it possible Clara put something in the food that made her sick? I've heard about a rare psychiatric condition where people make themselves sick just for the attention."

"I suppose anything is possible," Jan said, with a slight shrug of her shoulders, "but that doesn't seem to fit her. Not that either one of us knows her well. No one in this area does, as far as I know."

For a moment Jan wondered if that's what Clara liked about Chickadee Lake—a chance for some anonymity. She'd earned herself quite a reputation as a food critic in Portland, often making appearances on local news and radio shows.

Elaine pursed her lips. Then she tore a roll in half and set it on her plate. "Maybe we've got this all wrong, Jan. What if Clara is trying to avoid something—or someone—in Portland? That would be a reason to rent a cottage here."

Jan nodded. "I suppose that's possible."

"An overattentive beau, maybe?"

"Or a demanding editor," Jan said. "Clara mentioned having a headache from working too long on her computer. And the doctor did tell her to take it easy for a few days."

"And if she's negotiating for a better paying job with a possible syndication deal, she might want to lay low until it's done."

"You're right," Jan said. "That makes sense."

Elaine gave her wry smile. "You don't sound convinced."

Jan chuckled. "I know. My intuition just tells me there's more going on with that woman."

"My intuition has been working overtime too. Remember when I told you about my visit with the Murphys? And how happy Des was to have that picture of his grandfather?"

"Yes," Jan said, finishing the last of her soup.

Elaine reached into the bag hanging on her chair and pulled out a copy of the photograph and the rosewood box. Jan watched as Elaine opened the box, revealing the lovely sapphire ring that lay inside.

Jan arched a brow. "Do you think the ring is related to the picture?"

"Possibly. If nothing else, one of the men in the picture may be the key to finding out more about the ring."

Elaine paused a moment, her brow crinkled. "The Murphys didn't recognize the other two names on the back of the photograph, but one of them—or their descendants—might know about the ring. They all boarded here around the time this ring was probably placed in the wall."

"But how will we find them?"

Elaine sighed as she pulled out the ring and placed it on the table between them. The round sapphire caught the light from one of the pendant lamps overhead and glowed a gorgeous blue. "Well, the names Hawkins and Kershaw aren't in the local phone book, but Des thought they probably worked at the woolen mill with his grandfather, Arthur Murphy, so if we can find an employee list for the mill for 1933 and '34..." She let her voice trail off, and then chuckled. "Sounds like a long shot, doesn't it?"

"Maybe for some people," Jan teased. "But we each have unique detective skills that make us a great team. And I have faith that we can solve any mystery—as long as we work together."

CHAPTER SEVENTEEN

Elaine hurried into the east parlor of the tearoom on Friday morning, the long taffeta skirt of her green Victorian-style gown rustling as she walked.

With Christmas day only a couple of weeks away, she and Jan had decided to dress up for work today and celebrate by making special Christmas pastries. Jan and Rose were busy in the kitchen, filling the platters with Christmas favorites, such as sugarplums, gingerbread teacakes, and stuffed dates.

Jan had even devised a way to make miniature Yule log cakes, to the delight of many of their customers.

One of those customers, Macy Atherton, was waving her hand in the air, trying to get Elaine's attention. Elaine took a moment to place a refilled teapot on the table of another customer before making her way over to Macy.

Macy sat up straight in her chair, craning her head to look into the west parlor of the tearoom. "I need some service. Is Archie working today?"

"Yes, he is," Elaine said, knowing that Archie was one of the few people that Macy actually seemed to like. "He just arrived and is in the kitchen at the moment."

"Please let him know that I'd like a cup of white tea," Macy told her, folding her hands in front of her. "And one of those Yule log cakes."

"I'll do that," Elaine said with a smile. Then she turned around and surveyed both parlors to see if anyone else needed service. A lone woman, one Elaine didn't recognize, sat at a table in the west parlor, a dessert plate filled with sugarplums in front of her.

Elaine watched her for a moment, sensing something odd about her. She saw her take a bite of a sugarplum and then grimace, almost as if she was in pain. Then the woman's expression cleared as she took a second bite.

"Strange," Elaine murmured to herself, her mind flashing back to the day Clara had collapsed in the tearoom. The thought of something like that happening a second time gave her a chill and she tried to put it out of her mind.

But as she continued waiting on customers and pouring tea, she kept glancing over at the woman. She looked about forty, with long, raven-black hair that framed her face and reached just below her shoulders. The long curls nestled against a pine-green cardigan sweater adorned with a silver-filigree dove brooch on one side.

Elaine watched as the woman took another bite of the sugarplum and then stared intently at her plate. She shook her head, pressing her lips together, and then sucked in a deep breath and closed her eyes.

"Oh dear," Elaine murmured to herself.

Archie approached her, looking quite dapper in his Victorian-style cutaway suit. A teal silk vest provided a pop of color to the charcoal herringbone jacket and matching trousers.

"Is something wrong, Elaine?" he asked with his British accent as he adjusted the silver silk cravat at his neck.

"Look at that woman by the window," Elaine whispered. "Does she seem to be acting...oddly to you?"

Archie casually moved his gaze toward the window then, after a moment, turned his attention back to Elaine. "I'm not sure what you mean."

Elaine glanced at the woman, who was now reading a book as she speared another sugarplum with her fork. Relief shot through her, along with a tinge of embarrassment. "I thought the woman might not be feeling well, but it looks like I was wrong." Then she cleared her throat. "Macy requested that you bring her a pot of white tea and a mini Yule log."

He smiled. "I'll get right on it."

Elaine watched as he turned around and walked briskly toward the kitchen. She checked on some other customers and then soon followed behind him, feeling a little foolish about her concern over the woman at the window.

When she walked into the kitchen, she saw Rose bent over a dessert plate, with Jan standing at her side. Archie was at the stove, preparing a pot of tea.

"How's it going out there?" Jan asked Elaine, as Rose used the tines of a fork to carefully etch decorative lines into the chocolate frosting of the log-shaped cake.

"Busy," Elaine told her. "How are we doing on pastries?"

"We have plenty of sugarplums and stuffed dates, but the mini Yule logs are running low, so I'm going to have Rose make another batch. We might want to thaw some more cookies from the freezer later."

"Will do," Elaine said, making a mental note in her head.

"There," Rose said, stepping back from the dessert plate. "Does that look like a tree log to you?"

Elaine saw Jan study Rose's work.

"Very good," Jan told Rose. "And I love the knothole you designed in the center. That will be the perfect place for holly leaves and berries."

Elaine watched as Jan used a pastry bag to pipe green frosting into small leaves around the knothole, then added chopped dried cherries to resemble holly berries.

"Now for the finishing touch," Rose said, reaching for the fine mesh strainer sitting inside a bowl full of powdered sugar. Rose carefully lifted the strainer, holding it over the dessert plate, then lightly tapped it until a small flurry of powdered sugar fell on and around the Yule log cake like snowflakes.

"Well done," Archie told them, walking over to the table with a silver tray that already held the teapot and a cup and saucer.

Rose picked up the dessert plate and added it to the tray. "There you go, Archie. I hope Macy likes it."

"I am certain she will let us know either way," Archie said before turning around and heading out of the kitchen.

Elaine walked over to steep another pot of tea while Jan and Rose gathered supplies to mix up another batch of Yule logs.

"Flour, sugar, cocoa powder, espresso powder, vanilla extract, and salt," Jan said, reading off the recipe in front of her while Rose pulled the ingredients out of the pantry.

Then Jan walked over to the refrigerator. "I'll grab the eggs and butter..." Her voice trailed off. "Oh dear."

"What's wrong?" Elaine asked her.

"I'm not sure we have enough eggs. We need six." Jan opened the lid of the egg carton, then smiled with relief. "Looks like there are seven eggs here, so we've got one to spare."

"I can go pick up some up later," Rose offered, setting the dry ingredients on the counter. Then she froze. "Hey, wait a minute. I just remembered something from that day the food critic got sick."

Both Elaine and Jan turned to look at her.

"I didn't have enough eggs to make the third batch of white maple brownies. I was one short." She met Jan's gaze. "And you and Elaine were both busy, so I looked up food substitutions online."

"And?" Elaine prodded.

"And I found out that you can use half of a mashed banana in place of an egg." Rose blanched, raising a hand to her forehead. "I can't believe I forgot about that." Her brow crinkled in worry. "I didn't say a word about it during the police interview."

"I don't think the police are going to care about half a banana," Elaine assured her. "But what about Clara?" She turned to Jan. "Did she mention having any food allergies?"

"No, in fact, Clara said she'd never had a reaction like that to food. She is allergic to latex, but we don't have anything with latex here."

"So it probably wasn't the banana?" Rose asked.

Elaine smiled at her. "I don't think you need to worry, although I suppose we should let Clara know in case she's suddenly developed an allergy to them."

"Yes, I'll send her a message later this evening," Jan said. "Her e-mail address is listed on the Portland newspaper Web site and I know she has her laptop with her."

Elaine picked up the teapot and left the kitchen as Rose began mixing together the ingredients for another batch of mini Yule log cakes. A few of the patrons had left, but the woman in the green cardigan still sat at the window. She sipped at her tea, the book open on the table in front of her.

Then Archie walked up to Elaine. "I must say, there is something a little off about that woman. I saw her talking to herself."

"Really?" Elaine asked, holding the teapot in her hands. "I'd better go see if she's all right."

Archie nodded, then moved off to another table of customers.

Elaine walked over to the woman's table. "Would you like some more tea?"

The woman looked up at her. "No, that's never going to work. I've told you before that it's impossible."

Elaine didn't know what to do, realizing the woman was talking nonsense. She stepped back, preparing to make another call to the paramedics.

Then the woman held up one finger. "Just a moment, please." She tucked her hair behind her ear, revealing a small electronic device attached to her ear. "Yes, I need to go. I'll call you later."

Elaine bit back a smile, realizing the woman had been talking to someone on the phone through a device hidden by her long hair. That probably explained her earlier behavior too, if she was having a conversation with someone.

Elaine wondered if her detective skills were getting a little rusty.

The woman smiled up at Elaine. "Sorry about that—I was on a business call." Then she slid her teacup toward Elaine. "I'd love some more tea. I'm just driving through town, but when I saw your tearoom I had to stop in. It's lovely."

"I'm so glad you like it," Elaine said, as she filled the woman's cup. "And how were the sugarplums?"

"Delicious." The woman gave a happy sigh. "My grandmother used to make sugarplums for Christmas when I was a child, so it was a wonderful treat to find them here."

"You'll have to stop again the next time you're in the area."

"I will," the woman promised, reaching for her cup.

As Elaine walked away from the table, she caught Archie's eye. She walked over to him and explained the simple reason behind the woman's strange behavior.

Archie chuckled. "Well, that's a bit of a laugh. I'm glad she's well and happy."

"Me too," Elaine said as Archie headed back into the kitchen.

Elaine tended to the other customers, then enjoyed a long chat with the Yeatons. Julie was a selectman and had been a year behind Elaine and Jan in school. Her husband, Chuck, worked at the state office building in Augusta, and had quite the sweet tooth.

When she turned away from their table, Elaine saw Macy motioning to her. She swallowed a sigh of exasperation as she made her way over there.

"How was the mini Yule log?" Elaine asked her, noting that only a few dollops of frosting remained on the plate.

"Not bad," Macy told her, looking a bit grim as she scraped up the last of the chocolate frosting and licked it off her fork. "Although I thought the dried cherries were a poor choice for holly berries. Why not use marzipan? That would make more sense."

Leave it to Macy to find something to complain about— even while practically licking her plate clean. "I'll be sure and let Jan know your thoughts," Elaine told her. "But a lot of our customers like the cherries."

"There's no accounting for taste," Macy grumbled. "Now, will you please let Archie know that I'd like some more tea?"

"Of course," Elaine said, happy to turn over their perpetually disgruntled customer to the man she seemed to truly admire.

As she tended to other customers, Elaine kept thinking about her earlier fear that the woman by the window was having a bad reaction to the sugarplums. She didn't want to spend the next several weeks or months worried that someone else would fall sick at the tearoom.

She still didn't know the reason Clara became so ill, but the report from the police lab had made it clear that someone had added senna to one of the tea canisters. But how had someone gotten into the kitchen without being noticed?

Suddenly Elaine had an idea. She walked into the kitchen, where Jan and Rose were plating more desserts. "I've been looking at this all wrong," she announced.

Jan looked up, a quizzical expression on her face. "What are you talking about?"

Elaine moved closer, kicking herself for not realizing it sooner. "We've been looking for the person who put the senna in our tea canister. Maybe we should be looking at the senna instead—especially, where it came from."

Jan's face cleared and she gave a slow nod. "I see what you mean. The senna may lead us to the culprit."

"Exactly," Elaine said with a smile.

Rose looked between the two of them. "But how in the world do you investigate an herb?"

"Good question," Elaine replied thoughtfully. Then she walked over to the drawer and pulled out the phone directory. "Maybe I should ask an expert."

LATER THAT AFTERNOON, Elaine sat at the desk in her office with the phone book open in front of her. She'd found the number for the Maine Department of Agriculture, Conservation and Forestry earlier, but had decided to wait until the tearoom closed for the day to make the call.

After changing out of her Victorian gown and into a pale-green turtleneck sweater and jeans, Elaine had made a beeline for her office.

Now, as she dialed the number, she just hoped someone there could give her some answers.

"Department of Agriculture, Conservation and Forestry," a female voice answered. "How may I direct your call?"

"I'm looking for someone who has knowledge about local plants—especially herbs."

"That would be our botanist, Dr. Bixby," the woman said. "May I tell him who's calling?"

"Elaine Cook."

"One moment please."

She reached for a pen and notepad while she waited, writing the name *Dr. Bixby* at the top of the page. Then a man's voice came on the line.

"This is Walt Bixby," he said.

"Hello, Dr. Bixby," Elaine said, sitting up in her chair. "I'm Elaine Cook, calling from Lancaster, and I'm hoping you can answer some questions I have about plants. Specifically, how to trace them."

"How to trace them?" he echoed, his voice curious. "Are you talking about forensic botany?"

Elaine smiled, surprised it had a name. "I suppose I am, although this is the first time I've ever heard of such a thing."

He chuckled. "Well, it's not well known, but there's been a marked increase in its use and application the last few decades. Forensic botanists combine their knowledge of plant life, biology, and ecology for application to both criminal and civil cases."

"That's fascinating," Elaine said, intrigued by his comment about its use in criminal cases.

"Indeed it is," Dr. Bixby agreed. "But the science itself has been around a long time. In fact, it was used in the Lindbergh kidnapping trial to analyze the wood grain of a ladder."

"So it's a pretty specific science."

"Yes, it even involves molecular biology in some cases. All phases of plant life can help the police gain information about possible crimes."

Elaine circled Dr. Bixby's name on her notepad, sensing she'd found just the person to help her. "So it *is* possible to learn where a certain plant comes from? I mean, the exact location?"

"Absolutely," he said without hesitation. "We can look at seeds, pollen, and leaves—as well as fungal spores in the soil. One case in Arizona was solved when seed pods from a specific tree near the crime scene were found in the bed of a pickup truck of one of the suspects."

Elaine sat back in her chair. "That is impressive. And I'm hoping you can help me solve a mystery involving an herb called senna."

"Go on," he said cheerfully.

"Well, I don't know a lot about senna, but I was wondering if it's grown in Maine—specifically in the Lancaster area."

"Well, it depends," he began. "*Senna hebecarpa,* or wild senna, is listed as a threatened plant in New England due to habitat loss. When it does grow in the wild, it prefers to grow in moist areas, such as such as roadside ditches, meadows, and pastures, although it can tolerate drier growing conditions."

"So it's rare?" Elaine asked.

"Yes, locating wild senna in nature can be difficult. Although senna seeds are available for planting. In fact, *Senna hebecarpa* is often planted by beekeepers since its bright-yellow flower is attractive to bees."

Beekeepers.

Elaine jotted the word down on her notepad and then underlined it three times. She asked Dr. Bixby a few more questions just to make sure she had the information she needed.

"Thank you so much, doctor. You've been a tremendous help to me," Elaine told him.

"Happy I could help," he replied. "You have a good day, Ms. Cook."

"You too," Elaine said, before ending the call. She picked up the notepad and practically ran to the kitchen, where Jan was finishing up the last of the dishes.

"So I made the call and got to talk to a botanist."

"Wonderful," Jan exclaimed, drying her hands on a dish towel. "What did he say?"

"Lots of interesting things." She smiled. "Remember when Annie Richardson told us that Dori had taken up beekeeping to help earn money for college?"

"Yes," Jan replied, untying her apron. "Are you saying the honey we buy from the Richardsons is connected to what happened to Clara?"

"Not exactly. But I have a hunch that we might find some answers there." Then she told Jan what she'd learned about senna and beekeepers.

"It sounds like a good lead," Jan told her, "although I'm not quite sure how the senna would get from their farm to one of our tea canisters."

Elaine glanced at her watch, feeling a little tired after their busy day in the tearoom. "I'll make a trip out to the Richardsons' dairy sometime in the next couple of days and ask them about it."

"You can pick up some eggs while you're there—a couple of dozen at least. Rose bought a carton at the store to tide us over, but the Richardsons' eggs are the best."

"I'll do that," Elaine promised. "And that brings me to another subject. If you're free this evening, why don't we make a list of the menus for Christmas Eve and Christmas Day when your family comes over? Then I can pick up anything extra we might need at the dairy."

"That's a great idea." Jan walked over the cupboard and retrieved a can of cat food. After opening it with the can opener, she walked to the door and stepped out on to the enclosed back porch where Earl Grey sat next to the empty food bowl, waiting for his supper.

Elaine moved toward the doorway to watch as Jan emptied the can into the food bowl.

"There you go, Earl Grey," Jan told the cat. "It's chicken and rice."

Elaine smiled. "Should we make a Christmas dinner menu for Earl Grey too? He deserves something special."

"He sure does." Jan reached down to lovingly pet the cat as he munched on his food. "I found a recipe for catnip biscuits that I think he'll love."

"Sounds perfect." Elaine moved out of the doorway as Jan stepped back inside and closed the door. "And speaking of perfect, your mini Yule logs were a big hit. We might have to make those on Christmas Day for your kids and grandkids. It will be so nice to have children around at Christmas again."

Jan averted her gaze, not saying anything for a long moment. "Yes, it sure will."

"Is something wrong?" Elaine asked, as Jan grabbed a dishcloth and began wiping down the kitchen counter.

"Not at all," Jan replied. "I guess I'm just thinking about the menus. You know how much I love to cook."

Elaine laughed. "I sure do. It's a good thing the tearoom keeps me moving to work off those extra calories from your pastries."

"You and me both, cuz."

As they chatted and shared ideas for the holiday menu, Elaine knew that as much as she loved Jan's delicious pastries, the friendship and camaraderie they shared was the sweetest part of her life.

CHAPTER EIGHTEEN

Jan rose bright and early on Saturday morning, eager to start the day. She wanted to get a head start on baking the pastries and finishing the grocery list that she and Elaine had started last night.

When she walked into the kitchen, she was surprised to see Elaine already there, dressed for the day in black slacks, a black-and-white Christmas sweater, and stylish black flats. She was sitting at the table with a cup of espresso in front of her.

"Good morning," Jan said with a smile. "I didn't realize you were already down here. I was tiptoeing around upstairs so I didn't wake you."

"Well, that was nice of you," Elaine said, chuckling, "but I woke up around four this morning and couldn't get back to sleep. Too many things on my mind, I guess."

"I know what you mean," Jan said, thinking about Elaine's phone call with the botanist yesterday and the secret Jan thought Clara was keeping. She began to prepare a simple breakfast of oatmeal and tea. "Are you still planning to visit the Richardsons today?"

"Yes, this afternoon. Rose and Archie are both working today, so I'll finish up here around two o'clock and then head over to the dairy."

"Don't forget to call them first. They're not always open on weekends."

"You're right," Elaine glanced at her watch. "I'm sure they're up milking cows by now, but I'll give them a call around noon."

"Sounds good," Jan said, retrieving a handful of dried cranberries and walnuts from the pantry for her oatmeal.

As she ate breakfast, they chatted about the day ahead, which looked to be sunny and clear, but still quite cold. Jan knew weather like this would bring a lot of shoppers to the tearoom to warm up with some hot tea and take a break from the busy shops.

Elaine made herself a second cup of espresso. "I've already fed Earl Grey," she told Jan, "and prepared the tearoom for the day."

"My, you have been busy. Can you believe it's less than two weeks until Christmas?"

Elaine shook her head. "Don't remind me—I still have some shopping to do and I'm not sure when I'll find the time."

A knock at the back door interrupted their conversation. Jan glanced at the clock, noting that it was just past eight in the morning. "Maybe Rose or Archie are early birds today too," she said, getting up to answer the door.

Earl Grey greeted her with a friendly meow as she walked out on to the porch. "We have a visitor," she told the cat as he followed her to the back door.

When Jan opened it, she was surprised to see Bob on the other side, holding a large red poinsettia plant. "Hello, Bob. This is a nice surprise."

He smiled. "I took a chance that you'd be up. Sorry for not calling first, but I forgot my cell phone at home."

"I'm just glad you stopped in," Jan said with a smile.

He handed her the poinsettia. "I saw this and thought you might like it for the tearoom."

"It's gorgeous," Jan said, carrying it inside. Bob followed behind her, while Earl Grey sniffed at a leaf that had fallen from the plant.

"Don't eat that," Elaine called out, stepping out on to the porch and picking up the leaf.

"Thanks," Jan called to her as she and Bob made their way out of the kitchen and down the hallway to the tearoom. She looked around for a moment, then placed the poinsettia on a small table near the front door. "There, that's the perfect spot."

"It looks great there," Bob agreed. Then his gaze moved to Jan. "You look great too."

She could feel a warm blush creep up her cheeks at the compliment, especially since she hadn't put on her makeup yet today. But at least she'd gotten dressed before coming downstairs instead of wearing her bathrobe, as she usually did. "Do you have time for a cup of coffee or tea? We've got both."

He winced. "I wish I did, but I've got a meeting with a client this morning so I don't have much time."

Elaine joined them in the foyer. "I like the poinsettia. It really adds some Christmas cheer."

Bob smiled at her. "I couldn't resist when I saw it for sale. Especially since I was planning to stop by here anyway." He turned to Jan. "I wanted to ask you and Elaine to join me for dinner tonight—my treat."

Jan smiled as she met Elaine's gaze. "I think we're both free, right?"

Elaine hesitated and Jan could see the indecision wavering in her blue eyes.

"Let's just say yes," Jan told her, assuming Elaine was worried she'd be a third wheel. "We've been so busy lately we need a night out to have fun."

"Well," Elaine said, looking between them, "it would be nice to have dinner with the two of you. And I do have a new Christmas outfit I've been wanting to wear."

"Then it's settled," Bob said with a smile. "And it's a good thing too, since I already made reservations at the Odyssey for seven o'clock."

Jan clapped her hands together. "That new restaurant in town? I've heard great things about that place."

"So have I," Elaine said, sounding impressed. "It's small, but prides itself on using local produce and cooking gourmet cuisine."

Bob smiled. "Shall I pick you ladies up at six thirty?"

"That sounds perfect," Jan replied, looking over at her cousin. "Does that work for you, Elaine?"

Elaine hesitated. "I think I'll meet the two of you there at seven, since I have some things to do later today. But I promise not to be late."

Bob nodded, reaching into his coat and pulling out his black leather gloves. "Well, I'd better be on my way if I don't want to miss that meeting."

Jan escorted him to the back door, where he reached down to pat Earl Grey on the head before taking his leave. Jan stood in the open doorway, the cold air swirling around her as she heard him drive away.

Earl Grey looked up at her and gave a plaintive meow. She picked him up, cuddling him in her arms. "Were you happy to see Bob this morning too?" she asked, laughing softly.

The cat nestled against her, purring as she rubbed his ears. She was so happy that Bob had invited Elaine to dinner tonight. Nathan had been strangely absent ever since Elaine had told him she wasn't ready to start dating. She hoped it wouldn't affect their friendship, because Jan knew how much Elaine enjoyed spending time with Nathan.

Jan breathed a silent prayer for Elaine and Nathan, trusting that God had His own plan for all of them.

And she had a plan this morning as well—bake as many pastries as possible before the first customer walked through the door at ten o'clock.

"Time to get to work," she said, gently setting Earl Grey on the floor of the porch. "Something tells me it's going to be a lovely day."

LATER IN THE morning, Elaine stepped into her office and called the dairy.

"Hello," Annie answered after the first ring.

"Hi, Annie. This is Elaine Cook. I was hoping to stop the dairy this afternoon to pick up a few items."

"Oh, I'm sorry, Elaine," Annie replied. "We're not open today. We decided to make a college visit with Dori. We'll be open tomorrow afternoon though."

Elaine felt a tiny stab of disappointment but told herself she could wait until tomorrow to have her questions answered. "That's fine. I'll plan to see you then. Have a wonderful day."

"You too," Annie said cheerfully before ending the call.

Elaine stood in her office, not certain what to do next. They didn't really need her help in the tearoom and she'd already told Jan, Archie, and Rose that she was heading out for a few hours.

Then her gaze landed on the ring box on her desk. She hadn't put it away yet after getting it out the other day. Maybe she could use the rest of the afternoon to search for the identities of the two men in the photo with Des Murphy's grandfather.

She printed off another scanned copy of the old photo from her computer, then folded it in half and placed it in her purse. Then she grabbed her coat and headed for the door, eager to do a little sleuthing on a Saturday afternoon.

Two hours later, Elaine sat alone in the basement of the Lancaster Public Library, scrolling through microfiche of old newspapers. She'd done her shopping first, putting off the task of searching for information on the woolen mill during the Great Depression. After she finished up at the library, she would go home to change, then head straight to the restaurant.

She just hoped she could find what she was looking for. The microfiche collection of old newspapers and magazines was spotty, with several issues missing. But that didn't stop her from scrolling through them one at a time, looking for clues.

Elaine hummed softly to herself, trying to ignore the eerie silence surrounding her. There had been a few patrons upstairs when she'd arrived at the library and she'd had a lively chat with Priscilla Gates, the librarian, a frequent guest at the tearoom, before heading down to the basement.

She glanced at her watch, noting that the library was due to close soon. That meant she didn't have time to waste.

Elaine sighed as she leaned forward in her chair, her eyesight a little bleary after scrolling through three years of newspaper articles, many of them about the stock market crash and the worsening Depression. It had been a difficult time, and yet she'd found nuggets of charity and goodwill among some of the sadder tales.

She'd finally reached the year 1934 and didn't want to miss anything about a possible theft at the woolen mill.

It was the only clue she had that might lead her to more information about the men in the old photograph. A newspaper article about the theft might list the names of witnesses or employees of the mill—giving her a lead to someone who might be able to identify the other men photographed with Arthur Murphy.

Even as she scrolled through the articles, Elaine knew it was a long shot. And the sooner she could leave this dust, creepy basement, the better. There were no books in the basement, only a couple of older microfiche machines, a reference room, and a few classrooms. Priscilla had been kind enough to do some research for her before, but Elaine didn't want to ask her a second time. She doubted she'd even find anything, given Pricilla's thoroughness, but she had to give it a try, no matter how much she disliked spending time in this place.

She sighed, remembering the time she'd attended a genealogy workshop in one of the dimly lit classrooms and discovered the teacher was actually distant relative of her late husband, Ben. They'd gone for coffee afterward, comparing notes about the extended Cook family with the teacher. She enjoyed meeting new people, especially when they shared a common interest.

Then a headline caught her eye and Elaine stopped scrolling. She leaned even closer to the screen. "Ring Stolen at Mill," she said out loud, barely believing her eyes. She quickly began to read the short newspaper article.

A burglar broke into the local woolen mill in the dead of night and stole a valuable sapphire ring. The police have no suspects at this time, but are looking for anyone who can give them information about this case. The police declined to comment on why a ring was at the woolen mill or if anything else was taken.

Elaine sat back in her chair, stunned. She realized this had to be the theft Arthur Murphy was accused of. And it was too much of a coincidence not to be connected to the ring they'd found behind the wall. A sapphire ring had been stolen from the woolen mill. Arthur Murphy and other employees of the woolen mill had boarded at her house in the 1930s. A sapphire ring from that era had been found behind the wall in that same house.

Elaine wondered how Priscilla had missed this article before, then realized she probably hadn't gone as far as 1934 in her research. She printed off a copy of the article, then continued scrolling, but soon hit a dead end. There were several missing issues and she couldn't find any more information about the theft at the mill.

And, much to her disappointment, she didn't find any mention in the article about suspects or the names of any employees at the mill—nothing that would lead her to another clue. Still, this was a major step in solving the mystery of the ring.

She couldn't wait to tell Jan all about it.

ELAINE ARRIVED AT the restaurant exactly one minute before seven o'clock. She was out of breath after her brisk walk from the parking lot and could feel the tingle of a deep flush in her cheeks from the exertion.

The hostess was speaking with the couple in front of her, so Elaine took the opportunity to look around Lancaster's newest eatery.

The restaurant was small, but had an old-world ambiance that she found charming. The exposed brick walls and rustic furniture blended well with the antique wall sconces, high ceilings and open, airy atmosphere. White linen cloths covered the tables and the wait staff wore black and white uniforms.

"I'm so sorry," the hostess said, speaking to the couple in front of her. "All our tables are reserved this evening. Please accept this coupon and come back again." The hostess smiled as she handed the couple a small coupon. "Just call ahead first so we can save the perfect table for you."

"We will," the woman promised as she tucked the coupon into her purse. Then she and the man beside her headed for the door.

"Good evening," the hostess said, greeting Elaine. She was a woman in her early twenties with long brown hair, wearing a simple long-sleeved black knit dress. "I'm Kimi. How may I help you?"

"Hello, Kimi," Elaine said, appreciating the warm greeting. "I'm meeting a couple here. The reservation should be under the name Claybrook."

Kimi smiled. "Yes, Robert Claybrook," she said, after a quick glance at her reservation book. "He told me to expect you. I'll take you to their table."

Elaine followed the young woman around a half wall separating the entrance from the dining room. She was surprised to see only about a dozen tables there, which made the restaurant seem even more exclusive. *No wonder that couple needed reservations in advance,* she thought to herself. Then she saw Bob and Jan seated at a table near a stained-glass window.

"Here we are," Kimi said, waiting until Elaine sat down before handing her a menu. "Our special this evening is a braised short rib with creamy polenta and a porcini red sauce."

"That sounds delicious," Jan exclaimed, looking between Bob and Elaine after the hostess walked away. "I think I'll have the special."

Elaine took a quick glance at the menu. "Me too," she said with a smile.

"Me three," Bob chimed, making both women laugh.

After they ordered, the three of them chatted about their day and their preparations for Christmas.

"I can't believe Christmas is coming up so quickly," Jan said, turning to Bob. "Do you have plans for the holiday?"

He nodded. "I'm driving to Portland to spend Christmas with my mother. She's got all my favorite foods planned for Christmas dinner." An amused twinkle lit his brown eyes. "You'd think at my age, she'd stop spoiling me."

Elaine smiled at him. "I believe no matter how old our kids get, they're still our babies. And we love them more than anything in the world." Her voice tightened as she spoke, knowing she wouldn't be able to see her babies this Christmas. Then she took a deep breath, aware that all she really wanted—or needed—this Christmas was to know that her family was happy and healthy.

"I got a reminder of how blessed we truly are while at the library today," Elaine continued, reaching for her purse. "I was searching articles from the 1930s for news about the theft at the woolen mill. That was such a trying time for so many people." She retrieved the article she'd printed out at the library. "Look what I found."

Jan read the article first, and then handed it to Bob. "A sapphire ring was stolen? Is that the same ring we found?"

"It has to be," Elaine replied. "But who stole it? And why?"

They speculated on possible answers for the next several minutes, with Bob joining in and offering his perspective as an attorney.

"What I'm curious about," Jan said at last, "is what the ring was doing at the mill in the first place. What an odd place to keep it."

"Well," Elaine said, "the Wood family did own a similar mill at one time—although the property seems to have passed out of their hands—and their family crest was scratched on to the flue cover."

"For love and blood," Bob said, repeating the motto that he'd helped them translate. "I still wonder why that crest and motto were so important that someone took the time to etch it on to the flue cover."

"So do we," Jan agreed.

Elaine sat back in her chair, half lost in her thoughts. "I feel like we need just one more clue to help us figure it all out." Then her gaze landed on a couple at a far table.

It was Nathan. And next to him sat an attractive woman about Elaine's age. She watched in silence as the two of them talked and laughed together.

"Elaine?" Jan said, looking at her with concern. "Are you all right?"

Elaine cleared her throat and looked away from Nathan's table. "I'm fine," she replied. Neither Jan nor Bob could see Nathan and his date from their vantage point and she thought it best not to make mention of it.

Especially when she was still surprised at the thought of him dating someone. Which was silly, she told herself. A handsome man like Nathan would have no trouble finding a date, and she wanted him to be happy. She'd made it clear that she wasn't ready to start dating anyone.

So why did she feel disappointed at the sight of him with another woman?

Bob and Jan chatted amiably together, with Elaine chiming in from time to time, hoping they wouldn't notice that she was distracted. Then something even more startling happened. Nathan and his date started walking toward them.

"Hello," Nathan said as he and the woman approached their table. "This is a nice surprise."

"It sure is," Elaine said, with a nod of greeting toward the woman beside Nathan. "Have you two been here before?"

"No, this is our first time," Nathan replied, his gaze meeting hers. "But I like what I see so far."

Bob stood up and shook Nathan's hand. "Hello, Nathan. I'd ask you two to join us, but I'm afraid our table's not big enough."

"We appreciate it, but we're fine where we are." Then Nathan shook his head. "I'm so sorry—I haven't introduced you to Sheila." He turned toward the woman beside him. "Sheila, this is Elaine Cook, Jan Blake, and Bob Claybrook. They're good friends of mine."

Elaine held her breath as he finished the introduction.

"And this is Sheila Hendricks," Nathan said with a proud smile, "my cousin."

Cousin? Elaine almost laughed out loud. When she'd seen Nathan and Sheila together, she'd instantly assumed they were dating. *How silly*, she thought to herself. "It's nice to meet you, Sheila," she said, reaching out to shake Sheila's hand.

Jan greeted her too. "So you're Nathan's cousin. Do you live near Lancaster?"

"No, I'm from Rhode Island now," Sheila replied. "I'm moving into a smaller home there, so I'm delivering some family heirlooms that belonged to our grandparents to my cousins."

She clapped Nathan on the shoulder. "Nathan was the first one on my list."

"We haven't seen each other for a while," Nathan added, "so it's fun catching up."

At that moment, the waitress appeared with their braised short ribs.

"It looks like your meal has arrived," Nathan said as he and Sheila stepped away from the table. "We'll leave you to it."

"Nice to meet you all," Sheila said, giving them a small wave as she and Nathan made their way back to their table.

Elaine watched them for a long moment, still a little perplexed by her reaction when she'd thought Sheila was Nathan's date. Maybe she cared about him as more than a friend?

"This looks delicious," Bob said as the waitress set their dinner plates on the table.

"It sure does," Jan said, giving Elaine a wink. "And the company's not bad either."

"They say good company makes the best seasoning," Elaine said, winking back at her. She picked up her fork and admired the artfully crafted plate of food in front of her.

Then she glanced over at Nathan's table and saw him looking at her. They hadn't seen each other since that awkward meeting in Oldies But Goodies a few days ago. But now the awkwardness had faded and they smiled at each other like two old friends.

She might not be ready to start dating anyone yet, but tonight she knew for certain that she never wanted their friendship to end.

CHAPTER NINETEEN

S omeone is missing a halo," Elaine announced, holding a glittery white halo in one hand.

She stood in the middle of the church basement on Sunday morning, looking around the large room. It was filled with children ranging in age from three to eleven, dressed in a variety of costumes.

They were just about to start the Christmas program, presenting the congregation with songs and verses that told the nativity story.

Both Elaine and Jan had volunteered to help this year and had purchased the fabric for many of the costumes. Elaine loved the youthful energy surrounding her as she searched for the angel who had lost her halo.

Then she spotted six-year-old Marcella Edmonds talking to a little boy in a donkey costume, the image making her smile. "Marcella," Elaine called out, "I need you over here."

Marcella turned toward Elaine and then danced across the floor until she reached her. "I'm an angel!" Marcella announced, twirling around so that her angel's wings flapped behind her.

"You sure are, but you need your halo," Elaine said, setting it gently on the girl's long, blonde hair. Then she knelt down. "Now, do you remember your line?"

Marcella blinked once, took a deep breath, and then whispered, "'Do not be afraid. I bring you good news...'" Then she looked up Elaine, her blue eyes wide. "But I am afraid."

Elaine knelt down on the floor so she was eye to eye with the six-year-old. "What are you afraid of?" she asked gently.

Marcella leaned her head in closer, her sparkling halo touching Elaine's forehead. "I don't know. I just feel afraid inside my tummy."

"Well, that's a normal feeling when you try something new," Elaine said with a smile. "So it's okay to feel that way sometimes, because life is full of new things. Otherwise we'd all stay home and hide under our beds."

Marcella giggled. "That would be silly."

"Very silly," Elaine said, giving her a reassuring pat on the arm.

Marcella took a deep breath. "Okay, I'll try again. 'Do not be afraid,'" she said, her voice growing louder with every word. "'I bring you good news!'"

"You did great!" Elaine told her, giving the girl a hug. "And I'll be right in the front row, cheering you on. So you can look at me if you need any help, okay?"

"Okay," Marcella replied, bobbing her head as she skipped away.

Elaine stood up, her knees creaking a bit. Jan was upstairs helping the older kids prepare the songs and set the scenery in place. She glanced at her watch, surprised to see the worship service was about to start.

She clapped her hands together. "Okay, kids, time to get in line. We're almost ready to go upstairs."

One of the mothers opened the wide double doors that led to the stairs while Elaine arranged the kids in order. "Let's have the shepherds and sheep first, then the three kings, and then the angels." She motioned to the two sixteen-year-olds that were playing the role of Mary and Joseph. "Mary and Joseph and the donkey will follow behind."

A bit of chaos followed as Elaine and some of the mothers herded the kids upstairs, but by the time she took her seat in the front pew, she couldn't help but smile at the picture the children presented in their costumes.

There were smiles and laughter during the program, along with the beautiful Christmas message that touched Elaine's heart each time she heard it. Marcella said her line without hesitation, followed by a small, angelic curtsy.

When the service ended, Elaine leaned back in the pew, a smile on her face as she watched the children parade out of the church as the choir sang "O Little Town of Bethlehem."

It was the perfect beginning to a beautiful day.

AN HOUR LATER, Elaine drove her Malibu into the driveway as Jan sat in the passenger seat beside her. They'd stayed for cookies and punch after the worship service, taking the opportunity to visit with their church family.

"I'm not a bit hungry for lunch," Jan said, patting her stomach. "I shouldn't have eaten that third cookie."

"I'm with you," Elaine said. The she noticed a yellow paper taped to the front door. "Looks like somebody left a leaflet on our door."

"The yellow neon paper makes it hard to miss." Jan said, smiling as Elaine parked in front of the garage and they both got out of the car.

Elaine paused a moment to take in the crisp, clear day. The sun shone in the blue sky as a fluffy white cloud drifted overhead and a bird warbled in the distance. Even the snow in the driveway had melted, leaving damp patches on the ground that she tried to avoid she followed Jan to the front door.

That's when she saw her cousin staring at the paper on the door. "What is it?" Elaine asked, moving beside her.

"Not a leaflet," Jan said, her voice grim as she plucked the paper off the door. "It's a notice from the health department."

Elaine's jaw dropped as she stared at the form in Jan's hand. The letterhead at the top read: Maine Department of Public Health.

But it was the words below the letterhead, typewritten in big, bold black letters that sent a chill through her heart.

NOTICE OF CLOSURE: TEA FOR TWO
PERMIT SUSPENSION DUE TO
IMMINENT HEALTH HAZARD

"This can't be right," Jan said, flipping the paper over. "Do you think it's real? Anyone could have printed this."

Elaine took a deep breath, suddenly feeling a chill pass through her. "I agree. It doesn't look like any official document I've ever seen. The point was to scare us—or worse. This could be a warning that if we don't close the tearoom, something bad will happen."

"Who would do such a thing?" Jan asked, shaking her head. "We know someone doctored one of our tea canisters with senna. That little stunt managed to close us down for a few days. And now this?"

Elaine had never seen her cousin so angry. She was still in shock that someone had the nerve to walk right up to the front door and tape this ridiculous fake notice on it. Thankfully, the tearoom wasn't open for business on Sundays so none of their customers had seen it.

"I think this is just another ploy," Elaine told her, "designed to scare us."

"It did scare me," Jan admitted. "At first. Now I'm just so . . . "

"Mad?" Elaine asked with knowing smile.

"Well, yes," Jan huffed, "but I'm actually even more determined to find out who's behind this. Someone is playing a game with us—and with our business. We already suspect Clara may be involved somehow, as well as Scott Landon and Irene Kelly."

"And we know the motive Scott and Irene might have to sabotage us. They bought land from the Richardsons as a building site for Gram's Victorian Tea Company. So they must consider us their competition and are trying to drive us out of business."

"Or ruin Tea for Two's reputation, at the very least." Two pink spots burned in Jan's cheeks. "We can't let that happen, Elaine."

"We won't," Elaine agreed, taking a deep breath. She gave her cousin a wry smile. "You're an expert at puzzle books and I've always loved board games, so let's try to beat them at their own game."

"We need a strategy first," Jan said, unlocking the door and walking inside.

Elaine followed her. "Okay, let's put our heads together and compare notes. We'll write down everything we know about the three of them." She closed the door behind her. "And then we'll make our move."

A SENSE OF calm and purpose settled over Elaine as she drove to the Richardsons' farm on Sunday afternoon. She'd called ahead and given them her order, and now she just had to figure out how much she should tell them about the real reason she was stopping by.

As she turned down a gravel road, the bright winter sun made her wince. She reached into the console and pulled out her sunglasses, then slipped them on. She pushed on the radio button, the station already set to play Christmas music. She smiled at the sound of Elvis Presley singing "Rockin' around the Christmas Tree" and moved her shoulders to the fast beat of the music.

Her mood had improved immensely since finding that Notice of Closure paper on the front door of their house. It had come as a shock, and while they were 99 percent sure the notice was a fake, Jan planned to call the Maine Department of Public Health first thing in the morning just to make sure.

In the meantime, they intended to follow the plan they'd sketched out to stop whoever was trying to sabotage their business. It had gone far enough and Elaine didn't want anything else to mar the upcoming Christmas holidays.

The radio began to play "O Little Town of Bethlehem," reminding her of the Christmas program this morning. She had so many wonderful photos of the kids taken both before and after the program. She couldn't wait to watch the video Jan had taken from the choir loft so she could enjoy their performance again.

The children had been so cute in their costumes and recited their lines perfectly. And Marcella had done well too.

The advice she'd given the little girl had done the trick: It's okay to feel afraid when you try something new.

Her mind flashed back to seeing Nathan in the restaurant with Sheila, and her assumption that they'd been on a date together. She'd tried to ignore that tiny twinge of unease—to hide under the bed, so to speak.

"Maybe I should take my own advice someday in the future," Elaine said out loud as she turned her car into the Richardson's driveway, "and consider trying something new—even if it scares me a little."

As she parked her car near the Richardsons' barn, Elaine saw Annie at the open doorway of the dairy's shop, near the walk-in cooler. Annie wore a faded pair of blue jeans, cowboy boots, and an oversize gray sweatshirt with the words *Augusta College* printed on the front. Her hair was neatly parted into two braids.

"Hello there," Annie greeted her as Elaine stepped out of the car and approached the barn. "Isn't it a beautiful day?"

"It sure is," Elaine said, watching the Guernsey cow standing by the fence. She had a reddish brown coat dappled with white spots and chewed on a mouthful of hay as she watched Elaine with her big brown eyes.

"Gavin is putting your order together now," Annie said as they walked inside. "Sorry you had to wait a day."

"That's not a problem at all," Elaine said, letting the door close behind her. She could hear the plaintive moo of the cow outside, making her smile.

Gavin emerged from the cooler carrying a large cardboard box with handles on each side. "Here we go," he said, setting the box on the counter. "I think I have everything, Elaine, but why don't you take a look just to make sure?"

Elaine walked over to the counter and peered inside the box. "Eggs, cream, honey, butter, and cheese." She smiled up at Gavin. "You got it just right."

"Good," he said, moving toward the door. "Now I'd better get back to the house and print some more labels for the honey jars."

"We need more return address labels too," Annie reminded him, giving her husband a cheerful wave. Then she turned back to Elaine. "Is there anything else you'd like before I ring up the order?"

"Well, since you asked," Elaine said, sensing the perfect opening, "I heard beekeepers often grow senna near the hives. It's a medicinal herb sometimes used in tea."

Annie smiled. "It sure is. And we planted some last spring in the roadsides along our land. Too much senna isn't good for a cow's digestive system, so we kept it out of the pastures."

"And did the bees like it?" Elaine asked with a smile.

Annie laughed. "They did. I always saw them buzzing around the yellow flowers on the plants. We even harvested the leaves in the fall and dried them to sell in the store."

"Oh?" Elaine's heart skipped a beat. "And have you had many buyers?"

"No, although we haven't advertised it yet either. To tell you the truth, I'm a little hesitant about selling it since it can make people sick if they take too much. I've only had one customer buy it so far."

"Someone from out of town?" Elaine guessed.

Annie looked surprised. "Why, yes. Irene Kelly noticed the senna plants in the road ditch when she and Scott were looking at the piece of land they wanted to buy. I was surprised she recognized the herb since the plants were all withered and brown. But when we got back to the house, she asked if she could buy some of the dried leaves."

"I know senna is very popular in medicinal teas," Elaine told her. "Since Irene and Scott are affiliated with Gram's Victorian Tea Company, they probably know all about it—and how to use it."

The phone on the counter rang before Annie could reply. "Excuse me," she said, with an apologetic smile as she reached for the receiver.

Elaine stepped away to look at some of the products lining the shelves while Annie took an order over the phone from another customer. After a few moments, she located a small box labeled Senna. She picked it up and carried it back to the counter just as Annie ended her call. "I'll take this too."

Annie smiled. "All right. Just be sure and follow the directions on the label."

"Thanks," Elaine said, appreciating her concern. She was tempted to tell Annie the real reason for the purchase but didn't want to alarm her in case there was no connection to the senna that had been secretly placed in one of their tea canisters.

After paying for her order, Elaine chatted a bit longer with Annie, then carried the box to her car and put it in the trunk, where the items would be kept nice and cold until she got home.

As she climbed into the front seat, she waved good-bye to Annie and then headed down the driveway. Her heart beat a little faster with the knowledge that Irene had purchased senna shortly before showing up at the tearoom. It wasn't hard to put two and two together.

She just hoped they could prove it.

CHAPTER TWENTY

Jan tracked down Trooper Benson at Kate's Diner on Monday morning. She'd stopped by his house first to give him the senna that Elaine had bought from the Richardsons, but his wife told Jan that Daniel occasionally liked to have a cup of coffee at Kate's Diner before starting his shift.

"It gets a little hectic around here with the kids running around," Charlotte had said, laughing. "And he has such a demanding job that he deserves to read his newspaper in peace once in a while."

As Jan opened the door of the diner, she hated to interrupt the man's quiet time but she really wanted to talk to him before he went out on patrol.

Jan walked up to his table, where the trooper sat sipping a cup of coffee with a newspaper open in front of him. "Excuse me," she said, hoping those pumpkin cookies she'd given him a few days ago would make up for interrupting his breakfast. "Do you have a minute?"

The trooper looked up at her. "Jan Blake," he said evenly, setting down his newspaper. "Of course I have time. Please sit down."

She took a seat across from him, grateful that his table was far enough away from the other patrons so their conversation wouldn't be overheard. "I'm sorry to bother you like this," she began, "but Elaine and I need your help."

His brow furrowed. "Is something wrong?"

"We think so." She pulled out the fake notice they'd found yesterday. "This was taped to our front door when we came home from church yesterday."

The trooper took it from her, his mouth forming a frown as he read it. Then he looked up at her. "I've seen a lot of public notices, but this doesn't look authentic to me."

"It's not," she replied. "We contacted the Maine Department of Public Health earlier today and they assured us that we had no violations of any kind."

He gave a slow nod. "So someone was pranking you?"

"I think it's worse than a prank," Jan said. "Given what happened at the tearoom with Clara Hill a couple of weeks ago, we think this is related. Someone is trying to shut us down."

He sat up in his chair, his blue uniform pristine and his gold badge glinting off the pendant light above the table. "That's quite an accusation. Do you have any suspects? Any proof?"

She leaned forward and lowered her voice. "The most likely suspects are Scott Landon and Irene Kelly. They were in the tearoom the day of the incident and then made a big production about how someone had been poisoned there, according to the owner of Oldies But Goodies."

A waitress came over and refilled the trooper's coffee cup, then looked at Jan. "May I get you anything, hon?"

"No, thank you," Jan said with a polite smile, too nervous to eat or drink anything.

After the waitress left, she turned her attention back to the trooper, hoping he wouldn't have to leave before she could make her case. "Did Scott and Irene tell you that they're agents for the Gram's Victorian Tea Company and they came to Lancaster to buy land to build a tearoom?"

The trooper took a long sip of coffee, as if needing time to respond. "Their interview wasn't that in-depth. But are you saying they'd be in competition with Tea for Two?"

"Oh no," Jan replied hastily, afraid he'd gotten the wrong idea. "I mean, yes, I suppose they would be competition, in a sense." This was coming out all wrong. She wished Elaine had come with her. When they'd discussed it this morning it had all seemed so clear.

She took a deep breath, deciding to start over. "Here's our concern. Scott and Irene were in the tearoom the same day that senna was placed in one of our tea canisters—which the police lab confirmed. And we discovered yesterday from Annie Richardson that Irene Kelly bought some dried senna leaves from the Richardsons' dairy. Leaves from senna the Richardsons grew on their farm."

He arched a brow. "Really?"

She reached into her purse and pulled out the box of senna that Elaine had purchased yesterday. "According to Annie, they harvested the senna leaves last fall and dried them, then put them up for sale. If you could have the police lab examine this senna from their farm and compare it to the senna found in our tea canister…"

"It might be a match?" The trooper took the senna box from her and studied the label, then gave a small shrug. "It's worth a shot."

She detected a skepticism in his tone that surprised her. "You don't think the lab can do it?"

"On the contrary," he said, taking another sip of his coffee. "I think they can do it. But even if they prove it's the same senna, that doesn't prove Scott and Irene are guilty of a crime."

Despite her earlier apprehension, Jan found herself enjoying the back-and-forth of their conversation. The trooper hadn't immediately dismissed her, as she'd worried he might. Now she just had to convince him to see her side of it.

"They were at the tearoom that day, so they had opportunity," she began. "Irene bought senna before the incident happened with Clara, so they had the means to tamper with our tea and perhaps cause her illness. And they plan to open a competing business in Lancaster—which, I believe, is the motive in trying to damage their competition."

He smiled. "You'd make a good police detective. But there's one thing that missing."

"What's that?"

"Proof that *only* they could have tampered with the tea canister. As you said, the Richardsons sell it. Unless you have the names of all the other customers who bought senna, it's possible someone else in the tearoom that day could have placed senna in the canisters."

"According to Annie," Jan said, "there were no other buyers."

He gave a nod of acknowledgement. "Well, senna does grow along public roads, so anyone could have access to it." He tapped a finger on the table. "But this notice is troubling," he conceded, sliding the yellow paper back across the table, "even if it's just a prank. Do you have a witness who saw Scott or Irene place it on your door?"

"No, we don't." Jan took a moment to digest his concerns. He was right—they didn't have enough evidence to prove Scott and Irene guilty.

The trooper placed his broad forearms on the table. "Don't get me wrong, Jan. I think you may be on to something. You just need more evidence for me to reopen the investigation."

"I understand," she said, appreciating his candor.

He picked up his coffee cup, draining it before setting it back on the saucer. Then he placed some dollar bills on the table. "I need to go out on patrol now. But I think there's something else to consider."

"What's that?"

"That we were on to something before when we thought Miss Hill herself might be the target. As a food critic, she's probably made a few enemies along the way and causing her to become ill while she was conducting another review would be a twisted form of payback." He picked up the box of senna. "I'll get this to the lab right way and tell them to put a rush on it. At least then you'll know if it came from the Richardsons' farm."

"Thank you," she said, rising to her feet as he made his way to the door.

She watched him leave the diner, disappointed that she hadn't made her case, but grateful for his insight and that he was willing to test the senna. She glanced at her watch, noting that it was just past nine o'clock. If she hurried, she could stop in at Oldies But Goodies and get back to the house before the tearoom opened for business.

Jan zipped up her coat and headed outside, making her way down the sidewalk toward the antique shop. The weather had turned colder overnight and a few snowflakes drifted down from the sky.

As soon as she walked inside the store, she saw Fiona Latimore behind the cash register. Fiona looked up with a smile to greet her customer, but her smile flickered when she saw that it was Jan. "Oh...hello," she said.

Jan told herself she must be imagining things. "Good morning. I was hoping to find you open."

"Yes, it's such a busy time of year I like to open earlier than usual." Fiona cleared her throat. "I have to apologize to you, Jan. I just recently found the note Bree left for me—about asking me to look for a Meissen rose creamer for you. She told me you bought the sugar bowl we had in stock."

"Yes, I did," Jan said, feeling a little disappointed. She sensed that Fiona didn't have good news for her. "Have you had any luck?"

Fiona hesitated, then shook her head. "No, I haven't found a creamer for you. I'm sorry."

"That's all right," Jan said. "I've been searching online myself and even explored some other antique stores, but I'm not having any luck either."

"Is there anything else I can help you find?" Fiona asked her. "We just got some lovely lace doilies in stock."

Jan glanced at her watch. "I'm tempted, but I need to get back to the tearoom soon. I'll stop in again to take a look when I can stay longer."

"Sounds good," Fiona said with a smile. "And Merry Christmas to you."

"Thanks," Jan replied, heading out the door. "Merry Christmas!"

As she headed back toward her car, which was still parked in front of Kate's Diner, Jan couldn't help but wonder if something was bothering Fiona. She just seemed a little off today and Jan hoped she wasn't coming down with something.

As she neared her blue Camry, she glanced in the diner window. Then she stopped in her tracks.

Irene Kelly was seated at a table in the corner. She recognized the woman's fashionable, dark hair and red wool coat. And seated at the same table with Irene was none other than Clara Hill.

Jan stared for a long moment, taking a couple of side steps to remove herself from their view. She'd had no idea that Clara and Irene knew each other.

But judging by the way Irene was stabbing her finger toward Clara to make some kind of point in their conversation, they weren't friends. Clara's face was grim, her mouth pressed into a thin line. It looked as if Irene was doing all the talking.

"What's this about?" Jan murmured to herself. Then she realized there was only one way to find out. She straightened her shoulders and walked inside Kate's Diner.

Clara's face blanched when she saw Jan walk directly toward her table. Irene's back was to Jan, so she didn't glance over until Jan was practically standing beside her chair.

"What's going on here?" Jan asked, looking between the two of them. Then her gaze leveled on Clara and she decided to try the direct approach. "Are you conspiring with Scott and Irene to try and close down Tea for Two?"

Clara's eyes widened, her gaze flitting to Irene. "What? No! I…"

Before Jan could say another word, Clara leaped up from her chair and practically ran out of the diner. Jan watched her go, still somewhat stunned that the popular food critic might be involved in sabotaging their tearoom.

Irene smiled up at her. "How are you, Mrs. Blake?"

To Jan's surprise, Irene seemed calm and unconcerned about Clara's reaction. "I'm doing well. I talked to a state trooper earlier today."

"About Miss Hill?" Irene asked, reaching for her cup of tea and taking a dainty sip. "She does seem a little panicked about something, doesn't she?"

Jan recognized this kind of gambit. In the game of chess, it was a strategic move designed to sacrifice a pawn to gain an advantage. Was Irene trying to blame Clara Hill for everything?

"It might be better if you and Scott turn yourselves in now," Jan said, bluffing a little, although her instincts told her that Irene was behind the tea tampering. "Before things get even worse for you."

Irene's smile faded. "I'm not the one who needs to worry about things getting worse, Mrs. Blake. I can promise you that."

"I STILL CAN'T believe Irene said that to you." Elaine stood in the kitchen, washing out a teapot in the sink. The tearoom had closed thirty minutes earlier and Rose had already gone home.

As soon as Jan had returned home that morning, she'd told Elaine about her encounter with Irene and Clara at the diner. But they'd barely had a chance to talk about it, too busy attending to customers in the tearoom. They'd enjoyed a steady stream all day, but Jan still couldn't forget Irene's parting words to her.

"It sounded like a threat," Jan said slowly, reaching for a dish towel to dry one of the dessert plates. "But her tone was so relaxed and casual. It's very strange."

"I still can't believe Clara Hill is involved." Elaine shook her head, wiping a soapy dishcloth around the outside of the ceramic teapot. "She seems so nice."

"I don't know what to think. The way she ran out of the diner—something tells me that she's in over her head. I just wish I knew what was really going on."

"Oh, that reminds me," Elaine said, setting the clean teapot on the counter. "Trooper Benson called while you were busy with a customer. The lab report came back on the senna."

"Already?" Jan exclaimed.

Elaine nodded. "It's a match to the senna that was found in the tea canister. It came from the same plant."

"So what's our next step? Because the trooper made it clear that a match still wouldn't be enough evidence to investigate Scott and Irene."

Elaine sighed as she leaned against the counter. "We could call the president of Gram's Victorian Tea Company. Maybe he doesn't know he has two rogue employees causing trouble."

"Maybe," Jan agreed. "But what if he covers for them? Or makes them return to the main office in Portland? That would make it more difficult to find out the truth."

"There has to be something we can do," Elaine said, folding her arms across her chest. "Especially since Irene warned that things were going to get worse for us."

A knock sounded at the back door. Jan walked out of the kitchen and through the porch, glancing over at Earl Grey, who sat on a pillow, licking one paw. When she opened the back door, she was surprised to see Clara Hill standing on the other side.

"Are you alone?" Clara asked, peering inside.

"It's just me and Elaine." Jan opened the door wider. "Please come in."

Clara walked into the porch, her shoulders shaking and her eyes red. She met Jan's gaze and said, "I have a confession to make."

CHAPTER TWENTY-ONE

Elaine carried a tray into the west parlor, where Jan and Clara were already seated. Clara dabbed at her nose with a tissue, her eyes cast down toward the floor.

Jan looked up at Elaine and gave a small shrug, signaling that Clara was still too distraught to speak.

"I've got some nice chamomile tea," Elaine said, filling the cup in front of Clara and then doing the same for Jan and herself. She set the teapot on the table, along with a plate filled with stuffed dates and sugarplums.

But Clara barely seemed to notice.

"Drink some tea," Jan told Clara, pushing the cup a little closer to her. "It's wonderfully soothing. It will help you feel calmer."

Clara raised her head and reached for the cup. She blew lightly on the steaming brew and then took a cautious sip. After a moment, she said, "It's very good."

"Would you like something to eat?" Elaine asked, motioning to the plate at the center of the table.

"No, thank you," Clara said softly, "although it looks delicious. You both have been so kind to me. I don't know...where to begin."

"We'll wait until you're ready to tell us," Elaine said gently as Jan nodded in affirmation. "There's no hurry."

The words seemed to help Clara, as did the tea she kept sipping in silence for the next few minutes. Then she took a deep breath and said, "I did a terrible thing."

Elaine's heart sank, and in that moment she realized that she had never truly believed that Clara could be involved in sabotaging them. She'd always trusted her instincts about people and she'd sensed an inherent goodness in Clara.

How could she have been so wrong?

A long silence stretched between the three of them until Jan cleared her throat and asked, "What terrible thing?"

Clara closed her eyes and shuddered. "I took a bribe."

Elaine stared at her, noting the woman was clearly rattled. "A bribe? From Irene?"

Clara nodded, looking miserable. "Irene and Scott. They came to see me at my cottage the day after I came home from the hospital." She opened her eyes and wrapped her hands around the teacup, although she couldn't look Elaine or Jan in the eye. "I wasn't expecting them—I'd never even met them before."

Elaine glanced at Jan, feeling a small measure of relief at that news. It meant that Clara hadn't been in on the initial plan to tamper with the tea or—even worse—purposefully make herself sick.

"So they offered you money," Jan said, "for...a bad review of Tea for Two?"

Clara finally looked up at her. "Yes, that's exactly right. They offered me five thousand dollars for a scathing review of your tearoom. They even had it with them, in cash, in a sealed envelope."

"And you agreed?"

Clara bit her lip. "No, I was so shocked I didn't say anything. But they put the five thousand on my coffee table and just left. They didn't even wait for my answer."

Elaine shivered, not used to such hardball tactics. Irene and Scott had obviously thought it would be harder for Clara to turn them down if she had the money right in front of her—tempting her.

"You have to understand," Clara continued. "I grew up in a house where my father was very sick. The most vivid memories of my childhood are sitting in so many doctors' waiting rooms—one after another—as my parents tried to find out what was making him ill." Her eyes shone with tears. "They never did get a formal diagnosis, but his condition made it almost impossible for him to keep a steady job." She took a long sip of tea. "It was so hard on him—and on my mother. We struggled to get by. So when I collapsed in your tearoom and felt so sick..."

"You were afraid that what happened to your father," Jan said gently, "might be happening to you?"

Clara nodded. "Maybe it's silly, but when the doctor at MaineGeneral couldn't determine what made me sick, I didn't know what to think. And I worried I might have to stop working—and didn't know how I would support myself."

"But you're feeling better now, right?" Elaine asked her.

"Yes, I am," Clara replied, her expression softening. "I still don't know what made me so sick that day in your tearoom, but I'm feeling better and more rested. Just angry with myself that I even considered—for a moment—taking that bribe."

Now it was starting to become clear, Elaine thought to herself. "So you met with Irene to turn her down today? Is that what Jan witnessed between the two of you at the diner?"

Clara mouth twisted into a frown. "It wasn't a planned meeting. She found me there—or maybe followed me there. That's when I *tried* to turn her down—and told her that I planned to give her the money back, but she insisted she wouldn't take it. Irene told me a deal is a deal. And then, when I said I wouldn't go along with their plan, she threatened to tell my editor that *I* approached *them* for money in exchange for a bad review of Tea for Two."

Jan shook her head. "Those two are ruthless. And they shouldn't get away with it."

"I agree," Clara said, pushing away her empty teacup. "That's why I'm going to the police to tell them everything. I know I'll lose my job because I waited too long to come forward. Nobody would ever trust a restaurant review from me again." Her gaze moved from Jan to Elaine. "But it's the right thing to do."

Elaine breathed a silent prayer of thanks that Clara hadn't set out to sabotage their business. She'd been caught in a trap of fear and temptation, but she'd made the right decision in the end. "I think we can figure out a way to fix this without risking your job at the newspaper." She looked over at her cousin. "Right, Jan?"

"Absolutely," Jan said, tapping one finger on her chin. "And I think I might have an idea. But we'll need that envelope with the cash they gave you, Clara." She smiled at Elaine. "And an intrepid reporter."

"And another pot of tea, of course," Elaine added, intrigued by the gleam she saw in Jan's eyes. "While you tell us all about your plan."

ON TUESDAY AFTERNOON, Jan and Elaine sat in the lobby of the Corinth Hotel in Waterville. It was a modern hotel that sat on a hill overlooking the Kennebec River. The main lobby was long and large, full of abstract art prints and several seating areas with sleek, industrial furniture. A gurgling, horizontal fountain separated the center of the lobby and was filled with colorful glass beads.

"Are you nervous?" Jan asked, trying not to fidget in her molded plastic chair. She'd been anticipating this moment all day, but now she hoped they were doing the right thing.

"A little," Elaine admitted with a tentative smile. "I just hope we can pull this off."

"Me too," Jan murmured, looking around her, wondering if they'd be stood up.

The lobby was mostly empty, with a few people walking through it on their way to the elevators. River White sat at the opposite end of the lobby, reading a newspaper. He was well out of earshot, but Elaine knew that he'd be watching their every move. In fact, she was counting on it.

"Here they come," Jan announced in a hushed whisper. She pulled her purse closer on her lap, her gaze on the two people walking toward them.

Scott Landon wore a gray wool business suit with a crisp white shirt and a blue silk tie. He carried a briefcase and a confident air. Too confident, Jan thought to herself. Hopefully, they could use that to their advantage.

Irene Kelly walked beside her colleague, her black heels clicking on the Italian-tile floor. She wore a black blazer over a red sweater and a pair of stylish black slacks. Her hair was pulled back into a neat bun and a large pair of silver hoop earrings dangled from her ears.

They'd chosen the Corinth Hotel as a meeting place since Scott and Irene were currently staying there. Jan had hoped the pair would feel more at ease if they were on familiar turf.

"I'm sorry we're late," Scott said, taking a seat in one of the four lobby chairs that surrounded a small round table. He set his briefcase on top of it. "We were on a conference call." He looked between Elaine and Jan. "Now, what's this meeting about? Are you interested in selling your tearoom or perhaps you'd like to pay us to build somewhere else?"

Jan resisted the urge to laugh, amazed by the man's brazenness. It made her better understand how Clara had been bulldozed by the two of them—and also emboldened Jan to draw on her inner strength. "You're wrong on both counts, Mr. Landon. But I'll come straight to the point. We know you two are responsible for tampering with our tea supply by adding senna to one of our canisters. And we believe you put that fake public notice of closure on our door too."

Scott glanced at Irene, then shook his head. "I'm sorry, but we have no idea what you're talking about and are frankly shocked at the accusation. Perhaps you're simply looking for someone to blame for Clara Hill falling ill at your tearoom. We're not the only ones who saw her taken away by ambulance."

"You'll be lucky if she doesn't pursue legal action," Irene added. "Gram's Victorian Tea Company has a stellar reputation and—as far as I know—no one has ever gotten sick after eating at one of *our* establishments."

They're good, Jan thought to herself. After she and Elaine had finalized their plan last night, both of them had wondered if they should just contact Trooper Benson and let him handle it. But she wondered if they had enough evidence—other than Clara's word against two employees of Gram's Victorian Tea Company—and worried that the trooper might dissuade them from confronting Scott and Irene.

Elaine reached into her purse and pulled out the envelope of cash that Clara had handed over to them. "Here's the money you tried to bribe Clara Hill with to write a bad review for Tea for Two."

"We're going to give it to Trooper Daniel Benson for forensic testing," Jan added. "Clara told us the envelope was sealed when you gave it to her, so the lab might be able to get a DNA sample from whichever one of you licked the flap."

Scott smiled as he looked over at Irene. "There was an adhesive, self-stick flap on that envelope," he said with a chuckle. "So you've got nothing."

"Scott, be quiet," Irene hissed, shaking her head at him.

"We can also trace the serial numbers on those bills," Jan bluffed, "to the bank where they came from."

"Look," Irene said, leaning forward in his chair. "I think we can find a way to work this out."

"Irene, they're amateurs," Scott told her. "They can't prove we did anything."

"You were there that day," Elaine told them, not letting Scott's words deter her. "You were hoping to make people sick so they'd stop coming to Tea for Two. Then when Clara became ill, you decided to further help your cause by trying to bribe her to write a horrible review."

"I've had enough of this." Irene narrowed her eyes, her gaze moving between Jan and Elaine. "Look, there's been no real harm done. Take the money and keep it for yourselves. That should be more than enough compensation for your trouble." She stood up. "Scott, we're leaving. And if you two try to implicate us in a crime, our company will start a legal battle that will cost you so much money you'll lose everything you own before you even see the inside of the courtroom."

Scott rose from his chair and gave them a jaunty salute. "Good day, ladies."

"Not so fast," River said, walking up to them. "We're not done talking." He looked over at Jan. "Did you get it all?"

She reached into the purse on her lap and pulled out the tape recorder. "I think so." She rewound the tape, then hit the play button, where Irene's offer to bribe them into silence rang out loud and clear.

Scott paled. "You can't do that. It's…illegal!"

"Actually, we can." Jan couldn't believe Scott was suddenly worried about legalities—not after everything he and Irene had done. "It's legal to tape a conversation in Maine if at least one party knows it's being recorded." She motioned to Elaine. "In this case, both of us knew."

"She's right," Irene muttered to Scott. Then she squared her shoulders. "Look, ladies, let's renegotiate. We can work this out."

"The best way to work this out," Elaine said, rising to her feet, "is for us to take this tape to the police."

"Wait, please," Irene said, holding up one hand. Her voice was high and tight, revealing the fear hidden by her stoic expression. "There must be something we can do to make this right without getting the police involved."

Jan looked over at Elaine, still worried about what might happen to Clara's career and reputation if this all came out. "What do you think?"

Before Elaine could answer, River stepped forward. "Well, one option is that I could write a newspaper story that could put Gram's Victorian Tea Company out of business—especially when people learn how two employees of that company tampered with tea leaves and made people sick."

Scott swallowed hard, sweat beading on his brow. "I really hope there's a second option."

"The second option," River said slowly, obviously enjoying the moment, "is that you sell the land you bought from the Richardsons, preferably to a local farmer. Then you scrap the idea of ever building one of your company's tearooms in Lancaster. We don't like the kind of trouble you brew up." He grinned at Elaine and Jan. "I have a way with words."

Jan looked over at Elaine, who gave a nod of approval to River's suggestion. Neither one of them opposed another tearoom opening in Lancaster, but Scott and Irene had caused too many difficulties in the short time they'd been here. "And you leave Clara Hill alone. You've given her enough trouble."

Scott looked sheepish, then glanced at Irene. It was clear to Jan that Irene was the one in charge.

"It's a deal," Irene said at last, her face grim. "Now, can we have the tape?"

"No, I think we'll keep it," Jan told her. "And if we hear of the two of you causing trouble someplace else—like the kind of trouble you stirred up here, then we'll take this tape straight to the police."

Scott's shoulders sagged. "Look, we're not bad people. It's just so competitive at our company and they expect big results in a short amount of time. I guess we got caught up in the race to win—regardless of the cost."

Irene looked down at the floor but didn't say a thing. If Jan had to choose one word to describe the expression clouding the woman's face, it would be *ashamed*.

After a moment, the pair walked toward the elevators, taking the envelope of cash with them.

"We did it," Elaine said with a sigh of relief. She turned to River. "Thank you for letting us use your tape recorder. And for telling us that it's legal in Maine to record a conversation if at least one party knows about it."

"No problem," River said. "And I heard Clara turned down that job offer in Massachusetts, so I guess this story is over."

Jan pulled the mini cassette tape from the recorder and dropped it in her purse, intending to lock it away for safekeeping once she got home. "Thank you, River. We couldn't have done it without you." Then she handed the tape recorder to him, ready to put this saga behind them.

As they walked out of the hotel, Jan almost felt like she was floating on air. She couldn't believe their troubles were finally over.

Elaine turned to her with a wide smile and said, "We did it, Jan!"

"We sure did," Jan replied, chuckling to herself. "I wasn't sure it would work, but I think it all turned out well."

"Me too," Elaine said, hooking her arm through Jan's as they walked along the street. "And I think we should celebrate with dinner out tonight. I'm thinking burgers and fries at the Pine Tree Grill."

"I'm in," Jan said, ready to have some fun now that they wouldn't have to worry about Scott and Irene sabotaging their business anymore.

"I just wish..." Elaine let her voice trail off.

Jan stopped on the sidewalk, looking at her cousin. "What is it?"

"We still don't know what made Clara so sick. I know she said she's feeling better, but after she told us about her father, I'm sure she's still worried that it might happen again."

"So you don't think the senna caused her to collapse?"

Elaine shrugged. "I don't know. I'm certainly no medical expert. But everything we've learned about it only mentions digestive disturbances. Clara passed out—and had low blood pressure and trouble breathing. That seems pretty extreme."

Jan agreed, but they didn't have any other explanation. "Let's invite Clara to join us for dinner since she's leaving town tomorrow. We can tell her what happened with Scott and Irene so at least she won't need to worry about them anymore—or about losing her career."

"Great idea," Elaine said as they started walking once again. "I'll give her a call. What time shall we have her meet us?"

"How about seven? That will give us time to do a little shopping beforehand."

Elaine grinned. "You read my mind."

CHAPTER TWENTY-TWO

A short time later, Jan walked into the Bookworm, one of her favorite shops in Lancaster. She adjusted the two bags in her hands after a successful shopping expedition at the Sugar Plum. She and Elaine had parted ways after shopping at Sylvia's Closet, planning to meet up with Clara at the Pine Tree Grill at seven.

A cheery fire burned in the fireplace at the back of the store, where a young man sat reading a book. The Bookworm featured both new and used books, as well as some specialty magazines. Jan could spend hours in the shop—and she had in the past, just looking at the books on the shelves or paging through a magazine by the fire.

She approached the front counter, telling herself she'd have to save that treat for another day. Bristol Payson, the forty-something owner of the shop, stood near the cash register with a stack of books in front of her. She and her husband, Mark, were active members of Lancaster Community Church and had a son, Greg, in college.

"Hello, Jan," Bristol greeted her. "It's nice to see you on this fine day." She wore a bulky green sweater, jeans, and a red scarf around her neck, along with a dazzling smile. "If you're here for the latest edition of your puzzle magazine, you're in luck. It just came in."

"That's what I call perfect timing," Jan exclaimed, eager to get her hands on some new puzzles. Bristol had started carrying *Cryptograms* magazine after Jan had expressed an interest in it. Now she made a point to come into the shop at least once a month to get the newest issue.

"Do you mind waiting a few minutes?" Bristol asked her, looking apologetic. "I need to finish ringing up these purchases for a customer, and then I'll go to the back room to find your magazine."

"I don't mind waiting at all," Jan said with a smile. "It will give me a chance to browse a bit and see what new books you have in stock."

Bristol smiled. "Perfect. We do have quite a few new cookbooks, as well as some gently used ones, if you're interested."

"That's right up my alley," Jan said, before heading to the nonfiction section of the bookshop. She still had some time to spare before she was due at the Pine Tree Grill. Plus, she might find one or two cookbooks to give Rose for Christmas. They'd agreed not to exchange gifts, but a cookbook was more of a teaching tool, and she knew Rose would appreciate it.

As she perused the shelf full of cookbooks, Jan's saw several that Rose might like. She chose one written by a pastry chef and then began to page through it, admiring the colorful photographs and the step-by-step directions that were perfect for a baking apprentice.

She tucked the cookbook in the crook of her arm, then scanned the bookshelf once more. That's when an intriguing title caught her eye: *Secrets and Substitutions for the Savvy Baker*. Remembering Rose's ingenuity in substituting half of a banana for an egg while making the white maple brownies, Jan thought Rose might appreciate a cookbook with information about food substitutes and baking tips.

She pulled the book off the shelf, admiring its pristine brown leather cover. It wasn't until she started paging through it and saw a few notes and comments written neatly in the margins did Jan realize that she'd picked up a used book. She started to put it back on the shelf, then changed her mind. There was nothing wrong with a used book—and this one was in great condition.

As she began to slowly page through the cookbook once more, she became even more impressed with the information it contained. Everything from the history of baking to information about unusual foods and exotic cuisines. And even the comments handwritten in the margins were intriguing.

The former owner of the book seemed well traveled and had a sophisticated palate, judging by the tidbits that had been added to the book.

Jan knew Rose would love that, especially since it seemed apparent that the former owner of the cookbook also very comfortable in a kitchen.

"You can substitute mashed avocado for butter," she murmured to herself as she scanned one of the pages. "Imagine that."

Then she read a tiny handwritten note in the margin of that page that changed everything.

JAN HURRIED ALONG the sidewalk as she approached the Pine Tree Grill, eager to show Elaine and Clara the cookbook she'd found and the special tidbit inside. The night sky was filled with stars, and Christmas lights twinkled up and down Main Street. But as much as she enjoyed the scene and the nice weather, she didn't linger. And to her delight, Elaine and Clara were already seated at a table when she arrived.

Jan didn't waste any time as she walked over to them. "I know why you collapsed at the tearoom," she told Clara without hesitation. "It was the banana."

Clara blinked at her. "The banana?"

Elaine motioned for Jan to take a seat, a curious gleam in her eyes. "I think you'd better start from the beginning, because I'm confused too."

Jan pulled out a chair and sat down, finally noticing the festive crowd in the restaurant and Bianca approaching her.

"Hello there," Bianca greeted her, the gold bracelets on her arms jangling as she placed a menu in front of Jan. "Do you ladies know what you want to order?"

"I think we're all having a burger and fries," Elaine said, to nods of agreement by Jan and Clara.

"Well, that's easy enough," Bianca said, gathering up the menus. "I'll get your order in right away."

After Bianca walked away, Elaine turned to Jan. "Okay, spill it. What's all this about bananas?"

Clara nodded, her eyes sparkling with curiosity. "And what does it have to do with me?"

Jan took a moment to catch her breath, still a little winded from her brisk walk from the Bookworm. "Do you remember that e-mail I sent to you, Clara, about the white maple brownie and how we substituted half a banana for an egg in the recipe?"

"Yes, I think so," Clara said, her brows furrowing. "I appreciated you letting me know, but I couldn't even taste the difference. And believe me, I would have noticed, because I'm not crazy about bananas."

"So you don't eat them often?" Jan asked.

"No," Clara said without hesitation. "I can't remember the last time I had one." She wrinkled her nose. "It's the texture of bananas that bothers me more than the flavor. I'm just not a fan."

"Well, I found a used cookbook while I was out shopping and it had an interesting note in the margin about bananas. It said people who are allergic to latex shouldn't eat them, because there can be a cross-reaction."

Clara blinked. "So that's why I got sick? It was the banana in that delicious brownie?"

Jan nodded. "It appears so. You should double-check with your doctor, but that would explain your reaction after eating the white maple brownie. It was from the third batch—which is when Rose made the substitution."

Elaine folded her arms on the table. "So it had nothing to do with the senna in the cinnamon tea at all?"

"I don't believe so," Jan replied. "You didn't have any type of stomachache, did you, Clara?"

"No," Clara replied. "Although the other symptoms made me feel so awful that I might not have noticed a simple stomachache."

"So as long as you avoid bananas," Elaine said, "it shouldn't happen again."

Jan nodded. "And you might want to avoid kiwis, avocados, chestnuts, and stone fruits too, Clara. They were also listed as possible cross-reaction foods for people with a latex allergy."

"That is good to know," Clara said. "I'll definitely check in with my doctor." She breathed a sigh of relief. "Thank you so much—both of you. You've been so gracious about everything—and so helpful."

Jan almost asked Clara if she still planned to do a review of Tea for Two, but after everything that had happened, she thought it might be best just to let it go. The last thing she or Elaine would want was a biased review—either for or against them.

"I'm going to miss this place," Clara said, reaching for her milkshake. "I don't know if you've heard, but I'm staying on at the *Pelican*. Portland is my home. But now I know the perfect, peaceful spot to vacation whenever I need a break from work."

"Just promise you'll stop in to see us when you come back."

"I will." Clara smiled, looking first at Elaine, then Jan. "And I promise not to cause such a fuss the next time I visit your tearoom."

THE FOLLOWING WEEK, on Christmas Eve, Jan and Elaine started placing Christmas presents under the tree in their upstairs private parlor. The rays of the afternoon sun shone through the large windows, casting a golden glow along the polished wood floorboards. Despite the sunlight, there was snow forecast for later that evening and a white Christmas promised for tomorrow.

Elaine breathed a wistful sigh, so thankful to be spending Christmas in her beautiful home. She missed her kids and grandkids like crazy this time of year, but the fact that she'd get to celebrate with Jan and her family this year, in the house they shared together, still made it special.

"I can't believe it's Christmas Eve already," Jan said, setting a gift sack near the back of the tree. "We've been so busy with the tearoom, as well cooking and wrapping gifts and getting ready for a houseful of family, that the days have just flown by."

"They sure have." Elaine smiled, carefully setting a gift-wrapped wooden airplane under the tree. She'd picked it up from Des's workshop a few days ago, along with a box of other handcrafted toys. "And I'm thrilled that most of the gifts we're giving this year are locally made. I love those embroidered pillows from Dottie Ferrell."

"I do too. That was some date," Jan said, laughing, remembering her crazy date with Bob. "And those toys from Des for all the grandkids are wonderful—thanks to finding the photograph behind the baseboard and making a visit to the Murphys."

"And the jars of honey we bought to help Dori. They made a perfect gift to go with the variety of tea packs we gave to family and friends."

Elaine stepped back from the Christmas tree to admire their handiwork. "I just hope the presents I sent my kids got there in time for Christmas." She breathed a wistful sigh. "I'll find out when I call them tonight." She glanced at her watch. "Or maybe I should call them now."

Jan started to reply, but a knock at the front door cut her off.

"I'll get it," Elaine said, deftly moving around a large Christmas package as she made her downstairs. When she opened the front door, she found one of her best friends on the other side. "Nathan! This is a wonderful surprise."

"I was hoping to catch you at home." He flashed a smile, looking handsome in his black overcoat, his hair ruffled by the frosty breeze.

"Please come in," Elaine said, motioning him inside. "It's cold out there."

Nathan followed her inside the house, peeling off his gloves. "Where's Jan?"

"She's upstairs," Elaine said. "Her family is arriving later today, so we've been busy getting ready." Then she stepped toward him. "Here, let me take your coat."

"Oh, I can't stay," he told her, chuckling as he held up both hands. "There's a big Christmas weekend planned at my brother's house in Bangor. I'm on my way out of town but I wanted to stop and see you first."

His words warmed her heart. "Well, I'm so glad you did. We haven't seen much of each other lately."

He sighed. "No, and that's my fault. After our dinner the other night, I didn't want to make you uncomfortable. I know it's not easy telling someone you just want to stay friends." He gave her a wry smile. "Believe it or not, I've done that once or twice in my younger years."

Elaine grinned. "Oh, I believe it. You were always quite the charmer in high school. By the way, I enjoyed seeing your cousin Sheila the other night. Are you two close?"

"Very," he said. "She and her family lived in California while we were growing up, but we've spent a lot of time together since then and get along well."

She smiled. "I wish my grandchildren, Lucy and Micah, could spend more time around Jan's grandkids. They'd have so much fun together."

"Speaking of fun, let's plan to go to a concert after the holidays. I heard there's a traveling string quartet that plays lots of old favorites. Folks say it's a lot of fun."

"I'm in," she said, looking forward to spending time with Nathan again. "You know how much I like music." Then she told him about Jan and Robert's unorthodox Christmas caroling that led them to the Ferrells' farmhouse. By the time she was finished, Nathan was bent over laughing.

"I would have loved to see a goat chewing Bob's boots. What a sight!"

She also told him about the banana probably being the culprit for Clara's stint in the hospital and how they'd dealt with Scott Landon and Irene Kelly. Nathan hung on every word until she'd finished the story.

"I'm so happy it all turned out well." Then he glanced at his watch. "I wish I could stay longer, but I'm already running late."

"You'd better be on your way then," she said, smiling as she ushered him to the door. "And say hello to your brother for me."

"I sure will," he promised, then tapped one hand to his forehead. "I can't believe I almost forgot the main reason I came out here."

Elaine watched him pull a folded newspaper from inside his coat. "What's that?"

He grinned. "Something you've been waiting for. We can talk about it after the holidays. Enjoy, and Merry Christmas!" He handed the newspaper to Elaine, and then took his leave.

Curious, Elaine opened the newspaper, surprised to see it was the *Portland Pelican*. Then she noticed that Nathan had folded it around the Lifestyle section.

"Jan," she called out, staring at the paper, "you've got to see this!"

Jan walked slowly down the stairs, her gaze on the cell phone in her hand. "What is it?"

Elaine held up the newspaper. "Clara reviewed Tea for Two in her column."

Jan's eyes widened as she hurried toward her, slipping her cell phone into her pocket. "What does it say?"

Elaine cleared her throat, and then began to read the column out loud.

I started reviewing restaurants and eateries because I love food. As a food critic, I judge different aspects of a restaurant and the cuisine it serves, including taste, technique, presentation, service, atmosphere, and décor.

I've been to hundreds of restaurants and written hundreds of reviews. The science behind cooking fascinates me and I'm enthralled by the fact that something as simple as a carrot can be cooked a dozen different ways.

Which brings me to another food that's recently changed my life: The banana.

Now, I don't like bananas, but eating one inadvertently led me to one of the most unique experiences of my career as a food critic. There is a delightful establishment in the pleasant hamlet of Lancaster, Maine. It's called Tea for Two, and it changed the way I look at food.

I've always tried to be as objective as possible when tasting food and judging the creativity of the presentation—but I've never considered how certain foods might affect me personally.

The pastries at Tea for Two are enticing to both the eye and the palate. I chose a lovely white maple brownie, recommended to me by one of the owners and known as a local favorite by the patrons of the tearoom.

After just a few bites of the brownie, I fell head over heels—literally. You see, a banana was one of the ingredients in that delicious brownie—and that's when I discovered that I have a severe allergy to bananas. My experience at Tea for Two ultimately saved my life—thanks to the quick thinking of the two owners, Jan and Elaine. If I'd had a reaction anywhere else, I might not be here to write this review.

I'm perfectly fine now, and happier than ever to recommend Tea for Two to my readers. It's a cozy tearoom housed in a lovely Victorian manor. The atmosphere blends the nostalgic ambience of the past with the comfortable amenities of today. Tea for Two has won a coveted spot on my Top Ten List of favorite eateries—which you can find on my Web site.

My grandmother always said she seasoned her food with love. The two women who own and operate Tea for Two season their tea and treats with kindness and caring—and the type of personal service that we just don't see much these days.

If you want a great cup of tea and delicious pastries, then Tea for Two is the place for you. Give it a try—and tell them Clara sent you.

Elaine looked over at Jan, who had tears gleaming in her eyes. "Well? What do you think?"

"I love it," Jan replied, laughing as she blinked back the tears. "It was honest and fun and just...wonderful."

"I think so too." She stared down at the paper. "This is a fantastic way to start off our holiday weekend, isn't it?"

"It sure is." Jan arched a curious eyebrow. "And Nathan stopping by was a nice surprise. Did he bring the paper?"

"He did," Elaine said. "He's on his way to Bangor for the holidays, and I'm happy to say that our friendship is back on track. That's the best Christmas gift he could have given me."

"I'm so glad to hear it," Jan said, reaching over to give Elaine a big hug. "I could see a bit of awkwardness between you two that night at the Odyssey restaurant. And I just want you to be happy."

"I am happy," she said, feeling a warm glow inside. "And so excited and thankful to spend Christmas with you and your family."

"I feel the same way," Jan said, squeezing Elaine's hand. "Brian sent me a text while I was upstairs and said they're all on their way here. Amy, Tara, and the rest are right behind him."

"Wonderful!" Elaine exclaimed. "What do we have left to do?"

Jan thought for a long moment. "Believe it or not, I think we're ready. The food is prepared, all the gifts are wrapped, the beds and sleeping bags are ready, and Earl Grey is enjoying his catnip biscuits." Then a mischievous gleam lit her eyes. "But what do you think about opening our presents to each other before the kids get here?"

"Let's do it," Elaine said, setting the newspaper aside and walking over to the Christmas tree. Even at her age, she still got a thrill from opening Christmas presents and wondered what Jan had gotten for her. She was even more excited to see Jan's reaction to her gift.

Jan followed her to the tree, then knelt down to retrieve a red box tied with a gold ribbon. She picked it up and placed it on the nearest table. Elaine did the same with the decorative gift box she'd bought at Murphy's Store, with the red paper rose on the lid.

Then they sat down and traded gifts. "Shall we take turns," Jan asked, "or open them together?"

"Let's do it together," Elaine said, "like we do everything else." Then she carefully removed the gold ribbon from the red box, intending to save it to use later, and lifted the lid. Layers of white tissue paper lay underneath. She peeled them away, then stared at the delicate object inside.

"I don't believe it," Jan breathed from the other side of the table. She looked up at Elaine. "Did we...?"

Elaine smiled as she carefully pulled the Meissen rose sugar bowl from the box. "I think we did."

At the same time, Jan set the matching Meissen rose creamer in front of her. "You have no idea how much I wanted to find this creamer. I looked everywhere."

"And I searched for the sugar bowl," Elaine said. "I'd seen it in Oldies But Goodies, but when I went back for it, someone else had bought it."

Jan giggled. "That someone else was me! So where did you find the creamer? I looked everywhere so I could get you the matching set."

"I did the same. In fact, Fiona was helping me search for the matching sugar bowl."

Understanding dawned on Jan's face. "Well, that explains her strange behavior the other day when I asked if she'd found a creamer yet. She must have realized we'd each bought one half of the matching set, but didn't want to spoil the surprise for either of us."

"Well, I'm glad it worked out this way," Jan said, rising to her feet and carefully carrying the creamer over to the hutch and placing it on top. "Let's put the bowl and creamer up here for now, so we can look at them."

Then Elaine followed her lead, setting the sugar bowl beside the creamer, then stepping back to admire them. "A matching set."

"Just like us," Jan said, smiling as she circled one arm around Elaine's shoulders and gave her a warm squeeze.

Elaine laughed as a commotion sounded near the front door. "They're here!"

She and Jan hurried toward the entryway just in time to see Brian walk through the door carrying two suitcases and a large duffel bag.

"Are you moving in?" Jan teased.

Her son shook his head, setting the suitcases aside. "No, this is what happens when you live with three girls. Believe it or not, there's more in the car."

"I believe it. Just wait until Avery and Kelly are teenagers," Jan told him. "Then the fun really begins."

He feigned a groan, then reached out to hug his mother, before turning to Elaine. "Merry Christmas, Elaine. Are you and Mom ready for a houseful of company?"

"We've been looking forward to it all month," Elaine exclaimed, rising up on her toes to give her handsome young cousin a big hug.

Elaine saw Paula and the girls unloading pillows and sleeping bags from the car. Then she saw Amy and her family pull up in their minivan, shortly followed by Jan's youngest daughter, Tara.

"Looks they're all here," Elaine told Jan, greeting Avery and Kelly as they walked inside.

"Not quite," Paula said with a smile, reaching out to give Jan a hug.

That's when Elaine saw a big black SUV pull into the driveway, the windows shaded. She turned to Brian, smiling. "Did you invite extras this year?"

"Not extras, Aunt Elaine," Brian said with a grin. "I call them cousins."

Elaine was confused for a moment, until she saw her daughter, Sasha, step out of the SUV and wave to her. For a moment she thought she was dreaming. "I don't believe it."

Jan moved up beside her. "Merry Christmas," she said softly. "And remember when I offered to take your box of Christmas gifts to the post office to mail to your kids and grandkids?" Her eyes twinkled. "They're actually upstairs in my closet."

Elaine turned to stare at her, so happy it took her a moment to speak. "How long have been planning this?"

"Most of December," Jan admitted, laughing. "It was tough to keep a secret, but we all wanted it to be a surprise."

Happy tears filled Elaine's eyes. "The best surprise ever." Then she laughed and turned to run out the door, scooping Sasha into her arms. She gave her daughter a long hug, feeling like she never wanted to let go. "I'm so happy to see you."

"Merry Christmas, Mom," Sasha said, holding her tight. "You look great."

"So do you," Elaine said, holding on to Sasha's hands as she took a step back to take a good look at her lovely daughter. Sasha's blue eyes sparkled and her rosy cheeks and silky, nutmeg-brown hair all looked perfect to Elaine.

Then a male voice behind her said. "I always knew Sasha was your favorite."

Elaine looked up as she released her daughter and saw Jared approaching her. Tall and rugged, Jared was the picture of his father with the same dark-blond hair, green eyes, and square jawline. She ran over and embraced her handsome son. "Once I start hugging you, I might not let go."

He squeezed her tight. "I've missed you, Mom."

Before she knew it, Elaine was surrounded by Jared's wife, Corrie, and her grandchildren, ten-year-old Lucy and seven-year-old Micah. She escorted them all into the house, where Jan's children were already gathered in the east parlor.

Then Micah tugged on the hem of her sweater. "Grandma, are you surprised?"

Elaine sat down and pulled him onto her lap. His big green eyes looked up at her and she adored the flash of dimples in both of his cheeks. "This is the best surprise ever!" she told her grandson. "And I love you so much!" She wrapped her arms around him, thanking God for her beautiful family and the love that filled their house.

She met Jan's gaze and smiled, her heart bursting with joy. And now, more than ever, she knew the old adage was true: *There's no place like home for the holidays.*

ABOUT THE AUTHORS

Amy Woods loves nothing more than making up stories. Luckily, she's found the perfect way to justify spending all day doing exactly that by working as an author. When she's not busy writing, Amy can be found walking with her rescue dog, Maggie, or watching movies with her sweet husband of almost a decade.

Kristin Eckhardt is the author of more than forty-five books, including twenty-four for Guideposts. She's won two national awards for her writing, and her first book was made into a TV movie. Kristin enjoys quilting, traveling, and spending time with family and friends.

WHITE MAPLE BROWNIES

BROWNIE

1 cup sifted flour
½ teaspoon baking powder
⅛ teaspoon baking soda
⅛ teaspoon salt
½ cup walnuts chopped
⅓ cup unsalted butter,
    melted

1 cup brown sugar, packed
1 large egg, lightly beaten
1 tablespoon pure vanilla
    extract
½ cup white chocolate
    or butterscotch baking
    chips

ICING

¼ cup real maple syrup
¼ cup unsalted butter
⅓ cup brown sugar,
    packed

1 8-ounce package of
    cream cheese, softened
½ teaspoon maple extract
    or flavoring for stronger
    maple taste

Preheat oven to 350 degrees. Combine flour, baking powder, baking soda, and salt. Add nuts, mix well, and set aside. Melt one-third cup butter, add one cup brown sugar, and stir well. Add egg and vanilla extract, and mix well. Gradually combine with flour mixture, mixing well. Fold in white chocolate or butterscotch baking chips. Pour into a nine-inch square pan and bake for twenty to twenty-five minutes.

To make the icing, combine the syrup and butter, cook over low heat until butter is melted. Stir or gently whisk in brown sugar until dissolved and remove from heat. Add in cream cheese and maple extract or flavoring and whisk until smooth. Return to heat until it reaches desired consistency.

Read on for an exciting sneak peek into the next volume of Tearoom Mysteries!

On Thin Ice

Elaine Cook, co-owner of Tea for Two, the Victorian mansion in Lancaster, Maine, that she and her cousin, Jan Blake, had converted into a tearoom and their residence nine months before, was in the west parlor of the tearoom late on a February Sunday afternoon dusting a display of Nanking teapots their grandmother had left them. Outside the house, the Maine winter had a deep, inexorable grip on the landscape and the lake behind them, although for once there was no snow forecast for a day or two.

Elaine smiled as she worked, moving on to another teapot. She loved the teapot she was cleaning now. Although it was blue and white like many of the others, this one had what was known as a strap handle. Additionally, portions of it, including the spout, the handle, and the rim, were heavily covered in handsome gilt. It must not have been heavily used on a daily basis, because the gilt was still in excellent shape and hadn't worn away even in the areas where it would have been most commonly touched.

A distant shout from outside startled her, and she lifted her head, feather duster suspended in mid-air.

What was that? It had sounded like a man who was annoyed or startled. Angry, even. Cleaning equipment still in hand, Elaine went to one of the west windows, looking out at the back of the bookstore that was their nearest neighbor on that side and past it to the Pine Tree Grill. Nothing seemed out of place, and no one was moving around outside. Not unusual, given that it was a typical winter Sunday nearing suppertime. The sun was fast sliding toward the horizon; all too soon it would be dark. It was bitterly cold out there with below-freezing temperatures, although inside the old Victorian, Elaine and Jan were toasty and warm, particularly in the kitchen, where the oven often was on baking goodies for the patrons of the tearoom.

Frowning, she walked to the front windows and peered out. Again, nothing seemed out of place along Main Street. An SUV moved sluggishly past the library and on down the street, and she could see lights still on inside Gift Me, a Maine-items-exclusive gift shop beside the library. Even as she glanced, the light went out, signaling that it must be five o'clock, when the shop closed. The owner insisted on staying open from noon to five on Sundays even in the depths of winter when there was next to no tourist traffic.

She moved on into the east parlor, and as she did, she thought she heard another muffled shout. Quickly, she peered out the window. Frost crept around the edges, narrowing her view to an oval in the center of the pane, but she still could see in the other direction along Main Street, and her nearest neighbor, Sylvia's Closet, a vintage clothing shop, which, like Tea for Two, was usually closed on Sundays.

Concern deepened. Was someone out there hurt? She hurried into the commercial-grade kitchen. Jan, wearing an apron over her corduroy slacks and a white shirt with the sleeves rolled up, turned from the large granite-topped work island. A hair net covered her short dark hair. She glanced up from the stand mixer and saw her, indicated that she should wait, and after about ten more seconds turned off the mixer.

Silence fell. "What's up?" Jan asked. "I'm making raisin bread. It's so much easier to knead it in the mixer when I'm in a rush."

"I heard a sound," Elaine said. "A shout or something. And then I thought I heard it again. Did you?"

Jan shook her head. "I've had this mixer on several times. This last time, it's been kneading for nine minutes."

Elaine walked past her and peered through the kitchen door's half-pane of glass through the screened porch windows beyond. "Maybe it came from the lake."

"I doubt it," Jan said. "It's getting dark, and you know people don't go out on the ice when it's..."

"Hey, come look," Elaine interrupted.

Jan came to the door, narrowing her eyes. "There are a couple of people still out there, aren't there?"

"Yes. One, two men, right? Coming off the lake."

"The one on the right is pretty big," Jan said, "so probably men, but look. Did he just stagger? Is he hurt?"

"Oh, I hope no one was injured." Elaine was concerned. "He does look like maybe he's hurt, doesn't he? Or maybe he just had too much to drink. A lot of the fishermen seem to think alcohol is part of the experience."

"They do," Jan agreed. They continued to watch. The person helping the big guy along was not nearly as large, making his assistance unwieldy.

The two walkers had reached a public parking lot over by Green Glade Cottages by now. It seemed to take no time at all for the men to climb into a vehicle and head out of the lot.

"If he was hurt," Elaine reasoned, "they're probably going to the hospital now."

"And if he just had a little too much to drink, it's a good thing he's not driving. He'll sleep it off overnight."

"I imagine we'll hear about it tomorrow if it was anything unusual," Jan said. News traveled fast in the tiny Maine town of Lancaster.

"What smells good in here?" Elaine sniffed the air, distracted by the scent now that she knew she couldn't be of immediate service to anyone.

Jan grinned. "Pizza. I made whole-wheat dough in the stand mixer before I started the raisin bread. It'll be ready in about ten more minutes."

The pizza, which Jan had topped with spinach, banana peppers and mushrooms, was delicious. As they ate, the cousins firmed up their plans for Valentine's Day at the tearoom. Sweethearts' Day, as they'd called it, was coming up on Saturday, and they had planned several ways to promote the tearoom with a Valentine theme.

The discussion continued after they had cleaned up the remains of their meal and settled themselves in the sitting room upstairs.

Jan picked up a cross-stitch pattern she was working on; it was a lovely picture of a small round wicker table covered with a lacy cloth set for two with a charming rose-patterned tea set. Wicker chairs were visible, and a large Boston fern stood on a tall stand off to one side behind the table.

Elaine stopped to study it for a moment. "That's really coming along. You're going to be done in no time."

"Not really," Jan said. "This week I need to concentrate on getting our Valentine décor and costumes finished, and I need to finish Tara's birthday sweater. I was just excited about doing a little more of this."

"Wednesday is the cut-off date for photograph submissions," Elaine said. "So we can work on that display Wednesday night." They had decided to ask patrons to share Valentine photos, which they would place in a poster in the entryway.

"Yes, and..." Suddenly, Jan stopped. "What is that noise?"

Both women fell silent. From above their heads, they could hear something moving around in the attic. Goosebumps rose along Elaine's arms. "That's no mouse," she said in a low tone.

Jan nodded. "That's something bigger. Not human," she said hastily. "At least, I don't think so."

The sound came again, as if something was thumping across the floor. Then a skittering noise followed.

"A cat chasing a mouse? Maybe we'd better go look." Elaine rose. "I'll get a flashlight. Back in a minute."

When she returned from the kitchen with two large flashlights, the cousins quietly went to the attic door. Jan turned the knob and the hinges of the old door squealed as she pulled it open. "Well, that should scare anything up there into hiding," she whispered over her shoulder, as she began to ascend.

Elaine had to agree. "Between that and these creaky steps, we're not exactly going to be sneaking up on anything." She snapped on the light that illuminated the attic.

At the top of the steps, they paused and looked around. There were no further noises. The bare light bulb cast a pool of light around the center of the space, but there were deep shadows beneath all the eaves and behind assorted pieces of furniture that had been left up there over the years. Behind them, the brick column of the old fireplace chimney rose, casting a deeper shadow behind it.

Jan took the right side and Elaine the left. They trained their flashlights into the shadows as much as possible, but Elaine was quite aware that there were many hiding places up there for creatures of all sizes. Even a person could probably hide successfully up here short-term. Although, she assured herself, that sound definitely hadn't been human.

"Nothing over here that I can find," Jan commented.

"Not on this side either," Elaine said. "Daylight would help, but we may need to get a handyman or someone up here to try to figure out what that was."

"The go-to guy for wildlife is Jack Weston, the game warden. He's a jack-of-all-trades, so to speak," Jan smiled. "I'm sure he'll be able to relocate whatever it is if it's bigger than a field mouse."

"Whatever we heard was definitely bigger than a field mouse," Elaine said. "It sounded like a baby elephant rummaging around."

"I'll call Jack first thing in the morning," Jan promised. "After we get back from checking out the ice where that man was hurt."

"What? Why?" Elaine raised her eyebrows.

Jan shook her head. "I don't know. I just have a funny feeling about it. That tall fellow definitely looked hurt. You said so yourself."

"He did." Elaine couldn't disagree. "Maybe there was some sort of accident. He could have slipped and fallen on the ice."

"Unlikely," Jan said, "and you know it. It's not smooth and polished like an ice rink, and nearly everyone wears ice cleats. But it's possible that he had an accident. I would just feel better if we walked down there tomorrow."

"It's going to be frigid first thing in the morning," Elaine said. "Sunrise isn't until nearly seven, so I guess we'll go then."

As the cousins resumed their seats in the sitting room, Elaine said, "Have you thought any more about what we learned about the Wood family selling the land during the Great Depression?" She was referring to the cousins' ongoing interest in figuring out why a sapphire ring had been secreted in the wall of their home. They'd discovered it when they first began renovating, and they were determined to solve the mystery of how it had gotten there.

Jan pursed her lips. "The only thing," she said at last, "that I can think to do is to try to find out more about the sale of the house."

"And maybe the Wood Woolen Mill too," Elaine said. Something had been teasing at the back of her mind, but try as she might, she could not bring it into focus. "I wonder if the house and the mill were sold at around the same time."

"That's as good a direction to check out as any," Jan agreed. "Let's try to find a time this week to go . . . where? Probably not the library."

"The courthouse," Elaine said. "I think the courthouse would be the place for property records."

PROMPTLY AT SEVEN on Monday morning, the cousins met at the foot of the stairs. Both already had eaten. They were warmly dressed in turtleneck sweaters even before they donned long down parkas with hoods that would come up around their faces and high boots with removable ice cleats on the bottoms. Waterproof mittens and thick scarves Jan had knitted herself completed their outdoor gear, and a minute later, they stepped out the front door of Tea for Two.

In better weather, it would be an easy walk down the back steps of their house to Lake Chickadee. But in the winter, there was no need to constantly shovel off those steps and the dock, so there was no way to get to the lake that way. Today, they walked along Main Street until they reached the parking lot where the two trucks had been parked the evening before and then moved onto the edge of the lake.

Anyone born and raised around Maine lakes knew how vital it was to exercise caution and common sense when stepping out onto a frozen lake. Warm spells could rot even the thickest ice and make it unsafe. Fortunately, it had been well below freezing since the first day of the new year, so it was unlikely that there would be flaws or weak spots in the lake today.

Added to that, Bud Wattings, the owner of a fishing rental business in town, had several ice shanties placed at intervals in the area toward which they were headed. They knew Bud to be sensible and careful with his equipment; if his ice huts were out there, it should be safe.

Stepping onto the ice, Jan and Elaine headed directly for the hut farthest to their right. That one, closest to the tearoom as the crow flies, was the hut where they had seen the two men last night.

"You freezing yet?" Jan asked her cousin as they walked.

Elaine laughed. "Actually, since we've been walking steadily, I'm almost too warm. But better too warm than chilled. Did you notice the temperature before we left?"

Jan grinned. "A balmy ten degrees. As long as it doesn't get windy, that's not too bad."

As they drew close to the ice hut, Jan pointed. "No lock on the door, so it must not be rented out right now. If someone's fishing for a period of several days, Bud rents locks so fisherman can leave their gear in the shanty overnight instead of dragging everything back and forth."

The ice shanties Bud had out on the lake ranged in size from small ones, maybe six feet by five feet, designed for one or two people, to larger eight by ten ones that would accommodate three people and a small wood stove. Although they could be made of many materials, Bud had chosen to make his shanties of wood, which he then covered with vinyl siding. Each shanty had a single door and one or two Plexiglas windows. They stood on runners that would allow them to slide across the ice behind a snowmobile or an SUV. Elaine hadn't been in one for years, but she knew the ice shanties usually had a bench seat across one side.

There was no visible evidence of the men's presence at the narrow front door of the hut. Jan started around the side. Following her, Elaine nearly walked right into her cousin when Jan stopped suddenly.

"Oh no," Jan said.

"What?" Elaine stepped to the side. At the back of the hut was a dark brown-red frozen splotch the size of a grapefruit on the surface of the ice. "Is that blood?"

FROM THE
GUIDEPOSTS ARCHIVE

This story, by Tywana Totty of El Reno, Oklahoma,
originally appeared in *Angels on Earth*.

I inherited all of my mother's jewelry after she died. The piece
I cherished most was a ring my brothers and I had given her.

I kept my good jewelry in a velveteen pouch tied up tight.
Every few months I took out the items to clean them. I liked
knowing they were all in one place. One morning, I emptied
the pouch on the counter next to the bathroom sink. Blue sapphire ring, a diamond and emerald ring from my husband.
Where was Mom's ring? I looked everywhere, though it couldn't
have slipped through the tie I had knotted. I turned the pouch
inside out. No ring. The last time I'd worn it I'd put it back in
the pouch like always. I scoured the house, checked the car. It
was hopeless. *God,* I prayed, *I've lost the one thing that helped me
still feel close to Mom.*

I was exhausted. I made a cup of tea, and sat in the recliner
in the living room to try and relax. I woke up with a strong
sensation. *Check the pouch again,* a voice inside me said. I went to

get it. What could I hope? That an angel had dropped it down from heaven?

I got the pouch and spilled out the jewelry. Blue sapphire ring, a diamond and emerald ring from my husband...

There it was. Mother's ring. Sitting there plain as day, as if Mom or an angel had borrowed it for a special occasion and put it back in the pouch, like always.

A NOTE FROM THE EDITORS

We hope you enjoyed Tearoom Mysteries, published by the Books and Inspirational Media Division of Guideposts, a nonprofit organization that touches millions of lives every day through products and services that inspire, encourage, help you grow in your faith, and celebrate God's love.

Thank you for making a difference with your purchase of this book, which helps fund our many outreach programs to military personnel, prisons, hospitals, nursing homes, and educational institutions.

We also create many useful and uplifting online resources. Visit Guideposts.org to read true stories of hope and inspiration, access OurPrayer network, sign up for free newsletters, download free e-books, join our Facebook community, and follow our stimulating blogs.

To learn about other Guideposts publications, including the best-selling devotional *Daily Guideposts*, go to Guideposts.org/Shop, call (800) 932-2145, or write to Guideposts, PO Box 5815, Harlan, Iowa 51593.

Sign up for the
Guideposts Fiction Newsletter
and stay up-to-date on the fiction you love!

You'll get sneak peeks of new releases, recommendations from other Guideposts readers, and special offers just for you . . .

And it's FREE!

Just go to Guideposts.org/Newsletters today to sign up.

Guideposts

Visit Guideposts.org/Shop or call (800) 932-2145

Find more inspiring fiction in these best-loved Guideposts series!

Sugarcreek Amish Mysteries

Be intrigued by the suspense and joyful "aha" moments in these delightful stories. Each book in the series brings together two women of vastly different backgrounds and traditions, who realize there's much more to the "simple life" than meets the eye.

Miracles of Marble Cove

Follow four women who are drawn together to face life's challenges, support one another in faith, and experience God's amazing grace as they encounter mysterious events in the small town of Marble Cove.

Secrets of Mary's Bookshop

Delve into a cozy mystery where Mary, the owner of Mary's Mystery Bookshop, finds herself using sleuthing skills that she didn't realize she had. There are quirky characters and lots of unexpected twists and turns.

Patchwork Mysteries

Discover that life's little mysteries often have a common thread in a series where every novel contains an intriguing mystery centered around a quilt located in a beautiful New England town.

Mysteries of Silver Peak

Escape to the historic mining town of Silver Peak, Colorado, and discover how one woman's love of antiques helps her solve mysteries buried deep in the town's checkered past.

**To learn more about these books,
visit Guideposts.org/Shop**